THE APOSTATE

CLINT WESTGARD

ALSO BY CLINT WESTGARD

The Shadow Men:

   Realm of Shadows

   Council of Shadows

   Dance of Shadows

The Sojourners Cycle:

   The Forgotten

   The Apostate

   The Acolyte (forthcoming)

   The Double (forthcoming)

   The Sojourner (forthcoming)

The Maleficio Chronicles

The Devious Kind (a mystery)

Published by Lost Quarter Books
www.lostquarterbooks.com

This edition 2016

Cover image: © Agsandrew | Dreamstime.com

ISBN: 978-1-928035-21-3

For Mary Shelley

CONTENTS

PROLOGUE

The address, I saw when I arrived, was for a strip mall set off a busy street. There was laundromat, a barbershop, a pizza place, and a Chinese food place advertising its homemade jerky. There was another shop on the far corner with a faded sign and awning where it was not immediately obvious what was on offer within. A front of some sort, I thought. There was a payphone on the street corner—no phone box, just a pole bent at an odd angle with a phone attached—and a wide-eyed man was carrying on a loud and scattered conversation. "I just need twenty bucks man. That's all," I heard him say, and felt a familiar itch begin to work inside me.

I turned away, before it had a chance to grow more insistent, and went to find the entrance to the offices above the shops. It was around the side from the mystery store, and I went up the stairs, noting the well-worn carpet. At the top of the stairs there was a directory, which I scanned until I found what I was looking for: 214 Regency Services Limited. I followed the arrows down one of the hallways past closed doors to offices, disconcerted by the silence emanating from the hall. Was there anyone in any of these? I began to feel quite certain that this whole enterprise was a mistake, a waste of a precious free afternoon that I could have spent doing something else. I thought again of the man on the phone below and the itch returned. That was enough to push me on toward the office.

I knocked on the door and several painful seconds passed without any indication that there was someone within, during which I told myself again and again that I should turn and go. The door opened, revealing a young man about my age with a welcoming smile and shaggy mop of hair. "Welcome, Laila," he said. "I'm so glad you decided to come."

I could only muster a nervous smile in return as he ushered me inside. He continued to chatter away, trying to set me at ease, but I did not listen to what he was saying, my doubts about coming here returning sharply again. This was a mistake. My roommate had been correct. It was a cult and I was just one of the susceptible fools being drawn in. I was led into a large conference room overlooking the parking lot below, and the congenial Regent, as they referred to themselves, told me to make myself comfortable and that he would return in a moment.

There were three chairs in the room, looking oddly out of place in the rest of that empty space. I sat in the one facing the other two, understanding what was expected of me. A few minutes passed and I tried not to fidget or think about the man on the phone below or why I was here at all. Just as I was preparing to stand up and leave, the door opened and the man who had welcomed me entered, still smiling, followed by an equally gregarious woman. Both of them were dressed in bland white and black clothing, as though they were administrators in some office. I half expected them to launch into a discussion on supply chain or risk management.

The woman gave me a generous smile. She had long, tightly coiled hair that she had pulled back behind her head, and it danced behind her as she spoke. "My name is

Opal, and this is Hector. Thank you so much for coming today. We have so much to tell you about our faith. But first, what brought you to us?"

I squirmed in discomfort under their gleaming eyes. "I read some of *Mayan Codexes* and *The True Nature of the Multiverse.*"

"It is De Gofroy's finest work, in my opinion," Hector said with an encouraging nod.

"It was interesting. I...I guess I wanted to find out more." The room seemed uncomfortably warm, though the windows were tinted to stop too much light from coming in.

"Of course," Opal said. "We are happy to answer any questions you might have. First we'd like to find out a little more about you. You know how we do that?"

"The Protocol, yes," I said.

"What we will do today is not the Protocols," Opal said. "That only takes place at our Protocol Centers. For our initial meeting, we do what is called a pre-script."

"Oh," I said, and cleared my throat.

"It's something De Gofroy developed," Hector said. "The Protocols are too difficult for most new initiates to go through. It's overwhelming. The pre-script helps to open your mind to the Protocols. Helps prepare for the changes you will undergo. I will not lie to you—the Protocols of the faith are difficult. Not everyone is able to endure them. The pre-script will tell you if you have what is required."

"I thought this was all supposed to help me," I said. My throat felt dry, and I wanted to ask for a glass of water.

"Oh, it does," Opal said with the certainty of a true believer. "I cannot begin to tell you how. You'll have to experience it yourself."

Hector nodded firmly. "I was lost, completely adrift with my life. The understanding that I have gained from De Gofroy's teachings and the Protocols has completely reshaped me. I understand my place in the universes now and I know what must be done and the part I will play. You will be a magnificent vessel."

I looked from face to face, their eyes shining with belief, in a way that made me feel uncomfortable. I wanted that certainty. I wanted the vague sense of emptiness and unease that had haunted me for so long to dissipate. Yet everyone said the Regents were mad, a cult, with no greater understanding of the universe than any other religion. All of it lies. There was something about De Gofroy's book that had struck a chord in me, though, about our infinite selves. I felt that, and I wanted to understand more.

"Shall we begin?" Opal said.

I nodded.

ONE:

CROSSING OVER

1

The days drift, one into another, aimless and wandering as I am. The realization of my true identity, composite and shifting as it is, paralyzes me. After so long seeing myself as David Aeida, trying to stay free and survive long enough to regain my memory and myself, to face this new person, complete and whole, is almost too much. It is all there, all that I have done and all that has been done to me. There is no escaping it.

I tell myself I have the luxury of time, as I work to avoid facing the consequences of what has happened. The Travelers will not allow the Seeker to return to this world, at least not immediately. They will be more concerned with the damage that might be incurred by his return than whatever harm I might be able to manage. As far as they know, I am a native of this place.

And I am going nowhere; that much they know as well. They might send others to investigate. There is Osahi's extraction squad and the Watchers' Compound to be dealt with. But I feel confident I can avoid their grasp. I have done so before, in other times and other places.

Meredith, and whichever other of Molijc's foot soldiers are in this universe, presents a far more pressing concern.

How long, I wonder, will it take for her to escape the farmhouse and find some method of communication to the Watchers? There are not many with her, I believe. There was no one but her in the compound. The man who drove us to the compound was, I now recall, one of Aeida's fellow Regents from this world. There is Williams, whose apartment we used that first day. Who else?

I struggle with this thought until I realize it is of no consequence. I can avoid them as easily as I avoid the Travelers. They will need numbers, an extraction team, to find me, and they cannot hope to get them across now. Not after I escaped the Seeker. The Travelers will seal the universe, and they will be watching sub-signals for any channels that someone might try to open. Even communication across the universes will be difficult. Meredith will need the equipment in Lasinha's compound in order to manage it, and she dares not return there.

So I am safe for the moment, though I know that is illusory. I am not safe at all; I am trapped, and everyone—the Seeker and the Travelers, Meredith and the Watchers, and Molijc himself—can all afford to wait for circumstances to change, knowing that I will be here. It is clear I have to find some means of escaping this universe into another, if I am to have any hope of regaining my body and my life from the man who stole it from me. But doing so seems utterly hopeless. Not only do I face the impossible task of crossing from this universe, while avoiding the Travelers' notice, once I manage that feat I have to then find what the Grand Regent has done with my body and find an Acolyte who can extract me from Aeida and return me to my proper place.

It is all too much to think of, so instead I wallow in memory, chasing my thoughts down too-familiar byways. They all lead inescapably to despair. What a fate Molijc engineered for me. It is not torture enough to disappear me from the Church, put me in another's body in a forgotten universe—he made certain that Meredith would be there when I returned. He knows enough of the Acolytes' imperfect art to know that I would eventually emerge from whatever vessel he placed me in. And as I was born again each time, he wanted me to be faced with Meredith, knowing that neither of us would be able resist falling into familiar patterns.

Only I broke free this time, I defied him. I tore myself from the trap, leaving whatever limb remained behind, cauterizing the wound and going away. To where? Nowhere. I wander the city, going from place to place, staying nowhere long, refusing to do what I know must be done.

I have dreams of abandoning the faith, the center of my life for so many years, and finding my way in this new universe. If I could manage to squirrel myself away somewhere, the Society and the Order might lose interest eventually. Events would lead them elsewhere, would they not? And I could find peace away from this madness I am embroiled in. So much of it is of my own creation that I cannot even feel sorry for myself.

It is utter fantasy; I know that. Deep in these false bones, I know that. Aeida knows that too. We both understand Molijc all too well. Now that I have slipped free of his prison, he will not stop until he has me in his grasp again. He is beyond all reason, a monster. As is the Society. The Travelers' lust for power knows no bounds, and they will want to make an example of anyone like me who has defied them.

Am I any better than they? It is a hard question, and I fear the answer.

All I know is that the true faith has been central to my life for so long that I know nothing else. De Gofroy guided me. I sat at his feet and he taught me so much about myself and the universes. He told me I would be instrumental in finding the one true universe and in guiding the faith to its destiny. Part of me believes it still, no matter all that has transpired in the years since.

There is so much doubt in me now, where there was none before. How many have suffered as I have—or worse, perished—as a result of what Molijc and Lasinha have done in the name of the faith? And I cannot forget the extraction squad, killed by my hand, because in my vanity I believe I am central to the survival of the Church and the continuance of the true faith.

I am as mad as Molijc, and it is only my failure to topple him that has spared others from suffering the wounds I might inflict. What is this faith worth if all it leads to is destruction? Where is the light De Gofroy promised? Around me I see only darkness.

2

The only memories of my own that remain unclear, shrouded somewhat by the mists of Acolyte procedures, are of the last months—or years, perhaps, though I refuse to believe this nightmare has gone on that long—when I emerged from my slumber within the Aeida vessel. It is impossible for me to separate one instance from another, for they seem always to be the same. Inevitably I am drawn to the farmhouse outside Mission, my dimly remembered past taking me there, where I find myself acting out a charade of those half-memories with Meredith until the Acolytes do their work again.

Does he make her report all of it to him? He would and she would, in the desperate, impossible hope that he will forgive her and allow her to return to his graces. He is a madman. But she knows that and does not care. For a very long time, I did not either.

It is the thought of her reporting to him again about my escape, imagining his incandescent rage, that at last sparks the desire in me to act. I must escape. I cannot go back to the way things were. My only hope lies in leaving this universe. No matter how difficult it might be, I have to find a way. Two lives are at stake: mine and Aeida's.

He remains within me as well—what is left of him, anyway. His more recent memories, beginning from the time he joined the Church of the Regents, are there and mostly intact, or so it feels to me. Anything before that time is filled with gaps, half formed and cast in darkness. I can recall what his mother looked like, can feel the touch of her hand upon my shoulder, but her voice has disappeared. Her mouth moves, forming words, and I know what they are, but she does not speak. Her touch, so distant and so rare, still fills me with the strange amalgam of dread and need that sent me on this endless search for the shape of some meaning that might replace it all.

It is strange to think Aeida's thoughts as though they are my own, though I find myself doing it at moments when my guard is down. I will have to watch that. He is not a silent member of this partnership, as much as I want him to be. His knowledge of this Vancouver, a city I am only passingly familiar with in my own universe, is invaluable to me. It will be instrumental in what I must do, and on that we can both agree. It must be done.

I sidle up to my objective, circling toward it over the period of a day. Caution must always be my watchword, for it is only a matter of time before I am discovered. I must work to ensure that I give myself as much time as I can before the inevitable happens. Only when I am absolutely certain I am not being followed or observed do I at last approach the university campus on the peninsula's edge.

There is an old grey-stoned library there, towering and gothic, seemingly the repository of arcane and mysterious knowledge. I know that what lies within there is but a shadow of the truth, for no one here understands the true nature, the multiplicity of the universe and of existence. The library is largely empty, as is the campus, it still being several weeks before September and the start of term. I pass through the main entrance and into the narrow stacks, the stench of aged and damp parchment heavy in the air, and go below down a thin stairway. The lower levels are crowded with shelves, low-ceilinged and windowless, with a hint of mildew to the air.

The shelves are crammed with books of all sizes and shape, giving everything an appearance of disorder, even as there are signs posted at each row showing the call numbers stacked there. The numbers and letters mean nothing to me, it is like a foreign language, but I do not need them to guide me. I know where I am going. I head unerringly to the historical botany section, filled with monographs on Humboldt, Cuvier and their ilk. Crouching down, I run my hand along the bottom shelf until I find the books I am looking for, the many volumes of Humboldt's *Voyages in the New World* in the original French. None of them look as though they have been disturbed in a long while.

I count along to the fifth volume and pull it from the shelf. I have to brace myself to drag it free from what feels like a magnetic pull. With it in hand, I stand and flip it open to page 126, and am met by a wall of impenetrable text. Not seeing what I am looking for, I advance forward in the book, going by increments of three until I find the card slipped in between pages 194 and 195. Before looking at the card, I do the math: twenty-three days since I last replied. Twenty-three days since my attempt to cross over. It seems both too long and too short a time to have elapsed.

I am awash in the hum of vertigo, my legs trembling, and have to blink it away in order to focus on the card. The texture of it is very strange, feeling almost like cloth, though it is as stiff as regular paper would be. Drawn upon it is a sequence of three images: a seed just begun to sprout, a starling perched on a branch, and a table. I let out a steadying breath—all is not lost yet—and make my way, book and card in hand, to the center of the floor, where there are tables and chairs available. I borrow a pen from one of the students and sit down, studying the images again while considering my response.

My first image is a starling in flight, a signal that I am myself and ready to come across. The second image I draw is of a table that has been overturned, representing the transfer device I built in secret, and which Meredith destroyed. The third is a box with eyes upon it, which should indicate, I hope, the emergency transponder I stole from the Seeker. This is the means to get me across, if we can manage the channels without the Travelers becoming aware. Given that it is an emergency device, no doubt with beacon activation, that could prove difficult. I briefly consider adding a fourth image—another pair of eyes to indicate the universe is being watched—but they should know that already. We have people in the Society who will let us know such things.

When I am satisfied with my work, I return the card between the pages I found it and return the book to the shelf. Again I can feel the drag of something as I slip the volume into place. I linger for a moment after, though I know I should not, in case I have somehow been followed. I am confident I was not; no one has managed to find my trail yet, for I have been careful to move about the city randomly and without apparent purpose. But Meredith might know about the message drops in the library and set somebody to watch. I cannot discount the possibility, though no one is paying me any particular mind as I go about my business.

Tomorrow, when I return, will be the true test, or at the least the beginning of one. For now I will have to follow a pattern, returning here to send and receive messages, and no matter how I try to disguise it, the pattern will be there for someone to see—if they are watching, and in the Church of the Regents, someone always is.

3

I return to the university the following day, dodging among the film trailers set up along one of the pathways between the library and a gloomy, industrial-looking complex centered on a tower. It is raining heavily, the sky black with cloud and low overhead, so hardly anyone is about. I run from entrance to entrance, trying to find some shelter before rushing across the open plaza and up the library steps. I pause in the entryway to see if anyone is following behind and see only an empty expanse and a building all in glass in the distance. When I assure myself that no one is shadowing me, I go below.

I make a careful circuit around the basement floor to see if there is anyone I recognize before I dare to approach the botanical history section again. No familiar faces catch my eye, though my heart goes still whenever anyone meets my gaze. There is no flicker of recognition from anyone, or at least none that I see, and so I decide I am safe to proceed.

I make my way to the Humboldt books, and there on page 198 of volume five is the card. On it is a series of four pictures, as before. The first is a starling in flight, an almost exact replica of my own. The second is an apple, heavy on the branch, while the third is a house with smoke coming from a chimney. The fourth is a clock set to strike at midnight.

I stand and consider my reply for a moment, before sitting down to draw. I sketch a house similar to the one drawn on the other side and put a thick line across it. They want to use the farmhouse as the transfer point, which is impossible. It is compromised in this world, and probably theirs as well. I follow it with two clocks set to midnight and replace the card in the volume and put it back upon the shelf. I will return in two days, and by then our people in the Society will hopefully have found another point where a transfer can be managed. In the meantime, I will have to retrieve the transfer box from my apartment and stay out of sight.

I leave the library, though not without making one last circuit around the floor to look again at who is there. My nerves satisfied, I return to the rain and catch a bus back into the heart of the city. From there I make my way south to my apartment, taking a circuitous route, involving a taxi, several buses, and some time on foot. In all, it is well into the afternoon before I return to the sea-green building where I lived as Joseph Aurellano. I approach it from the alleyway after making a loop around the block to see if there is anyone at any of the entrances or keeping watch from a car.

There is no one that I can see, so I wander into the alley and slip into the car park in the basement of the building and take the stairs up to the third floor. As I approach the door to my apartment, I am brought to a halt, the hairs on the back of Aeida's head standing up, a strange tingle running up my hands. I stay frozen for a moment, listening for something that may tell me why my senses are warning me. I hear a shuffle of feet from behind the door of the apartment I am standing beside, along with the odd hum of the building, the sound of lights and pipes and whatever else might be running in the building.

I wait, hardly daring to breathe, for more than a minute, letting the sound wash over me. The television is flicked on in the apartment beside me, and I can hear muffled talk show applause. Still I do not move, trying to infer some presence from the silence emanating from my apartment. None emerges, but my disquiet won't leave.

I seem at war with myself. I know I must go into the apartment and try to retrieve the transfer box. It is my only hope of escaping this universe. But Aeida wants to flee, sensing some trap, and I trust his instincts.

At last I force myself to go forward, reasoning that I have already betrayed myself to whoever is waiting for me. I try the door and find it unlocked. As my heart races, I step within and see that a hurricane has descended. Everything is in disarray, seemingly every drawer, cupboard and closet emptied and spilled out onto the floor, every piece of furniture overturned. I step through the remains gingerly, going into each room to confirm what I already know. Whoever did this is already gone.

The destruction of the particulars of my life, false as they were, lands like a blow. My hands won't stop shaking, and I have to put them in my pockets to try to steady them. I've lived here for eight months, possibly longer, and all that I knew was here. That person still exists somewhere within me, moving about my mind like a ghost.

I leave the bathroom till the end of my search, dread clenching my chest. My worst fears are realized when I flick on the light and see that the tile where I hid the transponder is dislodged and the crevice below empty. Frantically I look around the bathroom for what became of it. There is no trace to be found. I am about to go back to the rest of the apartment, to sift through the detritus there, when a voice interrupts me, making me go cold with fear.

"Looking for something?"

I step into the hallway, expecting to see one of the

Black Robes or someone from the Order. Instead I am faced with a complete stranger, a young man, quite good looking, with dark eyes and hair and a carefully trimmed beard. In his hands is the transfer device.

4

I look at the stranger, unsure of what to say, careful to keep my face blank. The transponder looks whole, unbroken. I try not to stare at it, hoping not to give away how important it is to me.

"You don't recognize me, do you?" he says, his voice marred by bitterness.

Suddenly I do, or rather Aeida does, and I feel a flood of jealousy and rage surge through me. "Ana," I say, and he nods.

"You took her from me," he says. "Don't deny it. I know it was you."

"No it wasn't," I say, without thinking, as he shakes his head in disgust. It is the truth in a way, just as it is a lie, and there is no way I can explain that to him. For him I can only be David Aeida.

"I am not who you I think I am," I say, raising a placating hand.

"I know exactly who you are, David Aeida. She told me about you. She told me everything. She said if anything happened to her, I should find you." A surge of emotion ripples across his face, and he has to struggle to contain it. "It has taken me longer than I ever imagined, but I managed to."

"And what do you intend to do?" I say.

"I want answers," he says, lifting the transponder. "You'll give them to me, or I'll destroy this."

"Do that and you will never see Ana again," I say.

He smiles, knowing he has all the leverage he requires. "Tell me where she is."

"I don't know," I say.

"I don't believe you," he says, raising the transponder up as though to smash it.

I hold up my hands, pleading with him. "Are you a member of the Church?"

"No," he says.

This surprises me, for I assumed Ana would only consort with a fellow Regent, or at least insist upon his joining our brethren. Though I know her far better than the anguished Aeida believes he does, evidently there are still things about her that remain mysterious to me. It is a struggle at every moment to keep my emotions in check, and to approach the situation as I normally would, with an angle toward turning the situation to my advantage.

"What exactly has she told you about it? About us?"

"Enough," he says, "to know how important this is." He holds up the transponder.

"What does it do?" I ask. He hesitates, and I say, "I will tell you. It allows you to transfer to another universe."

He stares at the box, not quite believing what I said, and I see the thought as it begins to form in his mind.

"You could use it to cross over to her."

"You said you didn't know where she was."

"I don't, but I know who does," I say with a hard smile. "He is the one who is responsible for what happened to her and what happened to me." I have to fight the sudden revulsion I feel as I glance at the hands that are not mine.

Ana's lover stares at me in disgust. "What exactly are you proposing? That I ally with you? I don't think so.

You're the one responsible for what happened to her. Don't try to tell me otherwise. You can tell me what I need to know or I will destroy this. That is the only offer on the table."

"Don't be a fool," I say, some of Aeida's fury slipping free of my grasp. "That thing is the only chance you have of ever seeing her again."

"And I should just give it to you, I suppose, and you will help me find her?"

"Of course," I say, with far too much eagerness.

"I thought so," he says. "And I'm sure I will suffer the same fate as well."

"If you truly want to find her, you will need my help. And I will need that transfer box to be of any use to you."

I take a step toward him, almost without realizing it, and he backs away, holding up the box in warning. "How do I know you haven't killed her?"

"She is alive," I say. "What he does is much, much worse than death."

"Is that a threat?" the man says, incredulous.

As he speaks, I leap toward him, grabbing hold of the arm that clenches the transponder. He gives a shout and we grapple for the box, each of us throwing punches at the other, until eventually we fall to the ground in a tangle of limbs. The box slips from his hands, falling away from both us, and I try to free myself from him so that I can seize it.

Neither of us can gain the upper hand until I manage to roll on top of him, my hands clenching his throat. Though he flails against me in a frenzy, he is not able to dislodge my grip, and I hold firm until his eyes roll back in his head and he goes still.

I leave him on the floor and pick up the transfer box, looking it over to make sure there is no damage to it, while trying not to think about the man I have just killed. I did not intend to murder him, but Aeida's emotion overtook me and I was unable to stop myself from holding firm until the last breath was stolen from him.

First the extraction team, murdered without a thought, and now this. What am I becoming? It leaves me sick, but I know I have no time to lose to emotion. Someone might have heard our struggle, and I still am not entirely certain that Meredith doesn't have anyone watching the apartment. I can't chance staying any longer.

My hands are shaking so badly I drop the transponder, and as I bend over to pick it up I am struck in the head, blackness momentarily descending upon me. When I recover my senses, I open my eyes to see the man standing above me, the transfer box in his hands. He pulls the cables free of the box and smashes it against the wall until its plastic casing breaks open. I am unable to act, though I know my last hope of escaping is slipping away, and I watch as he pulls apart the insides of the device until it is ruined beyond repair.

5

I am numb with shock, unable to quite comprehend what just occurred. The man looks at me, his face a terrible mixture of hatred and triumph, and throws the ruined transponder into my lap. I cannot resist looking at it, trying to see if the device might still be salvageable. It is not, or at least it is well beyond my capabilities to repair it.

I should be furious or devastated. Something. Instead I feel nothing. This man has doomed me to this universe, condemned me to remain in this false body with these memories that are not mine, and I am left with only emptiness where my rage should be. I have no idea how to even go on from this.

For the moment I simply stand up, still holding on to the transfer box. The man is watching me cautiously, as though unsure himself what to do. I ignore him, picking up the cables and other stray pieces of the device and putting them and the box into a grocery bag I find on the floor in amongst my strewn belongings. *Aurellano's belongings*. They are not mine.

"What are you going to do?" the man says in a tentative voice.

I don't reply immediately, assuring myself that I have

collected every piece of the device. I don't want to leave anything here in case the Order or the Travelers come to search my apartment. Both will at some point; it is just a matter of time. There might still be parts I can scavenge from the box to help me create another as well, though I know I will, in all likelihood, not have the time to search the city for all that I will need. It took me months before, and I don't have months. For now it seems my only hope, faint as it is.

"What is your name?" I say to him when I am done.

"Sebastien," he says, after a moment's hesitation.

"What did Ana tell you, Sebastien, about the other universes and the Church?"

He runs a distracted hand through his hair, and I suddenly understand what attracted Ana to him. My own desire is followed quickly by Aeida's disgust and anger. Both must be visible upon my face, for Sebastien takes a step back, as though unsure of what I am going to do. I don't know myself. I raise a hand to reassure him and have to hide it, as it begins to tremble violently.

That seems to calm him, and he says, "She didn't tell me much at first. She wanted to keep me apart from all that. But when she got worried, when she started to think you were after her, she told me a few things. The multiverse. The Church and what you believe in."

"You don't?"

"No," he says. "I didn't believe any of it, to be honest. It just seemed too... But she was so frightened that I knew there had to be something to it. And when she disappeared, well, I had to find you and make you pay for what you did. It was the least I could do for her."

I smile at him ruefully. "Unfortunately, you cannot even do that. I am not who I appear. Oh, I know this is Aeida's body," I say, holding up a forestalling hand, and clamping down on Aeida's protests from within, "but I am not him. He was just a foot soldier anyway, following orders. The man who took Ana, the man who put me here in Aeida's body, he is over there, and you just destroyed your only chance at getting to him."

"You expect me to believe this bullshit?" Sebastien says.

I shrug. "I don't care. And I don't have time to stand here convincing you. Someone will have heard this and called the cops. They'll be here soon—or someone worse—and I don't intend to be here when they do."

I cast my eyes one last time over the ruins of this false life, making sure there is nothing else I need to take with me, and walk down the hallway past Sebastien. He looks as though he is about to stop me but he lets me pass, a look of absolute hopelessness crossing his face. Something in it makes me stop as I come to the door, and I turn back.

"You want to find her? You better come with me."

He hesitates, and I can see the war within him as he debates whether he can trust me, but in the end he follows me, as I knew he would.

6

Sebastien and I head across the city, back to the university library, so that I can let those on the other side know I no longer have access to a transfer device and that an alternate route across will have to be found. The journey this time is shorter, with Sebastien's car, though I still direct him on a winding path to our destination, my eyes on the mirrors to ensure no one is following us. Neither of us speaks, though I can feel Sebastien watching me from the corner of his eye as he drives. I can sense the doubt he feels as well, warring with his other emotions. He is unsure why he has come and fears a trap. I am too preoccupied to bother with reassuring him.

I make him stay in the car while I go into the library to send my message. I half expect him to be gone when I return, but he is still there, smoking a cigarette with the window rolled halfway down, ignoring the rain ricocheting into the car. He looks at me as I duck into the car, wiping the raindrops from my forehead, a question in his eyes.

"Drive," I say, not looking at him.

"Any place in particular?" he says, putting as much disdain as he can in his tone.

"Yours," I say. "But don't go straight there. Wander for

a bit."

"There's no way in hell I'm taking you to my place."

I turn to smile at him. "You want to find Ana, don't you? People are looking for me. And after the scene we created at my place, we can't go back there. We just need someplace to hole up for the day while I wait for my people to get back to me."

"And that's my place."

"Yes," I say. "Your place is perfect. No one knows who you are. Now drive. We shouldn't be sitting here for long. People will start to notice."

He opens his mouth to reply, but decides against it, starting the car and heading off campus.

"One night," he says at last, not looking at me.

"One night, and then we see what my friends have to tell me."

"What if there isn't another way across?"

This is my exact fear, but I don't say that. "There is always a way across. It's just a matter of how and how difficult it will be to manage it."

He appears to accept this, and the rest of our journey passes in silence. We arrive, after some wandering and backtracking on his part, at a condo building near Granville and Broadway, one of those square, glass-faced buildings, intended to look striking, but somehow appearing as blandly anonymous as any other apartment building. His apartment is on the second floor and is immaculately kept, furnished sparely in mid-century modern stylings.

"What do you do for a living, Sebastien?" I ask.

He gestures for me to sit down on a long couch. "What does it matter?"

I shrug. "Just curious."

"I have some questions of my own. If I'm going to be a part of this, I'd like them answered."

"That's fair," I say. "Why don't we get something to eat and then we can chat?"

"Sure. I suppose we'll be eating in, since you're so worried about being seen? And I imagine I'll be paying?"

"Well, it's the least you could do. You did trash my place."

"And you tried to kill me. I think we'll call it even."

I shrug, expressionless, and he shakes his head in disgust and calls a Chinese place for delivery, not bothering to ask what I want. I am careful not to let him see me smile.

We eat in silence, Sebastien refusing to so much as look at me. I don't mind his hostility; it gives me time to think through what my next steps will be. I still don't know what possessed me to invite him to accompany me. Is it guilt for my involvement in Ana's downfall? Is it Aeida's fury? I can't begin to sort through my emotions toward him. Surely, though, he has suffered enough losing Ana. He doesn't need to perish or fall into the hands of the Travelers or Molijc as well.

And that, I know, is the most likely outcome for both of us now. Time is quickly running out for me. It will not be long before another Seeker is sent across to hunt me. Or for Molijc to discover I escaped Meredith. It will be days, maybe hours, before someone picks up my trail again. His merely having spoken to me will implicate Sebastien in their eyes and doom him to my fate.

I can't worry about him, though. He made his choice and will live with the consequences. I have to see to myself. And there, Sebastien can prove useful, for any solution the other side provides me to escape my exile will be difficult to complete alone, especially given how little time I have. But with someone to help me there remains a chance, however slim, and I am determined to seize it.

When we finish eating, Sebastien retrieves two beers from the fridge and passes me one, a kind of peace offering.

"So," he says, "what's your plan exactly?"

I take a long pull from the bottle, trying and failing to

remember the last time I drank a beer. "I don't know. It depends what the other side says tomorrow."

"You must have some idea," he says. "You know what we need to cross over and what might be possible here."

"I know what we need, yes," I say. "But there's only one place I know of in this world where we could cross over. And it's impossible for us to use it. They'll be watching it."

Sebastien finishes his beer and begins to put away our leftovers. "Who? This Regent guy?"

"No. Well, he's not the one I'm worried about. It's the Travelers. They're watching this universe now." Sebastien looks blankly at me. "The Society of Travelers. They control the passages between the universes. They control many things. They know I'm here and they will be watching every transfer from this universe."

Sebastien ponders this a moment. "Can't you hide your crossing? Disguise it somehow?"

I finish my beer and he offers me another. I take another long drink and say, "That's what we do. But they know how, and what to look for."

"And because they're already looking, they'll spot you." I nod. "You'll just have to find another way of doing it, then."

"Yes," I say, not bothering to tell him that there is no other way, that even if we can somehow piece together the necessary equipment, I will still be arrested as soon as I step into the other universe.

Before despair at my predicament can overwhelm me, I get up to wander over to the window and look out upon downtown as twilight takes hold. The rain has stopped but the clouds are still heavy in the sky, promising more to come through the night.

"How far are you willing to go in this?" I say, not looking back at Sebastien, whose eyes I can feel upon me. He doesn't reply immediately, and I turn back to see him fighting with his emotion.

"I don't trust you, Aeida," he says.

"As I said, I'm not Aeida."

"I don't believe you. I don't believe any of this. And I don't trust you," he says. "But I'm willing to do whatever it takes to find Ana."

I nod. "She was one of my oldest friends, you know."

"I don't care," he says, echoing my own words to him earlier in the day.

I smile. "I don't blame you. I wouldn't trust me either in your place. But we need to come to some sort of understanding if you intend to find her."

"If you're my only hope of getting her back then I will help you to get back over. On the condition that you take me with you."

"I won't be going to her, you understand. You would be putting yourself at incredible risk as well. The Society of Travelers will arrest you for contravening their protocols, and there is nothing anyone can do to help you if they do."

"It hasn't stopped your Church from doing what you do," he says.

"No," I say. "We've made our choices and we've taken the risks that we have. For me, it makes no difference. They are hunting me in this world or any other I manage to get myself to. But they're not looking for you yet. You still have a choice to make, and you need to understand there will be consequences."

"I love her," he says. "It doesn't matter the consequences. I have to try."

I walk over to stand beside him, setting down my empty bottle. "Very well," I say. "If you help me here, I will take you across with me. And if we succeed, I'll give you what help I can in finding Ana."

I extend my hand, and, after a moment when he stares at me, trying to discern my thoughts, he puts out his own and we shake on our agreement.

7

I am exhausted, sleep still edging at my thoughts even with two cups of coffee in me, after a restless night spent on Sebastien's couch, as we make our way to the library to see if my friends on the other side have managed to conjure any miracles. It is fear of this moment now that kept me awake through much of the night. Fear, and guilt about Sebastien. Is the faith worth his life too?

The question may be moot. I expect my allies to say that there is no way for me to come across, that I will have to build another transfer unit in order to do so. They will know, just as I do, that such a plan will fail. There is not enough time. I will try, just the same. What else can I do?

It is this trepidation, combined with my fatigue, that leads me to miss the signs that something is awry. I know I am returning too often to the library, with too many messages being sent back and forth. It is a risk, along with all the others, that I am forced to take. I should be alert and focused, aware of the person watching me too closely. The Travelers will be watching for any ripples in the passages that should not be there, no matter how miniscule, and they are bound to see some signal from the notes going back and forth and wonder. And if they know, it is only a matter of time until the Grand Regent knows.

But I notice nothing untoward as I make my way up the steps to the library in the early morning glare. I hurry through the stacks to the shelf and pull the Humboldt volume out, seeing nothing that gives me pause. My reply awaits me, and I read the symbols and feel my heart sink, as what little hope remains in my soul leeches away.

I want to throw the book against a wall or push down the shelf. They are asking the impossible of me. They know I will fail, or that they will, which means that not only my options are dwindling. The Grand Regent is moving against us all.

I am still struggling with the message, staring at it in the hopes that the symbols will transmute themselves into something else, when I hear the footsteps approaching. There is one set on either side of the row I am in, perhaps three or four rows behind me. They are moving slowly enough that they might be scanning the call letters to find the shelf holding the book they are looking for, but I know better. I don't even bother to confirm my suspicions. I replace the volume on the shelf, keeping the note with me, knowing that will be message enough for those on the other side.

Picking up another book at random, I start moving along the row to my right, pretending to flip through it. Though they both must have heard me starting to move, neither set of footsteps changes pace, and they continue toward me in unison.

Three rows away. Now I am certain. I take a breath and step out of the row and into the corridor between the stacks, glancing to either side as though debating which way to go. The footsteps pause, a moment's hesitation, and then quicken toward me.

I turn to them and meet the eyes of a woman, innocuously dressed. There is nothing about her to signal who she is, but the laser focus of her gaze tells me all I need to know. As our eyes meet, she pauses again, almost imperceptibly, even as the person on the other side of the stacks quickens their pace. What happens next, I know, depends on how well they studied the layout of the library and how many of them are here to seize me.

I begin to walk toward the woman, pretending obliviousness, until I come to the next row in the stacks. She is one row away, her partner turning down the stack I am in to block my path back toward the stairs to the main entrance. In one motion, I throw the book at the woman as hard as I can and turn to sprint down the row away from the other pursuer. The woman cries out as the book strikes her, and I can hear the other mutter something, no doubt letting the rest of the team know where I am heading.

I dodge among the rows, angling away from both of them, and from where I assume the other members of the team will be stationed, heading to what appears to be the far corner of the basement, as far from the main stairway as possible. There is an old periodical collection there, which I hope my pursuers will be unaware of. I enter the room, kicking the door closed behind me, drawing stares from the two students studying at one of the tables. As I try to quell the urge to flee, though it still feels as though I am moving frantically, I grab a chair from the table and prop it under the door handle. It will only slow them for a moment, but I hope it will be enough to confuse them as to my plan.

With the door secured, I run to the far corner of the room, where there is a set of stairs leading to a door with a warning that it should only be opened in the event of emergency. I shove it open and the alarm immediately begins to sound, echoing loudly up the stairwell.

It is empty, which is a massive relief, for I half expected to be met by the rest of the extraction team here. The only question now is whether I have enough time to get up the stairs before they intercept me. If they are on the main floor watching the entrance and various stairwells, as I assume, I should have enough of a head start to be make it out of the building.

I sprint up the steps, taking them two at a time, and come to the first basement level, which on this side of the building is actually at ground level. There is an emergency exit, a small grey door, easily missed on a pass around the building, or so I fervently hope. A small stream of people are exiting from first basement level, and I join them, matching their pace, hoping to be lost in the flow. I don't look around as I follow the crowd along the path leading to the next building, knowing that the pursuit team will notify me of their presence, and not wanting to broadcast my own.

As I come abreast of the next building, I turn aside, heading across the road, making as though I am going toward the Student Union building. I still don't hear any sounds of pursuit, which makes me suspicious. They know by now I've left the library and they will have the Seeker's description of me as well, so I can't simply vanish. Maybe they are following me, keeping their distance, until a better opportunity to take me, with fewer witnesses, presents itself. I desperately want to turn around, to check and see where they are or if they have somehow discovered Sebastien.

The Student Union building is long and flat, with a broad staircase leading up to it. There are several people idling on the stairs as I go up them, none of them paying me any mind. Nor does anyone seem to be looking past me, telling me there is nothing untoward enough happening to draw their attention. As I duck into the building, I pull out my cell phone and turn it on. I was reluctant to keep it running for fear that Meredith, or whoever the Order has in this world, could use it to track me. Now I have to risk it, though. I dial Sebastien's number.

"What's happening?" he says without preamble, panic edging his voice. "Everyone's leaving the library."

"I pulled the fire alarm," I say.

"Where are you?"

"Don't panic," I say, glancing from side to side as I walk through the main part of the building. "Someone was expecting me."

"Did you get away? Are you all right? Should I come help?" These last questions come in a flurry, his voice rising.

"Stay calm," I say, keeping my voice level. "You need to get the car out of there before the fire trucks come and block you. Don't worry about me. I'm out of the building and I'm moving. Do you know the road into the bus loop by the campus entrance?"

"Yes," he says quietly, though I can still hear the nervousness in his voice.

"Good. Head there. Don't park. Stop somewhere where you can get out fast. I'll find you."

"What if they catch you?"

"Wait five minutes. If I'm not there, I'm not coming. Get out of here. If I'm still mobile I'll contact you and set up another rendezvous."

"And if you're not?"

"You want no part of that." I hang up, not bothering to wait for a reply.

My body is electric with energy and leaden with tension, rendering each step I take both propulsive and hesitant. At least, that is how it feels to me. I can only hope that I do not resemble the twitching, sweating, panicked maniac I can see in my mind. Damn this inadequate, unfamiliar flesh that I have been burdened with. Damn Aeida. And most of all, damn Molijc for condemning me to this fate.

It is the thought of my husband and the Grand Regent, author of my doom, that focuses me again. I have to get through this, get to the other side, so that I can see that he pays for all he has done. It is the only thing that matters.

There is a scattering of people throughout the main floor, and I weave through them on my way to the far end, where there is a cafeteria filled in the middle with tables and chairs. About half the tables are being used by students in pairs or on their own, all absorbed in their own worlds. I pass through them, floating along in my own universe, vibrating at a different intensity.

I still see no sign of the extraction squad ahead of me, and a quick glance behind reveals no one in obvious pursuit. At the cafeteria's far end, there is a bank of windows and a door leading out to a patio, from which there are stairs that join a path going across a broad, empty field, on the other side of which are some sports facilities. The bus loop is on the other side of those buildings, and that is ultimately where I am heading. I will be fully exposed as I walk across the field with nowhere to hide. If the extraction squad is going to pick up my trail again, it will be there.

The field is muddy from the rain in spots, where the grass was worn away by too many footsteps. I momentarily find myself in a panic as the mud pulls at my feet and I fight against it, the sensation of pursuers closing in on me heavy in my thoughts. There is no one there, I know, and I recover myself and continue on into the shadows that lie between the three sports facilities, and I feel that I can at last breathe again.

As I pass by the pool and the hockey arena, turning left toward the bus loop, where I can see the gleaming blue of the transit authority, I risk another glance back along my path. There are three people following the trail I took, each apart from the other, but clearly together, moving as one. I think I can recognize the woman who was in the library, but they are just far enough away I can't be certain. I have no doubts as to their purpose, though. They are on my trail, two-thirds of the way across the field, and moving fast, making no attempt to disguise their efforts.

Though I want to run, I force myself not to break

stride. I don't want to alert them. That there are only three behind me is a concern as well, for there has to be five or six on the team. Even the Travelers are not so arrogant as to send half a team to seize me, not after what I did to the Seeker.

There is always the chance these are Watchers, but I dismiss it. Molijc would not want many fingerprints in this world to point to my presence here, which is why Lasinha's compound was abandoned. Aside from Meredith, there may only be a trusted local or two observing me. The man who drove us from Stanley Park to the compound and Williams. He won't be able to send any others over now, not with the Society watching the universe so closely.

I force those thoughts from my mind, turning my attention to my surroundings. There are three others on the team, operating somewhere, sent to cut off my escape. Which means they will be ahead of me somewhere, expecting me to take one of the buses out of here. If they somehow know about Sebastien, then we are both doomed. Part of me, remembering what was written on the note and what lies ahead of me should I somehow manage to escape this predicament, hopes that is the case.

The bus loop is lined with several bays where buses idle or people stand, milling about, waiting for the next bus to arrive. The busiest bay is for an express bus where people are already standing in line. I head for there, thinking I might be able to draw out the rest of the extraction team before the three behind me arrive on the scene. As I come to the queue, a bus pulls up, opening all its doors. Everyone gathered begins to climb aboard, and I, after a moment's hesitation, follow suit, entering at the back. I linger near the door, which remains open as more students stream on, waiting and watching.

In the distance I can see my three pursuers arriving at the bus loop and starting into a run. I ignore them for the moment, scanning the crowd for whoever has alerted them to my location. One I see at the bus loop's edge, standing where she has a clear view of all the bays. She is staring at the bus I am on, but not directly at me, which tells me that at least one of the others is on the bus with me.

I cast my gaze into the distance, apparently staring at nothing, while allowing myself to watch from the corner of my eye, the woman standing vigil at the bus loop's edge and the three pursuers fast approaching. Only as the bus doors hiss and begin to close do I move, darting between them and onto the sidewalk. I feel the brush of a hand on my shoulder as I do so, but the doors close before anyone can follow, and the bus lurches into motion.

The lone woman takes a step forward in surprise at my sudden move before remembering herself. She looks to her left, away from where the other three agents are moving toward me—I presume at the final agent who is still in play. There is no point in subterfuge now; I whirl and duck behind the bus, running alongside it as it moves along the bay toward the street. Before it does, I turn and dart back through several other bays, dodging among buses and waiting students, as though I intend to escape on foot. As I go I scan the street, which I am now running parallel to, until I spot Sebastien's car.

I cut toward it, hoping that Sebastien has noticed me. There are shouts of outrage behind me as the pursuit team tries to cut through the bus loop to get to me. How far away are they? I don't risk a glance behind to see, keeping my focus on the car. Is the last, unseen agent, also in a car, moving now to cut us off? The thought causes me to break into a cold sweat, but the traffic on the street moves normally.

Sebastien has seen me. The passenger door swings open as I approach and he starts to pull out into traffic. I throw myself into the car and slam the door shut. As I do, Sebastien accelerates hard, tires squealing and the back of the car skidding as we race down the street, drawing stares from passersby.

"Where do I go?" Sebastien says in a panicked voice.

"Just drive," I say, as I turn to see where the extraction squad is.

The woman from the library comes running to the street, following along behind us until she trails to a stop, turning to look at her companions who are behind her. She is saying something to them, issuing orders, when Sebastien turns a corner onto another street and they disappear from view.

8

"Slow down," I say to Sebastien. "We don't want to draw attention to ourselves."

"What if they try to follow us?" he says, his hands gripping the wheel tight. We are on Marine Drive, heading east, having left the campus well behind.

"They will," I say. "But they don't know where we're going. They'll have to split up and get lucky. The only way they'll find us in this car again is if you get arrested for reckless driving."

He exhales loudly, and I see his hands are trembling on the wheel, but he slows down and the color gradually returns to his face.

"Who were those people?"

I shrug. "Travelers, most likely. It doesn't matter. Whoever they were, we can't be caught by them."

"So what do we do?"

"Get rid of this car, first of all."

"I'm not just abandoning my car," he says.

"Calm down," I say, looking at him steadily. "Head to the airport. You can leave it in long-term parking."

We drive on in silence, which I take as his acquiescence, and I turn my thoughts to what will come after we drop off his car. We'll need another, which means renting one. It will be a risk—the Travelers could track the car to the airport, assuming they got his license plate number, and then determine which car we rented—but that will take time, and there is nothing but risk to come.

I pull the note from the other side out to study it again, hoping that somehow I misinterpreted what is written there. That in my headlong flight from the extraction squad the symbols have been transmuted by some unknown force. Nothing has changed, though, and at the center of the page lies a castle atop a mountain.

"What does it say?" Sebastien says, interrupting my thoughts.

"It says we have to slay the dragon."

He looks at me and I shake my head. I need time to think, but time is the one thing I don't have. The Travelers have found me and the other side has just told me I need to be ready to go across by tomorrow. The clock on the note reads three. My stomach clenches as I look at it again. How can I infiltrate the Order's compound and access the transfer equipment there, without bringing the whole Society down upon me? This is assuming the Travelers haven't already dismantled the equipment, a thought best not contemplated.

A raid on a place under Society vigil is something that would normally take weeks of planning in order for it to be executed properly. Even then they are dicey propositions at best. This is something else entirely. The Society knows I am here, is looking for me, and they also know I will be trying to cross over. I have tried once before, after all. That the other side is suggesting such a course of action tells me their own situation must be precarious. Either Molijc or the Society is onto them—hardly surprising, given that our note passing has been discovered.

We leave the car at one of the long-term parking lots by the airport. Sebastien asks me how long he should keep it there for. I look at him and shrug. "A week," I say, not having the heart to tell him he will likely never return for it.

With some reluctance he agrees to rent a car in his name and we head toward downtown, neither of us saying much. Sebastien looks troubled; with the danger passed for the moment he now has time to reflect on the enormity of what he has involved himself in. He will be thinking about escaping this while he has the chance. No matter how much he loves Ana, is it worth his life? In the end, I think, but do not tell him, it never is. Only faith is, and even that I am beginning to doubt.

I cannot allow him to leave, I realize as I study him. The only chance I have of breaching the lock the Black Robes have put on the compound is with someone helping me. Sebastien is the only person I know in this world that I can trust, more or less. Beyond that I will need some tech, something to help disguise what I am attempting to do. I cannot trust that my compatriots on the other side will be able to do that for me. As I ponder how I might acquire what doesn't exist in this universe, it occurs to me that I need only do what the Church does in crossing over and hide myself behind another's attempt.

I look at Sebastien and smile, giving him directions to the apartment where Meredith and I stayed that first night after my memory was lost again, hiding ourselves from the Seeker. It is mad to be returning to this place, but insanity is the only play remaining in my hand. The Travelers might be watching the apartment building, knowing that I stayed here. I am counting on that. Now all that remains is their response.

We park out front on the street and go to the door, where I buzz the apartment number. There is a long pause, during which I grimace as I wonder what I will do if he is not home. The voice, when it at last comes, is tentative, but unmistakably his. "Yes?"

"It's Aeida," I say, and feel him stir within me.

Another lingering pause follows, during which I turn to

44

look back out on the street, studying the cars to see if anyone is in them. The door buzzes behind me, the lock clicking open, and Sebastien and I enter, heading up to the third floor. As I go to knock on the door, I recall the last time I was here, and my nightmare of Molijc. I begin to shudder and almost cry aloud.

"A price must be incurred for your betrayal," he said. Those were his final words to me before the Acolytes began their work. I was unable to respond by that point, able only to meet her eyes as she lay across from me, both of us knowing what was to follow.

Sebastien puts a steadying hand on my shoulder and is about to speak when the door to the apartment swings open and a short man with thick, round glasses peers up at me.

"Williams," I say, recovering myself.

"Yes," he says, running a hand through the frazzled tangle of his hair that inadequately obscures the bald spot forming at the back of his head. "What are you doing here?"

"You haven't heard?" I say. "They've taken Meredith."

He studies me closely, as though trying to determine whether I am telling the truth, while I do the same with him. Does he truly not know, or is he trying to play the part for me?

Williams steps aside and waves us in. "Who's this?" he says as Sebastien passes by.

"A friend," I say. "From this side."

Williams nods and takes us to his cramped living room, littered with his books, several of which he has open on the coffee table and the sofa. Sebastien and I sit on it while Williams takes a stiff-looking chair with a high wooden back.

"It's dangerous coming here again. Especially after the Seeker found you here."

"I know. I wasn't sure what to do," I say, trying to sound as though I am struggling through my thoughts. "I

45

wasn't even sure you'd still be here."

He shrugs. "There hasn't been time to move. And the Seeker wasn't coming back. He was only interested in you."

"I'm sorry," I say. "I didn't know what to do."

"It's fine," he says. "There's little here that's necessary. Tell me, David, what do you remember?"

The last is said nonchalantly, though I know it is anything but a casual inquiry. I shake my head. "It's so hard to say. Meredith was helping me get my memory back before the Seeker came after us. But—"

"Is he still here?" Williams says, a hint of panic in his voice that cannot possibly be faked.

"No. I stole a pulse weapon from them. They went back across, I think. Meredith said so, anyway."

"But they caught her?" Williams says, frowning.

"Just this morning. We got sloppy, I guess. They sent another team over. Not the Seeker. And they found us somehow. We managed to escape, but they got Meredith." I glance at Sebastien to see how he is reacting to all of this. His face is impassive.

"You're absolutely certain you were not followed here?"

"Yes," I say, and Sebastien nods.

"I need to know who this is," Williams says to me.

I don't want Sebastien to have to answer, certainly not to lie, so I say, "He knew the last Adjudicator."

"Ana?" Williams says, and Sebastien nods. "He was involved in that, then?" I shrug as though I don't know, trying to mask the swirl of emotion I can feel bubbling up from within.

"I was," Sebastien says in an even voice. "Meredith brought me in on this, before things went wrong."

"How much do you know?" Williams says, weighing his words.

"As much as I need to."

This seems to satisfy Williams, and he turns back to

me. "Do we know where they have her?"

"Lasinha's compound," I say, and hear him exhale.

"And you want to get her back, I assume."

"We have to," I say, trying to put as much desperation into my voice as I can manage.

"We can't. She's lost. You don't mess with the Society…" Williams looks as though he wants to say more, but then thinks better of it. "When Regents are taken, we accept the loss and honor their memory. It is the risk we all take in crossing over. You wouldn't understand."

I stare at him, making sure he meets my eyes. "She is not any other Regent."

"No," he says.

"What do you think he would want us to do?"

Williams sighs and runs a hand through his hair, looking away from me out the window that shows a dazzling blue sky speckled with clouds. "You are certain she is there?"

"It's where the Seeker said he was taking us when they captured us," I say. It is reasonable enough, or so I hope, that they would take over our former base of operations while conducting an investigation. It is unlikely they will have their own facilities on this world.

"You have a plan, I take it?" he says at last, after a long pause.

"We go through the tunnels," I say. "They won't have found the access point."

"They are not fools."

"Neither are we," I say. "The guards were in place. Unless they've managed to bypass them, any attempt to breach the tunnels will seal them off."

Williams considers this, his eyes not leaving mine. I feel Sebastien shift beside me, but I do not look away.

"I guess we'll know soon enough if they have breached them," Williams says at last, and I nod. He considers me for a few moments longer, and I think he will press me further, but instead he says, "When do you want to leave?"

"Time is short," I say, standing up. Both Williams and Sebastien rise with me, and we leave without another word.

9

The compound looks no different than it did the day Osahi's extraction squad invaded and met its fate and the Seeker and Black Robes seized us and locked it. The grass and plants at the front look a little disheveled from having not been cared for in some days. No one is visible through any of the windows, at least from down the street where Williams stops his car. They wouldn't be, though, not if they want to ensnare anyone in this trap. And I have absolutely no doubt this is a trap.

"We should get started," Williams says, shifting the car into gear, driving down the street, and turning left, heading down the mountain to the next neighborhood below the compound.

I study him from the corner of my eye as we head to the access point. It was entirely too easy for me to convince him to come on this journey. He accepted nearly everything I said, offering no argument, which is strange, given that what we are about to attempt will place all our lives in considerable danger. The question is why he is acquiescing. What does he know, or think he knows, that I don't? I have my suspicions, and I can only hope that they are correct.

Sebastien was quiet from the moment we entered Williams' apartment, taking a measure of the situation and offering little in turn. It was very impressive for someone with no training, and leads me to feel a little better about my present circumstances. If he can continue to keep his head about him for the next few hours, I might be able to slip from this world and begin to exact my vengeance upon all those who have wronged me. First, though, I have to find my way into the compound.

Williams pulls up in front of the access point, an innocuous maintenance shed on the edge of a park with football and cricket pitches on it. We open our doors and exit the car, almost in unison, and stand looking out at the few people using the pitches, children mostly.

"Someone should stay with the car," I say. "In case we need to leave fast."

Williams hesitates and then nods.

"It should be him," I say, pointing at Sebastien. "He's the only one who doesn't know the tunnels."

Williams looks at me and then Sebastien, doubt flashing across his face before disappearing. Sebastien, too, looks as though he is about to offer some form of protest, which is what wins Williams over in the end.

"All right," he says. "I've trusted you so far."

It is an odd thing to say, and I glance at him, saying only, "We are all of us Regents."

He hands his keys over to Sebastien who, at a gesture from me, goes to sit in the driver's side of the car. Williams and I proceed to the shed, which is locked with a combination key. Williams lets me punch in the code while he watches, a test of sorts. I use the one Meredith used to activate the compound's defenses, hoping that it is the same and that the Travelers haven't bothered to change it. Sweat beads on my forehead when the lock doesn't immediately click open upon my pressing the numbers. Here I have delivered myself to Molijc and the Society both, with nothing to show for it. A fraction of a second later, as darker thoughts assail me, the lock releases and I have to stop myself from exhaling in relief.

I look at Williams and he gestures to me. "After you."

I nod and step into the shed, blinking to adjust to the dimness as Williams closes the door behind me. Once I can see and have my bearings, I proceed to the shed's far corner, where I know there is a trapdoor concealed in the floor. I have to feel around for several moments before I find the latch. It lifts up silently on its hinges, revealing a staircase illuminated by a dim fluorescent glow. The tunnels Meredith and I tried to escape through lie beyond.

I descend with Williams behind me, our footsteps sounding dimly down the corridor. A vague sense of dread begins to take hold of me, a feeling that the walls are closing in around me and that I will be trapped in this underground warren forever. Williams moves to walk beside me, and I can see my own disquiet mirrored on his face. Does he understand what we are walking into? Unlikely, but he still is not to be trusted. The Grand Regent, I am certain, found some means to contact him once Meredith lost me, and now he is stalling for time, trying to ensnare me again.

The corridor leads to a door, sealed and with a single blinking light by a keypad. I glance at Williams and go to enter the code, the door hissing open in response. I go to step through but pause in the doorway, cocking my head to listen. The breach where Osahi's extraction squad entered the tunnels is somewhere ahead. The Travelers will have traced the tunnels, once they unlocked the defenses I enacted, sealing the breach. They might even have someone on watch here, although that is unnecessary. As soon as I opened this door, they will have been alerted we are here.

Williams moves up to stand beside me, glancing at me curiously.

"Do you hear that?" I whisper. He shakes his head.

"There's a hum," I insist. "It shouldn't be there."

Williams frowns and shakes his head again, taking a step forward and leaning his head out to better hear. I take a small step with him. The corridor stretches on, vast and dimly lit. Williams takes another step, peering into the gloom. He turns back to me and says, "I don't—"

His words are strangled in his throat as he sees that I have stepped back through the doorway and am already entering the code to seal the door and lock him within. He takes a step toward me, but it is too late and he knows it.

"Aeida," he shouts, his voice echoing back along the corridor.

"No," I say, and press the final command. The door slides shut and is armed. I enter in a new code to unlock it and walk back through the maintenance shed to where Sebastien awaits me.

10

Sebastien is leaning against the car, tapping his hand against it, trying, and failing, to look calm.

"Where's Williams?" he says as I approach after locking the shed behind me. "What's gone wrong?"

"Nothing," I say, gesturing for him to get in the car. "Now come on. We don't have much time."

Sebastien opens his mouth to ask another question, but thinks better of it, jumping into the car and starting it.

"Where to?"

"Back to the compound," I say, looking straight ahead. "Drive normally. We don't want to draw attention to ourselves."

As Sebastien drives, I glance at the clock of the car, trying to calculate how much time we have. It will take the Society's team ten or fifteen minutes to get from the compound through the tunnels to where Williams is, and another ten or fifteen minutes to come back once they realize what is happening. There will be six in the team, and the question now is how many will be sent in response. Four at least, five if we are extremely fortunate.

Sebastien pulls up just down the street from the compound and shuts off the car. I feel my pulse begin to race and force myself to breathe. The moment is at hand and my fate will be decided now. After so many months of attempting to escape the prison Molijc fashioned for me, I have another chance to return home. I will, or I will fail in the attempt and find myself in the hands of the Society of Travelers. I would be the agent of destruction for the Church of Regents, with all the secrets I know. I cannot let that happen. Better to die than to fail the faith so utterly.

I take a last steadying breath and glance at Sebastien, who is looking at me expectantly. I nod and look down at the clock one last time. It reads two forty. Twenty minutes. Twenty minutes to define a lifetime.

"Follow my lead," I say to Sebastien as we get out of the car and start toward the compound door.

"What the hell are we doing? Where's Williams?"

"He's the decoy," I say. "Hopefully he'll draw most of their attention so we only have one or two to deal with."

"How the hell are we going to deal with one or two?"

"Just follow my lead," I say. "You're doing well."

He nods and we go to the door. The lock the Black Robes placed there has been removed, which tells me, if I didn't know already, that a trap has been laid. With one hand I reach and grab Sebastien roughly by the shoulder, throwing him off balance, while with the other I knock on the door. There is a long pause, during which I glare at the door with what I hope is a suitable fierceness, still holding Sebastien by the arm. He struggles against me, but I do not let him go.

The door opens and I am brought face to face with a young man with a shaved head and the beginnings of stubble on his jaw. He has pulse revolver in his hand and he gestures for me to enter. I pull the still-struggling Sebastien within the compound as the Traveler keeps his weapon leveled at us, never taking his eyes from me.

"I want to make a deal," I say, glancing around as I do. The kitchen and living room overlooking the city below are empty, and the access to the stairs below to the rest of the compound is open. All good signs.

"What kind of deal?" the Traveler says, moving between us and the door. He shuts it with one hand, not taking his eyes from us.

"I'm not talking to some kid," I say. "I'll talk to whoever is in charge."

"You'll talk to me, or you'll talk to no one."

"Don't play with me," I say, pushing Sebastien toward him and nearly sending him stumbling to the ground. Only my grip on his arm keeps him from falling. "Do you have any idea who this is?"

"What does it matter?" the Traveler says, taking care to keep a safe distance between us. "You're the one we want."

"You're a fool, then," I say. "I'm nobody, just a sub-Regent in a false universe. This is the Adjudicator."

I am speaking loudly, hoping to draw out any other members of the team who might be nearby and staying out of sight. None emerge.

The Traveler takes his eyes from me to look at Sebastien, trying to see if he recognizes him from one of the dossiers they will have been given before coming across. It is only for a split second, but it is all the time I need. I shove Sebastien hard again, sending him sprawling into the Traveler, who tries to dodge out of the way. His eyes are not on me as he does so, and I leap at him, landing a blow on his temple that leaves him stunned and blinking. Sebastien lets his momentum carry him forward into the Traveler, toppling him to the ground and sprawling over him.

"Get his weapon," I say, as I swing with all my might, punching the Traveler in the head again. I feel bone give way beneath my hand and the man gives a terrible cry of pain.

Sebastien manages to tear the pulse revolver from his hands and kneels over the Traveler, staring at the weapon, his hands shaking.

"Give it to me," I say, and he hands it over. I help him to his feet, supporting him as he continues to stare at the writhing form of the Traveler, whose piteous cries are still filling the room. I raise the weapon and shoot him, even as Sebastien cries out. The Traveler goes still and silent and the blood drains from Sebastien's face.

"Why did you do that?" he says.

"He's not dead," I say, already moving toward the lower levels. "Come on. We don't have much time."

The second member of the team is coming to the stairs as I start down. I shoot him before he has time to raise his weapon. Behind me I can hear Sebastien's breathing coming in gasps.

"Slow down. Take each breath," I say, continuing down the stairs. "They'll be fine. It's just a pulse."

I don't wait to see if he follows me, heading into the corridor below, which is empty and unchanged from when I last saw it. The extraction team died here, but their bodies were removed by the Travelers. I don't have time to think about their deaths and my part in it. I continue on, heading back along hallways I did not look upon the last time I was here, using Aeida's memories to guide me.

The remaining four Black Robes will be aware of our entry, and when both of their agents fail to respond to communication, they will begin to move back through the tunnels. I have ten minutes, fifteen at the most, to get to the transfer room and set the parameters. It will be three by then, and whoever is on the other side will be expecting me.

The corridors are empty, but I keep the pulse weapon ready. Sebastien follows behind me, his breathing still heavy but under control. That is good, for he still has a part to play if I am to make good on my escape.

We are in the Acolytes' section of the compound, where they did their nefarious work on Aeida, myself, and Ana, among others. I can't bear to look at the sealed doors for fear that the memories of my time here will overwhelm me. My hands are shaking and Aeida's despair, to say nothing of my own, is nearly all-consuming. I force myself to go on, aware of the seconds and minutes slipping from my grasp. I can afford no hesitation, no doubts or second thoughts. Not now.

The corridor I am following opens up into a broad, spherical room with a tall ceiling, the walls lined with equipment. This is the nerve center of the Watchers' Order, where Lasinha and I, and the Acolytes, managed the transfers of hundreds of individuals across universes, all without the Society of Travelers knowing what it was we were about. Here we would piggyback on the Society transfers, disguising our own in their signals. With the equipment here, we were able to send and receive multiple people across universes in the same transfer.

Very few in the Society have access to such equipment, and I am somewhat surprised to see it all intact still. The Watchers' Order would have already scavenged every piece for its own use. But the Society is evidently unconcerned, or at least this team of Black Robes is. Unless they have disabled the equipment through some method I am unaware of, everything appears to be in working order.

The room is dark, the equipment silent, without the telltale hum of electronics. I wonder if the defenses I enacted cut the power to this room to ensure no attacking force could use it against whoever was in the compound. Or perhaps the Travelers shut the power off. Did they even make it to this room? How much time have they had to investigate the compound? I have been their goal; all of this is secondary. Or so I hope.

I find the fuse box and flip everything on, and see, to my immense relief, lights on all the equipment blinking to life. The computer to control the transfer equipment starts its boot-up processes as I count the seconds, unable to stop myself from glancing back down the corridor. Sebastien wanders about the room, staring at all the equipment, both strange and yet familiar looking, all the blood gone from his face. The channel indicators begin to blink at random as the transfer device warms. That will take five minutes at least, and then I have to synchronize the channels. Each second I stand waiting seems an impossible delay.

When the computer is ready, I begin to type in the transfer details. There will be two transfers, one that the Society will see and respond to, and the other, hidden within the first's signal, will take me to my compatriots. That is the plan, at least. The Travelers will notice the second transfer eventually, because, according to the message from the other side, they don't have a counterbalance to send across to further disguise it. But it should buy us enough time to make our escape from the transfer point. From there I will have to somehow find my way through my world, with the Seeker on my trail, for Aeida's body will be like a beacon for him there.

Sebastien is watching my preparations with suspicion. "What are you doing?" he whispers, as though fearing to disturb the quiet.

"Setting up the transfer," I reply. "Go down the hallway a bit and listen for anyone coming. But stay in sight."

He looks as though he wants to argue with me, but instead he turns and heads up the corridor and stands listening, glancing back at me from time to time. I ignore him. There is too much to do, too much to prepare, and not enough time to do it all. The transfer batteries seem to be taking forever to warm properly, the lights still blinking asynchronously.

My hands refuse to type the transfer details in, no matter how many times I try. There are mistakes, mis-pressed buttons, and other stumbles. Aeida seems to have risen up against me. I can feel him trying to seize my body and thwart my designs. It takes all my strength of will to steady my fingers and enter the transfer numbers.

At last the lights begin to flash in a recognizable

pattern, moving from green to blue. The sight of them makes me shudder in fear, even as I feel a jolt of exhilaration that I have managed this feat. I am going to escape this world, this prison, and reclaim all that is mine. And I will see Molijc pay for what he has done.

A hissed cry from Sebastien interrupts my thoughts. He is waving desperately at me to get my attention. When I turn to look at him, he points down the hallway, letting me know he has heard something. I motion for him to return and he comes at a run.

"I can hear them coming," he says as he approaches.

I ignore him, my eyes focused on the lights as they move nearer and nearer to synchronicity. When the pattern is almost there and I can sense the air around us beginning to change, I lead Sebastien to the center of the room.

"When you can see the other side, go through," I say. There is a shout behind us, and we both glance behind, but there is no one yet in sight. "Whatever happens," I say, "you have to go through."

Sebastien nods and we both turn to watch the room. As we do, I can see the other side beginning to take form. There is a room, not unlike this one, well lit, with the indistinct forms of a few individuals hunched over consoles.

"Five seconds and you walk," I say as footsteps begin to sound behind us.

Sebastien nods, his face twisted into a hard grimace. I glance over at the lights and see that the pattern has formed and held. The other side is clear, almost as if we are all in the same room.

"Now," I say.

Just as I speak, there is an echo from a pulse revolver and Sebastien collapses to the floor. I whirl, returning fire wildly, and see the approaching Travelers scatter to the ground. Still firing my weapon, I drag Sebastien's limp form and start toward the other side.

The Travelers are scrambling forward, trying to stay

away from my shots, while returning fire. I manage to hit one of their number, but, somehow, all their returning volleys miss me. I am blessed by De Gofroy. Adrenaline steadies my hands and I fire again and again, sending the Black Robes back.

As I come near the channel, the air feels electric, sending the hair on my arms alight. The faces of those on the other side are now clear and visible, a mixture of expressions and warring emotions flashing across them as I approach. Some of them begin to move in anticipation of my crossing. I come as close to the channel's edge as I dare and then shove Sebastien forward, sending him across and through. I have the satisfaction of seeing surprise ripple across their faces before the channel disappears and the second one materializes in its absence.

"Aeida," I hear behind me, along with the sour hiss of a pulse singeing the air beside me.

It is the last thing I hear in that universe as I step into the channel and go across.

TWO:

UAYEB

11

"We exist in a broken universe. Our very beings are shattered into an endless number of selves, stretched across all the universes of existence. The Society of Travelers, that plague upon all our souls, has dedicated itself to thwarting any attempt to reach across the universes, to unite our disparate beings. We must ask ourselves why that would be. Why would the Society, and its supporters in what remains of our feeble governments, be so set upon the dividing us from ourselves?

"Power, of course. Humanity is defined by two needs: the need to propagate and the need for the self to survive. We all know that instinctively. It is something that all philosophies and religions grapple with in some form of another. Many will create a strange orthodoxy to hide their own fundamental needs. But when you lay anyone bare, there it is. Or is it?

"Why do we all feel so empty? Why do even the most powerful and influential among us—and some of you gathered here today are among the most successful in your own fields—why do we all feel this ennui, this emptiness at the heart of everything we do? We know that none of this in the end matters. Christianity, Islam, Buddhism, all the others...they pretended to offer explanations. But when the true nature of the universe, that it was many, was revealed, they all faded away. Curiosities of another age. We all felt the cataclysms of that fading away. We all bear the scars. Many of us fought in those wars. I was one of them. I would have died, if not for this revelation."

De Gofroy paused, his eyes scanning the room, looking at the faces turned up at his. I felt an electricity run through me as his gaze lit upon mine, our eyes linking for an instant before he cast on. The hush as we all waited for him to continue had its own energy. Two hundred souls awaiting release. There was sweat glistening upon his forehead I could see from where I sat. He took a sip of water and continued.

"What does matter? Ourselves. Our souls. We know what emptiness is, that sense that there is more out there. It is because we are pieces, vessels for a part of a greater whole. We sense that greater whole, those millions out there who we are cut off from, who we yearn to be rejoined with. The Society will tell you the sanctity of the universes is absolute, yet they cross them daily. The Society will tell you that each of these others is its own being, unique and inviolate. I can tell you that is a lie.

"The Protocols I have developed, along with the Acolytes who have worked so tirelessly with me to bring this to fruition, will reveal the world to you as it is. You will sense those millions of souls; they will be revealed to you in all their glory. Why will you be able to sense those other *yous* in the other universes? Because you are connected to all of them. You are all Regents for a greater soul, a greater being. That being, your true and ultimate self, resides in another place. The Impossible Universe, I call it. The Society hates that. Their physicists will tell you that its existence precludes its impossibility. They do not understand.

"These millions of universes did not simply come into being. Something created them. These connections that we can sense, that the Protocols reveal to you on a level you cannot truly imagine, they are there for a reason. Our true selves left them there. They left them there so that we could find a way to them, to reunite and become our true selves. It is our duty as souls, as beings, to do this."

The electricity I had felt when De Gofroy had glanced at me returned anew at his words. I could sense everyone else feeling the same chord chiming within their minds.

"Remember the two needs. To survive and to propagate. Beneath them lies a far greater need, one that shapes and forms those two. The need to find our true selves." He paused again to scan the room.

"I am not the only one who understood these truths, as I have shown. The Mayans understood. It is there for anyone to see in their codexes, and most especially in their calendar. Anthropologists and archaeologists have long argued about the significance of that year when the long and short calendars coincide. Many have said that it signaled the end of one world and the beginning of another. As I have shown, the Mayans understood better even than we the nature of the universes, the nature of the battle we face every day. They knew there were times when the universes were pulled apart and times when they were drawn together, and in those moments there is a possibility that we must be ready to seize, of setting our beings to right. As we all know, we are on the precipice of such a moment.

"Make no mistake: we are at war. This is a war that has gone on for millennia, across all the universes. Every battle that has been fought on this earth, including the ones so many of us experienced not so long ago, has been a shadow war, just as we are shadows of our true selves. The true war is to reunite our true selves. To become. Not for power, not for greed, as our Society friends would have it. They will corrupt our governments, corrupt our universes. We will do it for ourselves. That is what I ask of all our initiates. To do this for yourself."

De Gofroy smiled. I looked around. Many of those gathered were staring in open-mouthed awe. Some were actually weeping, including, I realized as I touched my cheeks, myself.

I shifted uncomfortably in the chair where the Acolyte had gestured for me to sit. It looked like a dentist's chair, high-backed and capable of reclining, and like a dentist's chair it was always too tall or too deep for me to ever settle myself. Perhaps it was just the thought of the procedure that was to follow that made me uncomfortable more than the chair itself, although the straps dangling near my head, ankles, and wrists did nothing to settle my nerves. The silence of the Acolyte, who had barely acknowledged my presence, was disquieting as well. His focus was on a screen that faced away from me, to which he was making adjustments. As he did so, an orb—the Eye, I knew it was called—emitted what sounded like a sigh and began to float up from a table behind him.

The Eye was difficult to look at as it floated above me, rotating as if it were a planet, and emitting a rasping sound that I could have sworn was a breath. I resisted the urge to shudder. There were all sorts of stories about the creation of the Eye. De Gofroy said it had come to him in a vision as he had conducted the Protocols upon himself, and he had worked with the Acolytes to construct and perfect it.

Those who attacked the Church of the Regents, and there were many who did, claimed he and the Acolytes had stolen the technology from the Seekers' Guild. There was a whiff of truth to that rumor, for in seeing it, there could be no doubt the Eye was constructed from the same bio-technology the Seekers used to build their eyes. And there was no denying that the Acolytes' Guild had longstanding connections with the Seekers, though they had been severed when De Gofroy had convinced them to join his movement.

The break with the Seekers and the formation of a new

alliance with the Church of the Regents was shrouded in mystery as well, with the Acolytes having no obvious motive, beyond the faith itself, to abandon so profitable an association. The Society was mostly responsible for these lies, seeking to discredit the Acolytes and our faith. The Travelers would stop at nothing to secure their control of the passages between the universes, whether it was ensuring that governments were compliant, or placing spies within the midst of the Regent Church. That alone warranted the secrecy surrounding the Acolytes, the Eye and the Protocols. The faith itself was at stake.

As I tried not to contemplate the Eye, a well-dressed Regent entered the room, nodding familiarly at the Acolyte, who did not even glance up from the screen. He sat down beside me and smiled. "Hello. You must be Laila Johar. My name is Gabriel Arajuano. I'll be running your Protocols today."

I tried to return his smile but was unable to. It was a shock to realize that I recognized his name. He was one of De Gofroy's High Regents, a long-serving member of the faith. The Eye and the mute Acolyte had made me nervous enough about the Protocols, but the prospect of one of the High Regents running it was overwhelming. I had been an initiate for a year, as was normal, showing no particular promise I thought. Why had I been chosen for such an honor?

As if he knew the question I was asking, the High Regent put a reassuring hand on my shoulder. "The Grand Regent has noticed you. He thinks you will be a fine vessel and he wants a steady hand guiding your Protocols."

"Thank you," I managed to say.

"Shall we begin?" Arajuano said, looking at the Acolyte, who glanced up from his screen and nodded. "Good."

He went over to the table where the orb had risen from and retrieved a syringe, filled with a liquid that seemed to shift in color from blue to green as he held it up to the light. "This," he said, as he sat beside me again and rolled up my sleeve, "is just to help you achieve a state where you are more receptive to the Protocols. Once you've gone through it, you will find that you are able to achieve this state without the aid of this. But for the first time it is a necessity."

He looked at me to see if I was ready, and when I nodded he injected me. "We'll give it a few minutes," he said, and began to attach the straps.

Once that was done, he pressed a button on the chair and it reclined until I was lying straight back. I began to feel the effects of the injection almost immediately, a sort of anesthesia numbing my body while my mind remained alert. Arajuano pressed the button again and the chair began to lift up until I was held up perpendicular to the floor, face to face with the Eye. My instinct was to look away, but the strap did not allow me to.

Arajuano stood and moved to stand behind the Acolyte, his eyes on the screen. "First, I would like you to tell me about your parents," he said.

I answered with my usual evasions, but Arajuano allowed me no escape. He persisted in his questions, until I had revealed all of my broken life to this point to him. I was sobbing, tears streaming down my face. He asked me the same questions again, having me repeat my answers, until a kind of euphoria seized me. I was still staring at the implacable Eye as it rotated before me, but the questions from the High Regent began to sound distant, and though I kept answering them, a part of me stepped outside the bounds of my body. I was in the Eye looking upon myself in the chair. As the Eye rotated I saw not only my being strapped to the chair, but other versions of myself in other universes. Fragments only, glimpses of other lives that might have been mine.

There I was walking down the street in Medicine Hat toward the home where my parents still lived. There I was strung out and scarred, surrounded by refuse and despair. There I was being drawn into the embrace of a man. There

I was holding the hand of my child. On and on it went, a vast array of possibility. As it continued, I began to feel the connections that bound us, the invisible lines that still tethered us together even in these divided universes, despite all that had been done to tear us apart. I felt whole and complete for the first time.

At some point I realized that the questions had stopped and the Acolyte had left the room, the orb now settled back on its table. I was slumped into the chair, the straps loosened, a little drool touching the corner of my mouth. Arajuano was looming over me, smiling as he watched me emerge from whatever state I had been in.

"Welcome, Regent, to the One True Faith," he said, and extended a hand to me.

Initiates of the new faith were housed in the dormitories on the old university campus in Calgary, which De Gofroy had purchased from the city to establish as his base ten years earlier during the first florescence of the faith. It had been a tumultuous time, little of which I remembered, following the end of two decades of hostilities and the crumbling of institutions that had seemed impregnable. All because of the revelation of the multiverse and the Society of Travelers establishing their foothold in this world. Economies had been rewritten as well, leaving the oil-centric one of Alberta destitute for a time. Ripe ground for a new faith, which was why De Gofroy had chosen it.

In the years that followed, most of the campus buildings had been repurposed to support the work of the Church. The central towers had been remodeled to house the Hierarchy, those of the church who saw to its day-to-day running. The Acolytes had taken over the old engineering and science buildings, using the labs to continue their work in refining the Protocols and the Eye. There were whispers of other secret projects, as well, and the buildings were off-limits to all but the Acolytes and the elite of the Hierarchy. The other buildings had been given to the other arms of the faith: the Proselytizers and the Protectors. One worked to bring in new initiates, while the other worked to ensure that those who had joined the faith observed the tenets set out by De Gofroy.

As new initiates we were expected to attend a weekly lecture, usually given by De Gofroy, or one of his chosen lieutenants, in addition to being trained to conduct Protocols ourselves, as well as the other practices De Gofroy had outlined to connect us to our other Regent selves. The goal being to transmit our souls to the other universes, to gather ourselves in order to seek out the Impossible Universe.

Most initiates would leave after they achieved what was called the Second Order of the Protocols—being able to conduct a Protocol on others or oneself, without the aid of the Eye—returning to their lives while observing the tenets of the faith. For some of us, the faith was all, and we stayed on to study at the feet of the Grand Regent and to serve him and the Church. The fate of our beings and the universes themselves were at stake, after all, and the faith needed dedicated soldiers to serve.

The three years I spent ascending to the Second Order were among the happiest days of my life, belief giving me an identity I had long lacked, a solidity to my sense of self. There was also a cohort of us who studied and supported each other through the Protocol orders. Hector and Opal were both there, as was a middle-aged veteran, Morris Loverne, who adopted me as a sort of daughter. Others passed through or remained on the periphery, but all were welcome. I embraced them all, dedicating myself to existing in the here and now.

It was at one of De Gofroy's lectures that I first noticed a man, standing off to the side of the room, looking over the assembled initiates. Though he was near my age, he seemed much more sure of himself, possessed of a belief that made mine seem like a pale shadow. He had an easy, assured smile he wore as a guard against revealing any of his thoughts.

After that first time, I noticed him regularly attending the lectures and even some of the other classes I took, although he never participated, simply observing us with his watchful eyes. In spite of that, I was drawn to him, and I could tell others were as well. It was not just his perfectly styled hair, or his easy and unintimidating good looks. He had an innate charisma to him.

I asked Opal about him one day, and she smiled in a way that told me that she too was compelled by him. "That's Lasinha," she said. "He's one of De Gofroy's favorites, apparently. He's a Protector. Guardian of the faith."

One day he was waiting for me as I came out of one of my classes, materializing beside me as I walked down the hallway with Morris and Hector.

"Please come with me," he said, giving me a reassuring smile that somehow had the opposite effect on me. I could feel Morris and Hector go stiff beside me, which only increased my disquiet, but I followed Lasinha without question. I did not dare to defy a Protector.

He led me along a hallway through to one of the Hierarchy buildings. The corridors there were quiet, as opposed to those where the initiates spent their days, all the doors closed, which only added to my sense of impending doom. Lasinha stopped before one of the closed doors and unlocked it, ushering me in, and I found myself in what I realized was his office. There was a small desk with two chairs and a narrow window overlooking the campus' central courtyard.

Lasinha sat in one of the chairs, gesturing for me to do the same. His pants, I noticed, were finely tailored, fitting him perfectly, while his shirt was crisp and expensive looking. For some reason this made me even more uncomfortable, especially when I considered my own five dollar blouse and jeans.

"You have taken to the tenets of our faith quickly," he said, his stare intense.

"I hope so," I said, feeling myself go flush.

"Do no doubt it. I have spoken to your other instructors and they tell me much the same." He smiled, and I felt a mixture of excitement and trepidation. Why was this Protector spending so much time investigating me?

"I wonder," he continued, "what your thoughts are about taking a place amongst us in the Church when you have completed your courses. A mind like yours, with such capacity and enthusiasm, would be wasted outside these walls. Those are suitable paths, of course, for any sub-Regent. But you, I think, could be much more. The Third Order calls to you. The Grand Regent feels the same way."

He added the last almost casually, as though it were an afterthought, but I could hardly breathe, let alone find the words to respond. "I had not thought of it," I managed to say at last.

He smiled. "But you are interested, yes?" I nodded, and he said, "Good. Now is the time to think about such things, before paths are set."

"Of course," I said, still finding it difficult to fully comprehend the fact that the Grand Regent was not only aware of my existence but had talked about me with Lasinha.

"Good. For now, we would like you to do something for us," Lasinha said. The way he said it implied that the request was not his, but the Grand Regent's. "If you prove yourself capable here, your path will be set."

I nodded. "Of course. Anything you want."

"Wonderful," he said, standing up and indicating that it was time for me to go. "Someone will speak with you about it tomorrow and go over the details. Her name is Ana."

12

The blouse and skirt I had on were conservative in look, though they fit a bit too tightly. Ana had said that was good, nodding with satisfaction at the swell of my breasts in a way that took my breath away. Her clothes seemed to suit her better, though it was hard to imagine anything that would detract from her beauty. We had only been working together a few weeks and already I was hopelessly infatuated with her. She knew, I think; that was likely the plan in assigning us both to this task. Her job was not only to carry out this project, but to watch and assess me, bind me to the Church.

She was also Gabriel Arajuano's daughter, had been born into this faith, which was intimidating in its own way. De Gofroy had held her on his knee when she was a child.

"Are you ready?" she said, noticing that I was wiping the palm of my hand on my skirt. I took a deep breath and nodded. "It'll be fine," she said. "Just act like you should be there. No one will question us."

I attempted a smile, though I felt none of her confidence. We had spent the past three weeks establishing our bona fides as members of the International Trans-Universe Commission, a nonexistent body of experts on the ethics of transporting between the many universes. Though the Society of Travelers had managed to establish a monopoly in this universe and untold numbers of others, there was always tension between them and various governments over who actually had authority within their territories. Given their technology, and the need they had created for it, and the fact that only they could conclusively prove whether any of their agents were in fact of this universe and thus beholden to the laws of whatever state they found themselves in, the Travelers usually won such disputes. And if they failed to, they were not above putting moles in organizations or removing governments that were not properly compliant.

There was always hope, though, that some government would grow brazen enough to stand up to the Society and seize their facilities. The latest to make noises to that effect was the Independent Kingdom of Scotland, and so we had come to Edinburgh, purporting to represent a commission of the world's top physicists and other scientists opposed to the Society, willing to support their efforts at what we called Universal Independence.

We somehow had a meeting arranged with two junior ministers and the prime minister's chief of staff, and we, two women barely in their twenties, were to convince them to throw aside their careers and potentially their lives, and that the world would be at their side. It could not work, it was impossible, yet De Gofroy seemed convinced. He had been reviewing our plan every step of the way, I had been told, providing suggestions to Lasinha and Ana.

An aide stepped out of the conference room to where Ana and I were waiting, interrupting my thoughts. "They will see you now," he said, smiling brightly at Ana.

She returned his smile and I felt a pang of jealousy, which I had to smother. These next moments would be far too important to be distracted by petty emotions. We both strode into the room and introduced ourselves to the chief of staff and the junior ministers. I considered it a miracle they did not throw us out as soon as they laid eyes upon us.

Instead the chief of staff gestured for everyone to sit. "Well, I think we have a lot to discuss, so let's get started, shall we?"

Ana caught my eye as I settled into one of the chairs opposite the three government representatives, as if to say, "See, didn't I tell you?"

A hand on my shoulder pulled me from the dreams I had been embroiled in, the contents of which vanished as sleep ebbed from my mind, never to be reconstituted. I could smell Ana, feel her breath upon my neck, and for a tantalizing moment I was lost in a reverie of desire, imagining her moist lips finding my own. That fantasy was quickly snuffed out as Ana said in a low voice, "We have to go. We've been blown."

My mouth was dry and I was fully awake. I sat up in bed peering at the outlines of her body through the darkness. She was already dressed, I saw, and I got out of bed and struggled into my clothes.

"What's happened?" I said in my normal voice, drawing a sharp look of concern from her. She pointed at the door and raised a finger to her lips.

I nodded, thankful that the darkness did not show my face flushing, and set about putting on my clothes as quickly and quietly as possible. I avoided the ill-fitting skirt and blouse, opting for my usual uniform of dark jeans, a shirt, and a loose-fitting jacket. When I was ready, Ana motioned for me to follow her, and led the way to the door connecting our hotel room to the next. She had the key, or had already picked the lock, and we slipped within and crossed to the next door. Here Ana slipped something from one of her pockets and worked with painstaking care at the lock until it clicked, while I looked back across the darkened room.

It was empty, but the next room was not. I could just

make out the swells of prone bodies on both beds, their steady breathing unbroken for the moment as we moved with extreme caution to the adjoining door. Ana worked her magic on this door as well, and we stepped into another room just as its inhabitant stepped out of the bathroom. I did not even have time to see whether it was a man or a woman before Ana had taken hold of the person and pinched off their airways until they slumped to the ground unconscious. All of it had been done without making a sound.

I had to remind myself to breathe as Ana went to the main door and peered out into the hallway, before motioning for me to follow her. The corridor outside was empty, which meant that whoever had been outside our room was now inside and discovering that we had fled. In spite of that, Ana walked along calmly until she came to the stairwell and we started down the four flights of stairs. I desperately wanted to ask what had happened—how had we been blown and how had she gotten word of it—but I kept my counsel. Time enough for questions once we had made good our escape.

We avoided the lobby, heading for the parking garage, and there Ana deposited her phone in the garbage and motioned for me to do the same. She went to the nearest car and, using the same device she had on the hotel doors, unlocked and started it. We drove out of the garage—with me expecting cars to appear, cutting off our exit or in pursuit—and onto the street without incident, drifting off into the city. Only when we were three blocks away and, I thought, in the free and clear, did I venture to speak.

"What happened?"

"I don't know. De Gofroy messaged me that we were blown and had to get out. It's the Society." It was only with those words that I registered the panic in her voice, which she had done her best to hide. "We've got an hour, at best, to get out of here."

I glanced at her, fighting to control my own emotions.

"How do we get out?"

"De Gofroy sent one of the Church's airships. It's not registered to us, so the Society shouldn't recognize it. We just need to get to the airport."

The thought of slipping through an airport undetected was daunting. I checked my jacket pocket for my passport.

"No good," Ana said. "Those will be on their watch list. I've got backups on me."

We had no issue getting through the airport, to my surprise and relief. None of the Independent Kingdom's officials gave us so much as a second glance as we passed through security to the dock where the airship was berthed. Lasinha was there, grim-faced and cursing, to welcome us aboard. There was some nervousness among the crew even after we had boarded and the vessel had cast off, as if they half expected the Travelers to conduct a midair raid. None materialized, and we were soon out over the channel and on our way to France and destinations further south.

The airship docked again in the free city of Tangiers, a neutral port where we knew the Society would give us no trouble. There we took on two passengers: the Grand Regent and a young man with a familiar face whose name I would come to know only too well—Dejian Molijc.

He was of Slavic extraction, to judge by his features, with dark hair and startling blue eyes that seemed to hold both everything and nothing of the man. Aside from his eyes, he was an unassuming figure, drifting into the background whenever others were around. He was near my age, if I had to guess, and in the days that followed I noticed him looking at me several times in a way I understood. I was not interested and nothing came of it.

Despite the utter failure of our enterprise, the Grand Regent was in fine spirits, congratulating both Ana and I for our work. "We'll keep those bastards in the Society guessing, won't we?" he said on more than one occasion. I had my doubts that they would be much concerned, but I said nothing of the kind to anyone.

We stayed three weeks in Tangiers to no apparent end that I was aware of, though Lasinha was absent somewhere in the city at various junctures. I rarely left the airship, preferring to spend my time with Dejian Molijc and Ana at De Gofroy's feet. Here, far from the Church campus, he was in an expansive mood, offering continuous disquisitions on the faith and our place in it, as well as supervising us as we ran Protocols on each other. I was left giddy to be given such an opportunity, to be so near the Grand Regent, a recipient of his wisdom.

Though he knew Ana the best of us all, he was quite distant toward her, clearly favoring both Molijc and I. She did her best to hide it, but I could tell that his coldness hurt her. I wondered if he in fact blamed her for the failure of the mission. No doubt Ana did as well. One night, as I was returning from the city, I spotted her on the airfield, ducked behind some equipment away from the ship. As I was approaching to say hello and see what she was doing, one of the tower lights swung by, catching her in its glow, and I saw that her face was streaked with tears.

"What's the matter?" I said, rushing to her side. Though I desperately wanted to put a consoling hand upon her, I sensed that my touch would not be welcome.

"It's nothing," she said. "Stupid to think it wouldn't happen to me."

"He can't blame you for what happened," I said. "It wasn't your fault."

"That's not it," she said, with a sad smile. "You'll find out soon enough. Your time will come. He likes to play favorites among the disciples."

I nodded, unsure of what to say. It did not match with the De Gofroy I knew, but Ana had been with the Church far longer than I, so I left our conversation at that, returning to the airship.

After Tangiers we went to Madagascar for a time, and

then on to Goa. From there it was Singapore and Bangkok, our journey stretching to months. The exact purpose of these stops, and indeed our whole journey, was not shared with me. Nor was I told how long we were all to remain with the Grand Regent here. I did not care; I was simply thrilled to be included in any capacity. Never in my life had I dreamed I would be able to see as much of the world as I had in these last weeks.

Things changed as we grew nearer to Calgary and the Church's home, De Gofroy withdrawing from his three disciples. There were no more long discussions on the faith deep into the night, no more guiding of our Protocol sessions. He began to spend most of his time with Lasinha or one of his lieutenants, carrying on whispered discussions that the rest of us were not privy to. He became haggard and drawn, his eyes red from lack of sleep, seeming to age years in a matter of days. It was an unsettling transformation.

In Osaka, the day before we were set to leave for Calgary after nearly a year on the road, he disappeared, throwing the whole vessel into chaos, everyone fearing that the Society had seized him. Lasinha deputized me to assist him in the search, sending Molijc and Ana off together as well. Instead of conducting a search, though, Lasinha took me on the train to a small apartment complex on the city's edge and let me into one of the narrow, sparsely furnished apartments, telling me to wait. For an hour I paced the confines of the apartment's single room, going from the door to the window overlooking the street below to see if there was any sign of anyone.

I began to fear that De Gofroy's absence had been a ruse to draw me away from the vessel so that I could be abandoned here, though why they would do that I could not say. Nor could I begin to divine what I might have done wrong. Perhaps our failure in Edinburgh had resulted in more dire consequences than I was aware of.

I was well into a second hour of worry, and beginning

to contemplate leaving the apartment and returning to the airfield to see if in fact my worst fears had been realized, when there was a knock at the door. Before I could answer it, Lasinha opened it and stepped aside, allowing the Grand Regent to enter. He was haggard and unshaven, and looked as though he had been to battle with demons I could not begin to imagine. He sat in a chair and gestured for me to sit on the sofa opposite him. Lasinha shut the door and hovered behind the Grand Regent, moving at times to glance out the window at the street below.

I kept my face still, taking care not to show any of my agitation. De Gofroy put a finger to his lips in distracted thought, before bringing his attention to me. "You performed admirably in Edinburgh, I am given to understand," the Grand Regent said.

"I did what I could," I said in a neutral tone.

"Yes. A pity how it all turned out, but that couldn't be helped. Now I have another task to entrust you with. Are you a faithful vessel, Laila?"

"Yes," I said. "I have dedicated my soul to the Church."

"Indeed," De Gofroy said. "You do not realize, I am sure, how precarious our faith is. We are still a young religion, as these things are measured, and outsiders still question our belief. More than that, they are threatened by our existence."

He paused for a moment, as though expecting me to say something. "Why would they be threatened by us?"

"Because we reveal the truth behind their lies."

"The Society of Travelers," I said.

It was Lasinha who spoke next. "Yes. They have tried to place agents among the evangelized in the past, so we always review those new to the faith very closely."

He put a strange emphasis on the word *closely*, and I felt my mouth go dry. What had they found about me?

"Don't worry," De Gofroy said. "We have no doubts as to your faith or provenance."

"No," Lasinha said. "We are certain of you. There are others, though, whose pasts are unclear, shall we say. We want your help in ascertaining their allegiances."

I nodded. This was the sort of thing the Protectors would do, I realized, but I was still not entirely comfortable with the idea of spying on fellow Regents.

"It must be done," De Gofroy said, as if he understood my thoughts. "Recent events have made it plain that there are agents within our midst, hence our precautions in meeting you today. Before we proceed I must be certain of everyone's loyalty. The next years will decide the fate of the Church."

I watched as Lasinha went again to the window to look at the street, unsure what to say to all this. De Gofroy seemed lost in thought.

Lasinha turned back to me and said, "It is Molijc we are concerned about."

I could not disguise my shock. All those evenings with the three of us, and all along De Gofroy had been harboring suspicions about Dejian. It did not seem possible.

"I have noticed that he has taken an interest in you," De Gofroy said, causing me to flush. "I would like you to cultivate it. Get close to him. Get to know him."

"And let us know what happens," Lasinha said.

I considered this for a moment, palpably aware of both their gazes. "Why do you want me to do this?"

De Gofroy spoke. "You understand the Protocols in a way few do. If his belief is a pretense, you will be able to see it."

"And that is all you want?" I said, my voice trembling.

"That is all," De Gofroy said. He gave me a sad smile. "It is an ugly thing, but necessary if we are to survive. We must use the vessels we have at hand, and you are a fine vessel. Will you do this for the faith?"

It was no request, no matter how he phrased it, no matter how kindly he looked. If I refused now, I could never hope to join the Hierarchy and become a Protector. I would be set aside and another disciple would be found. What path did I seek? I did not know, only that I had yearned for more and that the Church had provided it for me.

"I will," I said.

De Gofroy nodded, as though he had expected my answer. "Go with Lasinha," he said, waving his hand. "He will tell you more. And do not speak of this with anyone."

13

After we returned to Calgary and the campus, Molijc and I became inseparable in the year that followed. It seemed he was infatuated with me and I had just been oblivious, too caught up in my own obsession with Ana to notice. I had no need to find excuses to spend time around him, he found them for me. I felt a certain amount of guilt at leading him on as I did, pretending interest that wasn't really there, all so that I could report what happened to Lasinha, as well as my own impressions.

I never spoke to De Gofroy about Dejian after our secret audience. He seemed to recover his spirits upon our return to the campus, throwing himself into lectures of the new initiates. He included both Dejian and I, and sometimes Ana, in these efforts. Molijc in particular seemed to thrive in such a setting. He demonstrated himself to be a compelling speaker and, in spite of what the Grand Regent had said to me, he was especially skilled at running Protocols. It seemed clear he was headed for a role as an Adjudicator, if not higher, within the Hierarchy.

It was clear that my role was to be in the shadows, as a Protector of the faith. Not only was I observing Molijc, Ana and I were assigned to other projects that struck De

Gofroy's fancy. These included spying on reporters who wrote false articles about the faith and trying to plant stories in the press about the evils of the Society. We also helped to subvert an investigation by the Calgary police into the Church, caused by apostates angry that they had been led astray by De Gofroy. Both Ana and I at various points dated the lead officers on the case and managed to discover that they were wiretapping the Grand Regent and most of the Hierarchy as they searched for evidence of tax violations.

Though I was not in the eye of the faithful, as De Gofroy and Molijc were, it was still gratifying to be thwarting attempts to persecute our faith, even if my efforts had to, by necessity, be unacknowledged. My compensation was that it gave me the opportunity to be closer to Ana. My longing for her seemed to grow by the day. She seemed oblivious to my desires, always friendly and genuine but never more than that, careful to keep a distance between us. It pained me greatly, yet I would still find excuses for us to be together, hoping against hope that she would somehow change her mind, even as I knew it was a fool's game.

Molijc must have been feeling the same about me, for no matter how much he contrived to spend time in my presence, I remained unyielding. Yet I had to continue to see him—it was my duty as a Protector. Part of me wondered if, in fact, Ana's friendship with me was of a similar sort, prescribed by Lasinha and the Grand Regent. It was an unsettling thought.

Most days, when I was not off campus on some other task for the Church, Molijc and I would meet for coffee in the morning between his Protocol sessions. We would talk of anything: our faith, how we had come to the Church, and what we hoped to achieve within it. He was easy to talk to, having that ability to look at you and make you feel as though you were the only person in all existence. I found it discomfiting, for it always seemed to me like a mask, behind which his real person was hidden. There was an emptiness, an absence to him, for all his charm, though I could not put into words what that was.

One day, several months into our friendship, he said to me, "What do you think the faith would be without De Gofroy?"

"There is no faith without him. He was given the understanding. He could read the codexes."

We were speaking the Mayan dialect De Gofroy had said was derived from the language of our true selves. The Mayans, having understood the true nature of the universes and war for our true selves, were obviously more closely descended from our true beings than most souls on this planet. I found it a difficult tongue to master and still spoke haltingly, although Dejian had picked it up seemingly without effort.

De Gofroy wanted those in the Hierarchy to speak the language, not only because of its holy qualities, but because it would hopefully thwart any attempts to wiretap the Church. We had managed to place one of our own, a Mayan native of Guatemala, as the translator for the latest wiretap effort, which meant we could take the investigation in whatever direction we chose.

"But he will be gone someday," Dejian said. "Unless we can manage to unite our true beings. And if he does go, someone will have to take over for him."

"He isn't that old, really, and he's in good health," I said. "The next baktun is in seven years. That is our chance to unite the universes. He will be alive for that."

"Life takes many strange paths," Dejian said. "Faiths are at their weakest after the founder dies. That is when so many fall. We must be certain we prepare for that day."

I frowned, annoyed at his certainty and wondering why he was discussing such borderline heretical ideas with me. He knew I was a Protector. He must at least suspect I was reporting to someone about him. So who was this intended for, exactly?

He smiled, his mood changing like quicksilver. "Forget about it. It's not important. Just a stupid thought I had. Are you free this weekend? A few of us were going to head off campus for drinks."

I said I would go if I could, and the conversation turned to other matters. I reported what Molijc had said to Lasinha, who raised an eyebrow but offered no comment. He never shared his thoughts with me on what I reported, his expression remaining the same at all times, his lips curved into his perpetual smile.

Our conversation turned to a project Ana and I were to embark on, investigating an apostate who was spreading lies about the Church and De Gofroy, but as I went to go Lasinha called after me. "I would like to hear more about what our friend Dejian thinks about De Gofroy and the end of the Church."

I turned back, but he was already looking at the screen of his computer, apparently oblivious to my presence, so I left the room.

It was near the end of the night, when we all had consumed a little too much beer, that I foolishly decided to act on what Lasinha had asked of me. Molijc, Ana, and I were sitting at one end of the table with some other initiates engrossed in conversation at the other end. Ana had been distracted all evening, half smiling and miserable, trying desperately to put a good face on whatever was bothering her. She did not want to be here, but had come and now stayed out of obligation, whether to me or to whoever had asked her to watch me I could not say, but I turned my anger and frustration on Dejian.

"What did you mean about what you said the other day?"

He blinked, giving me a confused smile. "What do you mean?"

"You know. About the Grand Regent." My eyes bored into his.

"That was nothing. Just a thought, you know. It's... Well." He seemed confused for the moment.

"Look, you know the Church is my life, and it's yours too. And Ana's. We're not like the rest of these people. Most of these people will get to the Second Order and go about their lives." He waved his hand vaguely at the initiates who were with us. "This is everything for me. I have dedicated myself to this battle and to this faith, and I think you have too. Part of what that means is that we have to think about things that others can't or won't. I don't know about you, but I plan on being an important part of this Church going forward. A faithful vessel. And that means making hard decisions. You can't do that unless you're aware they might come. You can't do that unless you're prepared."

He began in a jovial tone, but by the end of his speech he was speaking with a fierceness that took me aback.

"What are you prepared for?" I said, trying and failing to say it in a lighthearted tone.

"Someone will have to be the Grand Regent when De Gofroy is gone," he said, staring deep into my eyes. "I want it to be me."

I excused myself and went to the bathroom, not knowing what to say. When I returned to our table, Dejian was deep in conversation with Ana. They both burst into laughter as I came to the table, and I felt a surge of jealousy that he could turn her mood so easily when I seemed helpless to do so. I wanted to turn the conversation back to what he had said, but the words failed me and we all returned to the campus, where I was unable to sleep.

As I lay there, my thoughts turbulent and what felt like a fever running through me, there was a knock at the door. I stumbled over, wondering who it could be at this hour. I opened the door and Lasinha stepped inside without a word. I closed the door after him, feeling every ounce of the beer I had drunk in my movements. He looked me up and down, and I was certain he was going to say something about my state of dishevelment. Instead, he simply nodded toward my closet. "Put some clothes on. The Grand Regent needs us."

14

Lasinha and I moved through the darkened buildings of the campus, neither of us speaking. My body still seemed sluggish and uncoordinated, and I was preoccupied with hiding this from him. He was oblivious to me, however. I had never seen him like this before. His ease and smile had vanished and all that remained was a naked tension, his features struck tight with it. His obvious anxiety, which he was no doubt working hard to contain, began to permeate my consciousness as well. Why had the Grand Regent summoned us at this hour?

We made our way, not to the Grand Regent's tower, the central building on campus, but to the Protectors' building where Lasinha worked. Once there we came to an elevator. Lasinha uttered a voice authorization and selected the fourth basement level. I had not known there was a basement in the building, let alone four levels to it. I felt a mixture of curiosity and trepidation as we descended, wondering what was hidden below and why I was being brought here in the dead of the night.

We exited the elevator into a sterile corridor with fluorescent hospital lighting. After two or three turns down other similar hallways, I began to be unsure of where I was or if I could find my way back should it become necessary. There was nothing to distinguish any of the corridors, each with doors at set intervals, all without any sign or indication of what went on within. The sameness, the absence of anything distinguishing at all, began to grow more and more disconcerting, my imagination giving bloom to all sorts of terrifying possibilities as to what these rooms were for. It was hard to breathe, and it felt as if the earth above were pressing down on me.

I had heard the rumors—we all had—of what happened to apostates and heretics when they left the Church. I had never given them any credence. Since I had joined the Church, many people I had known had come and gone, all without anything untoward happening, to my knowledge. Things were a little different for those in the Hierarchy, of course, especially given the always real possibility that the Society of Travelers had turned them from the faith. I was involved in efforts to thwart some of those disgruntled apostates from spreading lies about De Gofroy and the Church. It was necessary to protect the faith. That was not what these rooms were for, though; it seemed obvious. The secrecy and anonymity spoke to something much darker.

We made another turn down a corridor and were met by an ostentatiously dressed man who glared at us with arrogant disdain. He was waiting outside a door, muted grey like all the others, and without a word he ushered us within. The lights flickered on as we entered, revealing a room with bare walls and a narrow table at its center with chairs on either side. An interrogation room. I broke into an immediate sweat.

Lasinha had gone very still beside me, which told me that he had not expected this either. I followed his gaze to the far corner of the room, where there was another chair. A man sat on it, his arms tied behind his back, and a hood covering his head. He did not move, did not even seem to breathe. As I tried to absorb what I was seeing, our guide, the man in the powder-blue suit, left, closing the door behind him. I turned to look at Lasinha and saw the same fear and anguish I felt on his face, which only disturbed me more.

Ten minutes passed and then ten more, each more agonizing than the last. Both of us remained standing where we were, as though we were soldiers called to attention. My legs began to ache from remaining in one position for too long and I stared longingly at the chairs. I could not seem to stop sweating, my hands and back damp, though it was not warm. We were being watched, I was certain, our reactions judged, though I could not have said why.

At some point my fear was transformed into a righteous fury. What was going on here? Why was I being subjected to this? My breathing sounded ragged, as though I had been running, and I tried to force myself into a state of calm, closing my eyes. As I did, the door swung open and Powder Blue stepped within, followed by the Grand Regent. Both of them ignored us, De Gofroy going to sit at the table, placing his hands one atop the other on it, while Powder Blue went to stand before the hooded man.

"Do you have anything further to add to your testimony?" Powder Blue said in a clipped voice, at odds with his immaculate dress.

There was a long pause before the prisoner spoke, his voice muffled by the hood, though his anger was palpable. "Do you really think you can get away with this?" When neither our guide nor De Gofroy responded, he said, "Do you? Answer me. I fucking know you're there."

A defeated silence followed, the man in the hood slumping into his chair. His voice, I thought, sounded familiar.

"Your testimony has been noted and will be put on the record," Powder Blue said, ignoring the prisoner's outburst. "A judgment has been rendered. You have been found guilty of betraying the faith and consorting with its enemies. This is the highest crime against the Church and the faith. The punishment in such cases is absolute excommunication. You will be removed from Church property immediately and forbidden from returning. You will not contact family or friends who remain with the Faith. Your life here is at an end."

The prisoner gave a bitter laugh. "You're not going to kill me, De Gofroy?"

"Murder is forbidden by the faith. It is a tool of the Black Robes alone," Powder Blue said. "Your excommunication is effective immediately."

He paused and looked to the Grand Regent, who was lost in thought as he gazed at the hooded visage of the prisoner. There was something in his expression that made me shudder, as though the veil had been lifted from the kind teacher who had spent so many hours with me, revealing the man himself. A moment later he was himself again, or at least the man I knew, and he stood, nodding to Powder Blue, and left the room without so much as looking at Lasinha and I.

Powder Blue looked at us and said, "Follow me."

He pulled the prisoner to his feet and led him by the arm from the room. We both watched them go, neither of us able to move as we struggled to sort through what had just happened. Lasinha was the first to emerge from his reverie, and he started down the hall after the two men, while I followed a step behind.

My heart was racing and I felt faint at what I had seen. It was as though I had been a witness at an execution, no matter what the man had said about murder being forbidden. My hands, I realized, were shaking. Why had the Grand Regent wanted us to see that and to be a part of all this?

We went back along the corridors we had traversed to arrive at this point—though perhaps they were new hallways; I had stopped paying attention—until we arrived at an elevator, which the four of us rode in silence. We disembarked onto another anonymous floor of windowless corridors and started again on a tangled path as though proceeding through a maze. No one spoke, and the only sound I heard was from our footsteps, the campus still asleep.

Lasinha seemed unperturbed, his mask of ease now back in place, his eyes intent on every last detail. I could not seem to find my equilibrium. Each step further seemed to take me toward a doom I wanted no part of, whether this Regent's or my own, I could not say. I longed to turn and flee, to return to my quarters and sleep so I might escape this nightmare.

That was impossible, of course. This was a test of De Gofroy's devising for Lasinha and me. He had chosen us for something, and despite my misgivings and fears I wanted to be a part of his design. I believed.

Eventually we emerged from the warren of corridors to a loading dock, which I vaguely recognized, though I couldn't at first believe we were still in the Protectors' House. There was a van parked on the loading ramp, clearly left for our purposes, into which Powder Blue thrust the bound prisoner and slammed the doors behind him. I jumped at the sound, which seemed to echo across the hushed campus.

"Take him to this address," the man said, handing Lasinha a piece of paper. "You know it?"

Lasinha studied the paper and nodded.

"Good," the man said, and handed me a set of keys. "Release him there. Bring the van back here. I'll be waiting."

He did not wait for us to say anything in reply, disappearing within the building. Lasinha and I watched him go before turning to stare at each other, as though waiting for the other to voice their thoughts. But there was nothing to be said, and we both got into the van. I maneuvered us off campus and onto the freeway, starting back toward the heart of the city, Lasinha directing me.

There was little traffic on the streets, the night still holding sway around us. The clock on the dashboard said it was just after four, and I felt exhaustion beginning to work upon the edges of my being as all the tension and emotion from the last hours began to dim. I had a headache, whether from the alcohol I had consumed earlier or this ordeal, I could not tell.

"Up here," Lasinha said, as I turned onto a dimly lit street near downtown. I pulled to a stop where he indicated, in front of a large building, set back from the street, of indeterminate use. A factory or warehouse at one point, though with the oil booms a thing of the past, it was likely empty or repurposed now.

"This is the address," Lasinha said, glancing down at the paper again.

"Let's get this over with," I said, and he nodded.

We climbed out of the van and proceeded to the back, each of us glancing down the street to assure ourselves it was still empty. I opened the door and Lasinha crawled in the back and got the prisoner to his feet, both us helping him down. It felt odd to do so, given our circumstances. We both hesitated for a moment, wondering if we were to simply let him wander bound and hooded. Our guide had given us no instructions on the matter.

Our eyes met, and even in the darkness we reached a wordless agreement. Lasinha began to untie his wrists while I worked to loosen his hood. Lasinha was done before I, and the man pushed my hands away and ripped the hood free. Both Lasinha and I took a step back. It was Gabriel Arajuano.

15

The months that followed were a mixture of ecstasy and misery in equal measure. Following Arajuano's exile, I was inducted into the Protectors, to stand watch upon the faith. Lasinha was my sponsor, though I knew such an honor would not have been granted me without the Grand Regent's approval. Both of them were at the ceremony, along with the fearsome man who had led Arajuano's interrogation, Toma Osahi. I now reported to him, as did Lasinha, both of us standing as equals, more or less.

It was not the ceremony I had imagined, for it was all done in secret, and I was told I could tell no one that I was now part of the Hierarchy. After he blessed me, De Gofroy said, "You will do more than any others before you to achieve our dreams, I am sure." He embraced me, and I felt like weeping.

The need for secrecy was soon made apparent to me. None of my duties were changed. Ostensibly I still worked with Ana on the same projects I had before, though, unbeknownst to her, I was her superior tasked with watching her every move and reporting back to Osahi. I was still to watch Molijc, though my reports now went to Osahi as well, not Lasinha, whom I only saw when he was giving Ana and I our assignments. Those were of marginal consequence, Ana not being trusted with anything now that her father had been banished and accused of apostasy.

There lay my misery, for Ana was devastated beyond measure by her father's excommunication. No word was given on what had happened. Another High Regent was appointed and nothing said about the fate of Gabriel Arajuano. Everyone was left to draw their own conclusions, which they readily did. Most initiates would have nothing to do with the daughter of the excommunicated, making it all the more difficult for her to deal with what had happened.

It did not help that Ana's own mother had disappeared some years earlier, leaving her utterly alone in the Church now. I had heard various whispers about that before—people saying that she had been a Society agent, or other outrageous claims—and they reached a fever pitch now that Gabriel was gone as well, under similarly mysterious circumstances. Ana had never spoken of her mother. It was as though she did not have one, and I wondered if it would be the same with her father eventually.

Ana continued to be professional in her work and toward me, though I knew she must be grieving her loss. It was difficult to tell, for she betrayed little emotion, mechanically going about her duties. We had begun surveilling an apostate to the faith, a minor figure in the Hierarchy whom I had not been aware of when he was part of the Church. He had been bitter about his treatment and had launched a series of revelations about the supposed inner workings of the Church, describing it as a cult to anyone who bothered to stick a microphone in front of him.

Lasinha had asked us to find out what we could about him, which meant discovering anything that could be used to discredit him. As Protectors, we were allowed to view his Protocols and make note of any personal revelations he had given. There was little of use there, and so we had begun to tap his phones and set up a keystroke log of his computer, so that we had access to all his communications. He was aware, or at least suspected, that he was under surveillance, and as a result was very careful in what he said and did, making the hours we spent observing him tedious in the extreme.

Ana betrayed no signs of boredom, though, fastidiously going about her work. She would know better than anyone that she would be under scrutiny now that her father had been cast from the Church. I desperately wanted to ask her what she believed had happened to him and what he had done, but her manner told me such questions would not be welcomed. During the second week of our observation, the apostate received a phone call from a reporter for a webmedia service asking about Gabriel Arajuano. Both Ana and I went still, she unable to look at me, I unable to stop myself from staring at her.

"The High Regent? He was De Gofroy's chief lieutenant. A nice enough fellow in his way. What about him?"

"He's gone," the reporter said. "Disappeared. No one seems to know where or why. I was wondering what you knew." Ana flinched at the mention of her father's disappearance, but otherwise betrayed no sign of emotion.

"What are you hearing?" the apostate said. Ana leaned forward in her chair.

"Nothing much. The Church has said nothing. They just appointed a new High Regent. It's as if Arajuano never existed."

"That's what they do. That's what they did to me."

"There are rumors," the reporter continued. "According to one of my sources, De Gofroy forced him out. Others say he was like you, and skipped out."

"I don't think so," the apostate said. "Most of the people who leave the faith contact me or some other apostate. We have a bit of a support network. His wife, Arajuano's wife, contacted one of us when she left. She hasn't heard from him. Anyway, I don't want to talk about that too much on the phone."

"Okay. If you hear anything about this, you let me know."

The apostate agreed and the call was ended. Ana recorded it in the report we would send at the end of the day, while I created a tape of the call to be included with it. Neither of us said anything, and I did my best not to look at her for any reaction, knowing she would be very conscious of my looking at her. I tried to think of something to say to break the agonizing silence that only grew more stifling as time went on, but nothing came to mind that didn't sound trite. The last thing Ana would want was pity from me.

When I looked up from my work creating the tape, I saw that she was weeping. I stood up and went over to her, but she waved me away. "Don't," she said, in a tone that broke my heart.

I stood over her watching, helpless. Here was my chance to prove my feelings for her, to demonstrate how deep my caring was for her, but I could not. My secret knowledge lay between us, an unbridgeable gulf casting us apart.

"Couldn't he have said something? Left a note? Did I mean nothing to him? I can't believe it. I can't believe any of it." Her voice was so raw with emotion it was painful to hear.

I shouldn't be here, I told myself, and I shouldn't be listening to this. But I had to stay. It was my duty. It was torture, and I wondered why I had been given this task. But I knew. It was exactly because of my relationship with Ana that I was set to watch her. It was a test, to see if I would give in.

It was all too much for me. My guilt at what I was keeping from Ana, the closure I was denying her, would not let me sleep. I began to lose weight, my face becoming haggard and drawn. All the signs of anguish that were becoming visible upon me remained hidden on Ana, who maintained her cool reserve. Yet I knew she suffered, and that somehow made her stoicism in the face of it all the worse for me. I began to question my faith and the Church. What was this all worth if it left us in misery?

I no longer trusted myself to be alone with Ana, outside of the projects we conducted for the Protectors, where I could let the work consume me. I should have just stayed away from her, but I felt I couldn't. How many of her friends had given in to the rumors and decided it was better not to be associated with the daughter of an apostate? She needed friends now, no matter how strong a front she maintained. I made it a point to invite her to everything I did, sometimes insisting over her objections that she come, while always making sure that someone else was there to help guard me from myself.

Most often this was Dejian, who proved to have a gift for saying the right thing to Ana. He could make her smile and laugh, and set her seemingly at ease. It was wondrous to see her at peace for those brief moments, though I furiously resented his ability to do so. He was the one who at last got her to open up about the struggles she was enduring.

It was during dinner one evening at the cafeteria. The three of us were sitting at one end of a long table occupied by several other initiates, who noticed Ana and began to whisper loudly amongst themselves. I paid no attention to what they were saying, but something must have caught Ana's ear, for she abruptly stood up and left the cafeteria, leaving her tray and half-eaten plate of food behind. Dejian and I looked at each other and then stood to follow her. I shot the initiates a glare and was met by several uncomprehending faces, which only made me angrier.

We found her in her room weeping uncontrollably. I sat beside her, putting an arm over her shoulder, looking helplessly at Dejian with a paralyzed tongue. Why was I so hopeless in these situations, I wondered? Dejian filled the void again.

"You cannot worry about what anyone says about your father," he said. "Your heart is your own truth. He raised you and guided you into the faith. You are the proof that he was true to it, whatever else he might have done. You are his greatest accomplishment."

"None of that matters. They will never see me like that," Ana said. "They will only see the daughter of the man who betrayed them and the woman who abandoned her faith. How long before I am cast out like them?"

"They wouldn't," I said, too quickly.

"No," Dejian agreed. "They have no reason to. You have demonstrated your faith to De Gofroy himself."

"My father did too," she said. "Right up until he didn't anymore."

An awkward silence followed. The questions about her father's disappearance lay unspoken between us all. They festered at Ana's mind, doubt worming into all of her thoughts. She would never be free of them so long as they remained unanswered. I could provide those answers, but I dared not. Why was the Grand Regent doing this to her and to me? That was not a question to be asked though, for o question him was to question the faith itself.

Ana gathered herself somewhat and pulled away from my touch. Looking at us both, she said, in a barely audible voice, "I'm being watched."

I felt the air go from my lungs. "Do you know who?" Dejian said.

Ana shook her head. "No. There's been different people. They've been following me wherever I go."

"It's to be expected," Dejian said. "Things will be ugly for a while. But it will end soon enough."

"Will it? How can you be sure?" Ana stared at me. *She knows*. I could only hope my face did not betray my thoughts.

"It will," I found myself saying. "And no matter what,

we will be there with you."

At my words, Ana again collapsed into my arms in tears. Molijc stood, squeezing my shoulder, and left. I stayed with Ana, comforting her and seeing her to bed. When I left, I wanted to weep myself. I could not bear this anymore. It was all too much. I felt myself trapped in a cell, the walls slowly drawing in until the air was gone from the room. I screamed but no one heard my cries.

I started back for my own quarters, and found myself thinking about Dejian. Anything to distract from the morass I found myself in. My thoughts were so tangled and confused, and my despair so heavy, that it frightened me. I did not want to be a part of the Church any longer, I realized, not if I was made to feel this way.

I knew I needed someone to speak with, and for once I wanted it to be him. I made my way to his quarters, but as I reached his door I hesitated. What did I want here, really? I was so much at sea I did not know.

I knocked upon the door, and after a few long seconds, during which my thoughts warred with each other and I nearly turned and left, he opened it. He was in a t-shirt and underwear, sleep in his eyes. He looked concerned, but as soon as he recognized me it vanished, transformed into a smile. I opened my mouth to speak, but could not seem to find the words. He stepped aside from the door and I went in.

16

There was the smell of rain in the air, a huge bank of clouds sitting low and heavy in the sky above. We were alone on the beach, but for a few joggers who passed by on the trail that snaked along the shoreline. I watched the waves lap against the beach, the rhythm deeply satisfying, letting my thoughts drift away from all that had haunted me these last months. It was good to just be here, in this moment, in Dejian's arms. The Church and my role as Protector could be forgotten. All that mattered was this moment now.

Dejian shifted into a more comfortable position, and I moved to match my contours to his. "What are you thinking about?" he murmured, kissing my neck.

"Absolutely nothing," I said, after a moment, smiling as his lips found my ear.

We had come to Vancouver the day before so that Molijc could lay the groundwork for what eventually would be a Protocol Center in the city. For now the Church was just leasing an office space above a coffee shop, which Molijc had arranged, and he had come to Vancouver to train the two Regents who would be running the pre-scripts on potential initiates. He had invited me to accompany him, saying that I needed a break from the campus and my duties as Protector. I knew what he really meant was that I needed a break from Ana and the anguish that continued to haunt all of my days.

I had, of course, told him nothing of that night, but he knew me intimately enough now to suspect that I knew some of the details that surrounded Gabriel Arajuano's disappearance. He also knew enough not to press me for them. The only person I could talk to about that was Lasinha.

I had only tried to ask him about it once, after one of our meetings with the always-imperious Osahi. He continued to be as obsessed with Ana as I was, seeing in my every report evidence of her betrayal of the faith. I was desperate to show that he was wrong, and he sensed that need in me as well, so our discussions became interrogations that always ended with me nearly in tears. All of this Lasinha bore witness to, silent and with his perpetual half-smile.

After one of these sessions, when I had had enough of Osahi hounding me, I turned to Lasinha as we made our back from the bowels of the Protectors' House where Osahi kept his offices, and said, "You don't believe Ana is an apostate, do you?"

He glanced at me, raising an eyebrow, the only indication he gave that he was surprised by my question. It was dangerous for us to be discussing such things, especially within these corridors. There was no doubt Lasinha was reporting all he observed of me to Osahi and perhaps even De Gofroy. I simply no longer cared.

Lasinha seemed to be running some inner calculus to determine how to respond. "No, I do not," he said at last as we came to the elevators.

He shot me a look, indicating that I should not say any more, at least for the moment. We rode the elevator in silence and then he led me from the building out onto the main lawn of the campus. We settled into a stroll, heading toward a pond surrounded by trees that was the centerpiece of the lawn and where Regents would often gather when the weather was nice. It was a brisk spring day, and so the lawn was empty of all but a few people hurrying on their way to one building or another.

Lasinha broke our silence, speaking in a low murmur, so that I had to lean my head toward him in order to be able to hear. "Ana is not an apostate. I don't even know that Gabriel was. But De Gofroy has determined that he was, and that is all that matters. I know you have feelings for Ana, but you cannot tie yourself to her. If they decide she is an apostate then they will start looking at anyone close to her. That means you."

"I can't just stop spending time with her. I'm supposed to be observing her." My words sounded hollow to me. We both knew that wasn't why I was spending so much time with Ana. His words had unsettled me deeply, though. Did he really believe that Gabriel wasn't an apostate? Or was he just saying that to judge my reaction?

He stopped and turned to look me in the eye. "Be careful, Laila," he said.

"I will," I said, and we left it at that.

Despite what I had said, I changed nothing. I continued to spend more time with Ana, trying to help her cope with her loss, and I continued to argue for her before Osahi. He had clearly grown tired of my efforts, and when I came to him with word that Dejian had asked me to accompany him to Vancouver, Osahi readily agreed.

"I have something for you to occupy yourself when your *boyfriend* is busy," he told me, putting a derisive emphasis on the word. He did not think much of Molijc, in part, I suspected, because De Gofroy did.

"One of our informants in the Society has let us know where Arajuano is living. He's working for the Travelers now, you know." I nodded as though I did, and Osahi continued, "I'm not sure I trust this informant, so I want to follow up on this. See if Arajuano is there. See what he's doing, who he's meeting with."

"We're only going for three days," I said.

"You'll have a week," Osahi said. "I'll see that something comes up."

When Molijc told me, as we sat on the beach together, that we would have to extend our stay, I was not surprised.

"That's not a problem, is it?" he said. "I can arrange for the airship to take you back if you want, but I thought you might like staying out here a little while longer."

"That would be wonderful," I said. "There's no problem, is there?"

"No, no," Dejian said, putting his hands over mine. "They just want me to head out to Abbotsford and run some Protocols. There are people from the interior who can't afford a trip to Calgary. But you don't need to come with me. Just relax in the city."

"That's what I plan to do," I said, wondering if he knew I was lying and if he had any idea that I knew that he was as well.

The building where Arajuano was allegedly living in was a luxury condo in Vancouver's west end, a few streets down from busy Granville. I took a taxi by it in the afternoon to get my bearings, having the driver pass by the front of the building twice as well as going down all the connecting streets. Arajuano's apartment was at the front of the building on the second floor, overlooking the street. Across from it was the back of a hotel, where I had the driver let me off. I took a room for the rest of the week that gave me a view directly across the street into the apartment, and settled down to wait.

It was a strange place for Arajuano to find himself, I thought, given that he was an apostate of the Church and had to know we would be trying to find him. The entire apartment building was sheathed in glass so that I could see into the living room and kitchen of everyone's apartments. This was a place for people who wanted to be seen and expected it. One of Arajuano's neighbors was a beautiful woman who spent the afternoon lounging about in a short robe, the better to display her exquisite legs. As there was nothing going on in Arajuano's place, I watched her through the crack in the hotel room's curtains as she went about her day.

Darkness had settled upon the city, and the food I had ordered had just arrived when someone entered the condo, the lights blinking on through the main room. I had to turn my own lights off, eating in the darkness, so that I could see what was happening. As I watched, I saw Gabriel pass through the main room in full view before heading upstairs to where the apartment's bedroom presumably was. It was kept safely away from the windows—displaying one's assets apparently only went so far. After several minutes he returned downstairs, having changed his clothes from what had been a rather formal dress to more casual wear.

He puttered about in the kitchen for a few moments, pulling some food out of the refrigerator and opening a bottle of wine, while I resisted a sigh. A night in alone. What, I wondered, did Osahi expect of me here? More than just confirmation that his source had been correct, I knew. But there were limits to what I could discover on a solitary operation. Did I follow him, assuming he left the apartment tonight or tomorrow? Or did I stay behind and risk breaking in to his apartment to see what I could discover there? Following him was its own risk, not only because I was operating alone, but because he would certainly recognize me. It all threatened to turn into a nightmare, which led me to wonder why, if Arajuano was still so important, I was left to do this alone.

I received my answer a moment later as Gabriel rose to his feet to answer the door. I could not immediately see who followed him into the room, but when I did I felt my whole body go numb. The food I had just eaten threatened to come right back up, and my hands shook violently as I watched Frederik de Gofroy wander into Arajuano's living room and sit himself comfortably on the couch. My horror only grew as Gabriel joined him on the couch, passing him a glass of wine and putting a familiar arm over the young man. They kissed and I had to look away, to put my head between my legs to try stop myself from fainting.

This was what Osahi had wanted confirmed, not Arajuano's location. That he would have known, or could have discovered easily. This was of far more consequence. When I managed to look again they had stopped kissing, but Arajuano's arm was still around Frederick as they spoke. I shut the curtain. I could not watch any more.

I stumbled to the bathroom and threw up all the food I had just eaten, sprawling against the tub, holding my head in my hands. My fate in the Church was now in doubt, I knew. Everything. If the Grand Regent were made aware of this, he would do anything in his power to hide it, including removing me. Frederik was his son and presumptive heir, and he was having an affair with an apostate. This was a nightmare.

Osahi had known. He had to have known. This had been going on for a long time—there seemed no doubt to me that this was why Arajuano had been exiled from the Church—and Osahi had wanted me to bear witness to it. Did he want someone else who could stand beside him when he confronted De Gofroy with this sordid knowledge? It was impossible to know how De Gofroy would react to his own son's defiance. Would he cast him out, or would he turn on those who had knowledge of it?

Osahi's actions told me what he thought. He wanted someone else to share this terrible knowledge, someone he could shift the blame to in the event it became necessary. As it would. If Osahi could discover this, someone else could as well. It was only a matter of time.

I felt as though I had been put into a vise whose crank was being turned steadily tighter and tighter. What did Osahi expect me to do with this information? If I reported it to him, my life was in his hands. If I did not, and it came out, as it would inevitably, then he could blame me for failing to investigate Arajuano properly. It was an impossible choice, and I did not know what to do.

My thoughts chased themselves in these circles for some time, before I managed to gather myself and go back to the window. Frederik and Arajuano were gone, though I could still see their wine glasses, now empty on the living room table. There was a glimmer of light from the hallway upstairs, presumably leading to the bedroom. Without another thought, I got up and left the room and the hotel, leaving my key on the desk. I would not be returning.

Though it was at least an hour to the house Molijc and I were staying in, I walked, heading south over the Granville Bridge, the air cool in my lungs, my thoughts thunderous and incoherent. At some point a shower passed, but I hardly felt the rain. Still, I was shivering and cold by the time I reached the house the Church was renting. There were still lights on, which surprised me, given the hour. When I entered I was met by Dejian, worry and anger warring in his features.

"Where have you been?" he said in a voice so loud I took a step back.

"Why are you back?" I said. "I thought you weren't coming back until the end of the week."

"Answer the damn question," he said, looming in my face. "Don't try to put this back on me."

"I wasn't," I said, raising a placating hand. "I'm just surprised, is all."

"You're surprised? I've been sitting here all night wondering where the hell you are. You're not answering your phone. Nobody here has seen you since this morning. They had no idea where you were."

Molijc was practically spitting he was so angry, his face worryingly red. In the year that we had been a couple I had never seen him so angry, so irrational. I almost didn't recognize what I saw. I took a deep breath to control my own frustration. "I didn't realize I was supposed to be reporting my every move to them. I told them I would be gone for the day."

"Where were you?"

I looked him steadily in the eye. "I'm a Protector. I can't tell you."

"Damn you, don't pull that shit with me. What did Osahi have you doing? Were you following me?"

I blinked, taken aback. "Why would I be following you? You were just going to run some Protocols in Abbotsford, right?"

He went very still, as though remembering himself at last. Out of the corner of my eye I saw one of the Regents staying in the house duck her head around the corner to make sure everything was fine. I nodded to reassure her that nothing was the matter, and she disappeared. Dejian's face had gone pale, and he swallowed.

"You're right," he said. "I have no right to question you. I'm sure you had your duties to the faith."

"I did," I said, reaching out and taking his hand in mine. "And now I need to sleep. We can talk about it in the morning."

I did not wait for an answer, heading straight to the bedroom we were sharing and throwing myself on the bed, not even bothering to take my still-damp clothes off. I was asleep before Dejian even entered the room.

17

I did not tell Osahi what I had seen that night. When he asked, I simply said that Arajuano had spent the night alone and that Molijc's early return had restricted my attempts to observe the apostate. He knew I was lying, but he said nothing. Someone would have been following Frederik and told him that he had entered the apartment building. That person would not have known whose apartment it was. Only Osahi and I knew that, I suspected. For the moment he was allowing my lie to stand, waiting for the moment when he would need to use his leverage against me.

The knowledge that he was biding his time left me uneasy. I was forever waiting for the sword dangling above my head to fall. It did not help matters that later that spring the Grand Regent made an ostentatious show of anointing Frederik one of his High Regents, establishing beyond any doubt his intention to have his son take over the Church when his spirit had cast off the veil of his Regent form. The move was met with derision within the Hierarchy. More than one Protector whispered scornfully to me, "All the boy does is drink and fuck, and he's going to be Grand Regent." I had to resist a shudder at those words, for I knew far better than they what drinking and fucking Frederik had been doing.

Dejian and I had reached an uneasy truce following our argument in Vancouver. We were both unsure if we could trust the other entirely. If he had known the Grand Regent had asked me to observe him at the beginning of our relationship, any trust he had in me would be gone. For my part, his rage that evening had been frightening. It had seemed to come from nowhere, exploding to the surface and leaving him beyond even his own control. He had seemed capable of anything, so unlike his normal persona, which led me to doubt whether what I saw of him was real or just affectation.

It was in the midst of this unsettled atmosphere that De Gofroy disappeared. Immediately those of us in the Protectorship knew something was amiss, and eventually the rumors and speculation spread beyond to the Hierarchy, as the Grand Regent failed to make several of his regular appearances, replaced by the High Regents. No explanation was given, and any concerns were dismissed by those in his inner circle. Something had come up that required his attention, or there had been a mistake in his scheduling. All reasonable enough explanations on their own, but added together they could not stand and the edifice began to crumble, revealing the void where the Grand Regent should have been.

Any number of rumors began to spring forth, wildflowers blooming in the spring. The Grand Regent had been arrested by the Society of Travelers and was being held for questioning at one of their black sites. There had been a coup within his inner circle and he had been deposed, the High Regents not willing to accept Frederik as the future Grand Regent. Some said he had abandoned the faith, absconding with the Church's wealth and disappearing to parts unknown. All of them were outlandish, stories that fell apart when examined closely, and yet the longer De Gofroy remained absent, the more credence they seemed to gain.

Though Dejian had been very close to De Gofroy, he knew nothing about this absence. I could tell from his pinched, worried face that he was at sea in the world, unsure where to cast his sails. He was a man desperate to rise in the Hierarchy, and had tied his fate to the Grand Regent's. If any of the outlandish scenarios being whispered were at all true, his future in the Church was grave. He understood now some of the anguish I had endured these last weeks, and I took an odd satisfaction in seeing him suffer.

I had little time to gloat, though, for Osahi was also left panicked by these developments, and he decided to act on what he knew about Frederik. The Grand Regent had been missing for a little more a week and the rumors had begun to spread beyond even the Hierarchy to Regents of the Third Order and even initiates on campus. A maelstrom seemed certain to erupt, and yet the Grand Regent did not appear and none of the High Regents made any announcements as to what was going on, acting as though nothing out of the ordinary was occurring. It suggested they did not know what to do either, and were hoping that a simple front of normalcy would be enough to calm the troubled waters. Instead it only fed the rumors and fears, ensuring they would gain more credence.

It was during my weekly report on Molijc that Osahi confronted me about Frederik. "Forget this shit," he said, waving his hand in disgust. We were in the basement warren that was his domain. "It's not important now, and we both know it."

I nodded, not daring to say anything. I knew what was coming next. He stared at me, and I forced myself to meet his gaze. "I know what you saw that night in Vancouver."

I shook my head. "I don't know what you're talking about."

"Yes you do. Do you know why I know?" He paused, but I did not acknowledge the question. "I know because I saw the same thing the month before."

A fan clicked on, sounding like a gunshot in the silence that enveloped us. I told myself to breathe.

"You have nothing to say?" Osahi said.

"I have no intention of changing my report, if that is what you mean."

Osahi smiled, looking past me, as though lost in thought. "I know what you think you're doing. You think you're protecting yourself, but you aren't. What you are doing is dooming the Church. The Grand Regent may not return." Osahi paused, exhaling slightly. I desperately wanted to ask him what he knew about that, but I held my tongue.

"If he does not, Frederik will become Grand Regent as it stands right now. We all know those are De Gofroy's wishes. Who would stand against them? No one, unless we make known what we both know."

I found a spot on the wall behind Osahi where the paint was dull and fixed my eyes upon it. "And what if De Gofroy does return? What then?"

"I don't think he will," Osahi said. "The High Regents are frightened. They don't know what to do. They don't want to give power to Frederik, but if the Second Order finds out that De Gofroy is gone for good, they may have to. Unless we can give them a reason not to."

"What's happened to him?" I said. "Why wouldn't he come back?"

"I don't know," Osahi said with a grimace. "Everyone's gone dark. No one knows what to do."

I frowned. It seemed impossible to me that Osahi was unaware of what was occurring with the Grand Regent. All our orders and projects flowed from the Grand Regent through Osahi. He was De Gofroy's secret hand. For him not to know…it did not stand to reason. He was either lying, or the stories of the coup were true and Osahi was attempting to cling to his position by using what he knew of Frederik to buy him or others off. All the more reason for me not to be involved and tie myself to him, if he were sinking in this new world.

Osahi could see the doubt on my face. He shook his head. "Everything is at stake now—don't you understand? If De Gofroy goes, his son will be Grand Regent. The son who we both know is having an affair with an apostate."

I shrugged, careful to keep my face neutral. "I've wondered if the only reason Arajuano was exiled was because of the affair. The Grand Regent did not approve of it, clearly."

"No, he did not," Osahi said. "Because Arajuano was a Society agent. He always has been. For years we wondered how they were always aware of what we were doing, how they were always able to thwart our attempts to get our hands on their technology so that we could cross over. It was because of him. Make no mistake: if Frederik becomes Grand Regent, the Society will control the Church."

"Even if I accept that," I said, "and I'm not saying that I do, what good is revealing this going to do? Will anyone accept it? Or will they just turn on you?"

"None of that is your concern. This is not your element, so do not pretend that you know what is happening. At the moment I require some leverage, and I intend to use this to get it."

I stood up. "I want no part of this."

Osahi laughed. "It is too late for that, Laila. Far too late."

"You can't make me do this," I said, turning to go. "You have no leverage on me."

"Don't I?" Osahi said. "I have enough information on Gabriel to show he was conspiring with the Society, and I will reveal it all. How long do you think Ana will be allowed to remain in the Church if I do? The only reason she was not exiled with her father was that the Grand Regent feels some affection for her."

My expression must have revealed my feelings in that moment, for Osahi gave me a grim smile. I left the room without uttering another word.

I went to find Lasinha as soon as I left Osahi. There was little time, I knew, for me to act if I was going to save Ana. Dejian was with Lasinha in his office, which surprised me. They were both taken aback as well, looking uncomfortably at each other after I burst through the door. At any other time I might have had some sharp questions for them, but I ignored their awkwardness and looked to Lasinha.

"I need your help," I said.

He nodded and gestured for me to close the door and sit, which I did. Dejian made no move to leave, and I glanced at him, hesitating for a moment, before concluding that I would need all the help I could get in the coming days. "I'm in trouble," I said. "And so is Ana."

As they listened intently, I told them about Frederik and Arajuano, how Osahi had entrapped me, and how he intended to expose Frederik and Gabriel and cast Ana out of the Church to protect himself. Both were quiet when I finished, until Dejian said, "De Gofroy would never declare Ana an apostate. He loves her like a daughter. He even hoped she would marry Frederik, but he obviously had other thoughts on the matter."

"Does anyone know what is going on with the Grand Regent?" I said, looking from face to face.

Lasinha shook his head. "We were just discussing that. I'm not even sure all the High Regents know what has happened. I assume Osahi does, or at least has some idea. He has tentacles everywhere. If he doesn't think the Grand Regent is coming back, then we have to assume he isn't."

We all fell silent as we mulled our future without the Grand Regent, our expressions mirroring each other, the disquiet plain. Lasinha was the first to speak. "I have a suggestion, but you won't like it."

I gave a helpless shrug.

"If we assume that what Osahi says is true, that

Arajuano was a Society agent—and he may well be right; I have not seen his evidence—then our best option may be to send Ana to the Society."

"What do you mean?" I said, hating the emotion that I heard in my voice.

"She goes before Osahi can exile her, but we send her. She's our agent. If her father is already an agent, they'll be more likely to trust her. And if they suspect her, when they investigate, what will they find out? That the Protectors think she is an apostate. It would be the perfect cover. Only we three would know the real truth. And if De Gofroy returns, or things change here, we can bring her back."

"It could work," Molijc said, looking at me. "It could definitely work. And if De Gofroy does somehow return, we would be the three who saved Ana."

"And she could be extremely useful within the Society," Lasinha said. "She has done fine work for the Protectors. If she could find out anything about the crossings, it could be monumental. Everyone is disappointed in our progress on the matter."

"It is essential to the realization of the faith. How can we expect people to follow and believe if we cannot realize what the Grand Regent preaches?" Molijc said.

I wanted to dispute what both of them were saying, but I could see the logic in it. If Ana was exiled, the Society would certainly approach her and attempt to coopt her, especially if Gabriel was in fact one of their agents. And if by some miracle she could manage to find something about the crossings, though so many of our other agents had been unable to make any headway in this regard, it would be a triumph beyond all imagining. It would not matter who was Grand Regent then—the four of us would be secure.

Still, I hesitated, sensing that this was just another trap into which I was being drawn. Osahi had ensnared me, and now I would be bound just as tightly to Molijc and

Lasinha. It was dangerous to carry so many secrets.

"We would all do anything to see the faith realized," Lasinha said in a gentle voice.

"And Ana will as well," Dejian said, putting a hand on my shoulder. "I really don't see any other way."

I opened my mouth, desperate to find anything to contradict what they said, but nothing came. At last I nodded, and Lasinha said, "We will speak with her together."

I arranged to meet Ana in my quarters with Lasinha later that evening. She arrived before he did, and I poured her a glass of wine.

"What is this about, then?" she said when my small talk had dwindled to uncomfortable silence.

"We should wait for Lasinha," I said.

"I'm being exiled," she said, setting down her glass and standing up. "I've failed whatever little tests you've set for me."

"No, no," I said, rising to my feet as well. "It's not that at all. But we should wait for Lasinha. Please, sit."

She did, glaring at me and refusing to say anything further. I could not meet her eyes, and sat miserably, staring at the floor, praying for Lasinha to hurry his arrival. When he did, he nodded at me confirmation that everything had been arranged, and turned to Ana.

"What is this about?" she said before he had a chance to speak. "Will you be straight with me?"

I bit my lip, wanting to tell her that I had been honest with her, but knowing it would do no good right now.

"Of course I will," Lasinha said, giving an easy smile.

Ana snorted. "Just get on with it."

"Very well," Lasinha said, looking at me as though he thought I had mishandled the situation. "As you know, the Grand Regent has disappeared. The situation is very much in flux at the moment, and Laila has discovered that you are in danger."

They both turned to me, and I swallowed. "Osahi claims to have proof that your father was a Society agent. He is worried about his future in the Church if De Gofroy is truly gone for good, and he is going to use what he knows about your father to secure his position."

"Everyone suspects that already," Ana said. "How does he think this new information is going to make a difference to his fate?"

"I don't know. He wouldn't tell me what information he has exactly. But it must implicate others in the Church in some way," I said, not exactly lying.

"The point is," Lasinha said, taking up the case in earnest, "it doesn't matter what the information is, or even whether or not it is true. If your father is implicated, you will be too. And if De Gofroy is gone, there will be no one in the Hierarchy to protect you."

"Except you, of course," Ana said. She smiled to herself and shook her head.

"No," I said. "We have no standing in the Hierarchy."

"Laila is correct," Lasinha said when Ana looked to him. "We will be hard-pressed to maintain our positions in the Protectorship, depending on how things go."

"But you will find a way to protect me."

"Not exactly," I said, unable to stop a heavy sigh from escaping.

"We have something of a proposal for you," Lasinha said. "It will keep you safe from Osahi's maneuvering and leave an avenue to return to the Church once these troubles have passed us."

"So I am to leave the Church?"

"A temporary measure," Lasinha said. "And a necessary one, for more than one reason. We want you to join the Society."

Ana laughed, though there was no mirth in it. "You want me to confirm everyone's suspicions?"

"Not only the Church's suspicions, but the Society's as well. You would be the perfect double agent. Your defection is completely believable," I said, hoping that I sounded more confident than I felt.

"We have agents in the Society now, working to find out how they manage the crossings, and how we might do so as well," Lasinha said. "But we've been stalled in our progress. No one can get close to anyone who is working directly on the crossings. And we can't turn any of those people either, it seems. They are true believers."

"And you think I will be able to infiltrate them where others have failed."

"I do," Lasinha said. "Your story is more believable than any of theirs. And you have a knack for this type of thing."

Ana smiled distantly, looking past both of us. Lasinha leaned forward to press his point home further. "You'll have to tell them something about our inner workings. Something about us. But once you've gained their trust, you should be able to move up and make the right friends."

Ana would still not look at either of us. I glanced at Lasinha. "More importantly, being away from here will protect you from whatever Osahi or anyone else in the Hierarchy has planned. It will seem like you've been cast out, but really you'll be working for us. Once things improve, we can bring you back."

"And if you succeed, no one will doubt you again," Lasinha said.

Ana finally roused herself from her thoughts, turning her gaze from Lasinha to me. "I'd be putting my life on the line for you."

"You'd be doing it for the faith," Lasinha said. "We two, and Molijc, will be the protectors of your secret here. You know what it would mean to be able to cross over."

"It is what our faith is for," she said, her voice distant again.

"Yes," Lasinha said. "And we know you want to be part of the faith. We have no doubt. But others do. If you were to make this sacrifice, it would remove all doubts forever. Your father—"

Ana raised a hand and Lasinha fell silent. I reached out and put my hand on her knee. Was I imploring her or trying to comfort her? Even I could not say. She looked at us both and nodded.

18

Ana disappeared the following day. Coming as it did on the heels of the Grand Regent's own mysterious absence, her vanishing led to a flurry of speculation among those in the Hierarchy and beyond. There were rumors, encouraged by Osahi, no doubt, about the reasons for her disappearance, all of them revolving around her father's betrayal of the faith. It was implied by all that she herself had become an apostate, and there were even further whispers that she had defected to the Travelers.

Osahi was furious at Ana's desertion and summoned both Lasinha and I to his office, where he berated us for our failure to stop her flight.

"You warned her," he said to me, his eyes bulging from his head. I had never seen him so angry, and it was difficult not to smile in satisfaction at how we had put one over on him.

"I don't know what you mean," I said.

"You know exactly what I mean," Osahi said.

"I feel as though I am not privy to the entire discussion here," Lasinha said, allowing himself a small grin.

This only infuriated Osahi even more. "It is none of your goddamn concern and you know it," he said, and turned to me. "And you. I will not forget this."

"What does it matter?" I said, with a shrug. "You can still do what you were planning to do. It proves what you were saying."

"Exactly," he said, slamming one of his finely manicured hands on the table. "Exactly. And now she is with the Society telling them our secrets. She worked in the Protectorship. She knows all our secrets."

"We don't know where she's gone or what she's doing," Lasinha said, and Osahi yelled at us both to leave.

By the end of the week, one of Lasinha's sources in the Society had reported that Ana had presented herself as a defector from the faith, offering to them all that she knew.

"He is in a panic," Lasinha said with some satisfaction. "They are accepting everything she says."

"For the moment," I said. "What if they decide they need a Seeker to have a chat with her?"

He shrugged. "If they do, then she can't infiltrate them, but she will still be useful. And it will still give her cover and protect her from Osahi. I seriously think he was planning an execution in the main square. And maybe we get lucky."

I did not feel lucky, but I consoled myself with the thought that at least I knew where Ana was and that she was relatively safe. So long as I still breathed, a pathway for her return to the Church remained.

Ana's situation became a secondary concern several days later when the truth about De Gofroy's absence—which had by this time stretched to almost three weeks—was revealed. He was gravely ill, though the exact nature of his illness was still not clear. He had been lying in a coma all this time in chambers atop the Grand Regent's tower.

The Acolytes had been tightly controlling access to his quarters—even the High Regents had been kept in the dark about his situation. The secret had been kept until the Grand Regent had emerged from his coma and asked to speak with several of his closest lieutenants, including both

Osahi and Molijc.

Osahi's audience was first, followed by Dejian's. He practically vibrated as he dressed and prepared himself, though he could never hope to be as immaculately made up as Osahi was with his powder-blue suits and ruffled collars.

When he returned an hour later, he was practically ecstatic. "Find Lasinha," he said, pulling me into an embrace. "We all have been summoned to speak with the Grand Regent again this afternoon."

"All of us?" I said. "What for?"

"I told him about our apostate and he wants to know more," he said, smiling and kissing me.

"But there's nothing to tell. We don't know any more."

"We can't tell him that," Dejian said, taking hold of my shoulders and peering into my eyes. "You will see. It is not good. Not good. I don't know if he can bear it."

I did not truly understand what he meant until we three were ushered into the Grand Regent's chambers by an unsmiling Acolyte. They were vast and hushed and, despite the vast windows that let in the afternoon sun, somehow dim and shadowed. At the center of the room lay the Grand Regent on a bed surrounded by a terrifying array of equipment with various tubes connected to his body.

"We will awaken him soon," the Acolyte said in a low voice, the only words he spoke to us. His face was dark and shadowed, full of crags, that made him look, at a glance, as though he were badly scarred. Molijc nodded while Lasinha and I gawked, unable to hide our curiosity and surprise.

It was hard to see a man who had once been so vibrant and alive reduced to this hollow shell. I could not stop looking at him, watching his shallow breathing, the rise and fall of his chest. He seemed very delicate, a wisp that might just float away into the ether above. The full implications of what was happening here dawned on me.

De Gofroy would not survive, or if he did by some miracle, it would be as a shadow of his former self. He could not continue as Grand Regent. That time was over.

The question now was what would follow in his wake. The High Regents had been maneuvering for some time to try and settle the future, but now that De Gofroy had awakened, he would have his say as well. And he wanted to talk to the three of us. It was clear now why Molijc did not want us to tell the truth to De Gofroy. What we had to say would determine all our futures in the Church, including Ana's, I realized.

"What would you have us do?" Lasinha whispered, his eyes still on the Grand Regent, his thoughts apparently mirroring my own.

"I have told the Grand Regent about Ana," Dejian said. "I have said that you two are in command of the operation. He wants to know what there is to report."

"You know as much as we do," Lasinha said.

"We can't tell him that," Molijc said in an earnest whisper. "This is his life's work. She was his favorite." He looked from one face to another, compelling us.

I nodded, and Lasinha said, "I understand."

We waited an interminable time for De Gofroy to awaken, the Acolyte busy at his side fiddling with the tubes that led from his body. It seemed a monstrous operation. *Let his soul find its peace*, I wanted to say, but I knew what the Grand Regent himself would say. There would be no peace for any of our souls until we could cross over and find the true universe. This, then, was a necessary sacrifice. At last the Acolyte looked up to Molijc and nodded, and Dejian approached the bed and kneeled so that he was face to face with the prone De Gofroy.

I had to fight back tears as I saw De Gofroy blink into a dim awareness. He did not even seem alive. There was no spark or color to him. It was as though he were an automaton, set to come to life at certain hours, only to return inevitably to his inanimate slumber. Dejian whispered something to him and gestured to Lasinha and I, and the Grand Regent smiled and gave a slight nod. Molijc gestured for us to approach, which we did, kneeling on either side of him so that there were three of us supplicating ourselves by the Grand Regent's bed. It must have been a strange sight, but we were alone, the Acolyte having withdrawn.

De Gofroy smiled distantly. Now that he was awake, his illness was all the more evident. His eyes had that unfocused dimness I had seen in my mother in her last days, the glimmer of life slowly being strangled from them. I noticed that my hands were trembling, and I took De Gofroy's in mine, clutching it to hide my own discomfort.

He smiled at me. "You three are the best of us," he said, his voice strained and frail. "I am so happy that you will remain to help guide the faith."

A rasping cough erupted from within and would not subside. I worried that he was going to choke, but eventually it quieted, though his breath continued to come wheezingly forth.

Lasinha waited until he was settled again before speaking. "As Dejian told you, the apostate is a false one. She volunteered to go to the Society and we agreed to protect her secret here. She has contacted us through the channel we established. She has let us know that she has gained entry to the inner circle of the Society. It's only a matter of time before she has their trust. The knowledge of crossing over will follow soon enough."

"It will be ours," Molijc added, and I forced myself to nod.

De Gofroy was silent for a time, emotion clearly overwhelming him. "It lightens my heart to hear this. You have no idea." He took an unsteady breath before continuing. "I knew that what I had been told of Ana could not be true. She has been like a daughter to me all these years, and she was as betrayed by her father's actions as I was."

"We were all betrayed by him," Dejian said.

The Grand Regent appeared not to have heard. He continued in the same broken voice. "This is the central work of our Church. Nothing is more important. I want you two, Laila and Lasinha, to lead it. No one else can be trusted with it."

"You honor us," Lasinha said, and I squeezed his hand, trying to hide the sense of vertigo I felt. The Grand Regent had done more than honor us; he had, in essence, made us High Regents. We answered to no one but him. I could only imagine Osahi's fury once he discovered it.

De Gofroy pulled his hand from mine and reached out for Molijc, who extended his own. "As you know, it is my wish that Frederik continue the work that I have begun. The High Regents do not want it. Osahi argues against it. I will see it done, if it takes my last breath. But you must help him and guide him, stand with him as you have stood with me."

"I will," Dejian said in a fervent voice. "I will."

The Grand Regent seemed to lose focus after that, slipping back into whatever sea he was adrift in. We watched him, none of us daring to break the silence or so much as move until the Acolyte emerged from somewhere, gesturing for us to stand back from the bed.

"He must rest now. He does not have the strength for any of this," he said as we clambered to our feet, feeling somewhat self-conscious.

"Thank you," Dejian said, and the Acolyte bowed to him. Dejian gave something of a nod as well, an acknowledgement of a shared understanding. What kind of understanding, I wondered?

I had little time to ponder the question, as Dejian led us from the room. We emerged from the Grand Regent's chambers and made our way down the corridor, passing a woman idling to no apparent purpose. She looked vaguely familiar, and I glanced back at her as we went. It was only as we entered the elevator that I remembered I had seen her with Osahi before. He was watching us closely, it seemed. There would be strange and difficult days ahead.

19

De Gofroy lingered on, barely alive, his flesh surviving as his spirit slowly absented his body. The Acolyte who tended to him would raise him from the coma he was kept in when required, though it seemingly became more difficult each time, the Grand Regent struggling to maintain his awareness for shorter and shorter periods. Still, even in this feeble and fragmented state, he managed to continue to rule the Church, none of the High Regents daring to defy him while he was still alive, however contingent his life might be.

Word by then had spread from the Hierarchy to the Regents and initiates of his current health, mostly as a result of Molijc, who had very carefully begun to whisper of what had befallen the Grand Regent and what must follow for the Church. That included adhering to his final wishes that Frederik be named Grand Regent, following his death. There was little Osahi, or his allies among the High Regents, could do once this became widely known. Tarnishing Frederik with what Osahi knew would only stain the Grand Regent, as well as the other High Regents.

For our part, I arranged for Morris Loverne to watch Frederik and his continued affair with Arajuano, to make certain that we knew exactly what was happening in the event that Osahi decided to move again. We all knew he would not simply accept that Frederik would become Grand Regent, not while he still believed Arajuano to be a Society agent. At some point he would act, and we would have to be ready to counter him.

Loverne reported that there was no evidence he could find of the apostate's supposed masters. "If he is a Society man," he told Lasinha and I, "he is hiding it well. Deep, deep cover. I have no idea how he would be reporting to them, or they to him."

We were in Vancouver at the Protocol Center, where we usually arranged to meet. Lasinha had arranged for Loverne to have a position there, though he did little work, spending most of his time observing Arajuano.

"Osahi is blind here for whatever reason," Lasinha said, nodding that Loverne could go.

"Maybe his collars are getting too tight," Morris said as he left, and we all laughed.

When the door had closed behind him, I turned to Lasinha. "Any word?"

"No," he said with a shake of his head. "None of my sources have heard or seen anything. It's like she never existed."

I sighed. It had been nearly a year since we had sent Ana to the Society, and there had still been no word from her through our agreed channel, and no evidence whatsoever of her existence.

"We sent her to her death," I said, giving voice to the thought that kept me awake many of the nights since we had sent Ana away.

"You don't know that," Lasinha said, standing up in preparation for leaving.

It was rare that we spent time in the same place anymore. Molijc, through his influence with Frederik and the Grand Regent, had facilitated our rise through the ranks of the Protectors. We were now Osahi's equals, if not his superiors, though the inner workings of the Protectors' House had always been somewhat opaque. For the moment we were ascendant, and with that came new responsibilities to see to the protection of the faith.

Now we cultivated sources and agents within various government agencies and guilds, and directed subordinates to flush out the spies within our midst. If the Society was to have its fingers everywhere, reaching into the very structure of the world, then so would we. It was dizzying to have such responsibility, and one or the other of us always seemed to be away from the campus, seeing to our duties.

Lasinha, with his contacts in the Society and elsewhere, was in charge of what we loosely understood as external relations, while I was left to watch those within the Church. Counterintelligence, it might have been termed, though I found it distasteful work. Largely it consisted of using men like Morris to ensure that those within the Hierarchy were beyond reproach, and when they weren't, to ensure that we had proof that could be used against them when it became necessary.

"It is not necessarily a bad thing," he continued. "None of my sources are deep in the Society. It is a many-tentacled beast, as you know. If Ana has been successful, this is exactly what would happen."

"This is also what would happen if she had been disappeared," I said, refusing to let him just leave. "What if they brought a Seeker in to question her?"

He shrugged, taking a step toward the door, his hand outstretched to grasp the handle. "We would know. They would have arrested the agents she knew about, or at least be watching them. There's been no sign of it."

"Maybe they're waiting," I said.

"Maybe they are," Lasinha said. "That's all we can do too."

He gave me a nod, and before I could say anything further he was out the door and gone.

In many ways, the months following Ana's exile were among the best that Dejian and I shared together. He was exultant that the Grand Regent had chosen him to be Frederik's counselor. And not just Frederik's counselor—he was De Gofroy's conduit to the rest of the Church, passing along what the Grand Regent said to the High Regents and others in the Hierarchy. He, along with the Acolyte who tended to De Gofroy, was always present when the Grand Regent awoke from his artificial slumbers, the only constants in his existence.

The flashes of anger and the mistrust that had crept between us following our trip to Vancouver seemed to have resolved themselves now that Dejian had what he most desired. And while I was still consumed by Ana's absence, and what I feared had befallen her, I was happy in the work we had embarked upon together, convinced of the rightness of our cause. We were the inheritors of the Church, the best of it, as De Gofroy himself had said.

It was only right that we should guide it, then, and the three of us set about making sure that we would be able to. Frederik was pliable enough—and could be made more so once we revealed to him that we were only too aware of his continuing affair with Arajuano—and not at all versed in his father's teachings, despite having been brought up in them. Dejian would be the Grand Regent in all but name, and soon enough, I knew, he would see his way to the title itself.

But for the time being, we needed Frederik as much as he needed us. There was still much anxiety among the rank and file of the Church about life following De Gofroy. Frederik was our link to the founder, the reassurance that though the Grand Regent was gone, his works would continue. It was also our protection against those in the Hierarchy who might oppose our influence.

There were five High Regents, three of whom—Guadalupe Des Rosas, Nikos Annestol, and Javrung

Hammelltharup—we knew were allied to some extent with Osahi. They had kept an uneasy peace as De Gofroy clung to life, but once he died we were certain they would act to ensure their own future, and we would have to be ready. I spent a great deal of time on this project, finding out everything I could about the High Regents that might be useful. Most had been with De Gofroy a very long time, yet there seemed to be little of note that could be found on them in the Church records beyond the usual hagiographies. They were circumspect in their actions now, careful to ensure they made no missteps. Any questionable activities that might be tainted by apostasy or subversiveness were carried out by underlings, so that they might easily deny any knowledge of what was done in their names.

I discussed this problem with Lasinha one day in the fall as the Uayeb neared. These were the five nameless days from the Mayan calendars when all Regents fasted and carefully observed the rites of the faith. No Protocols were completed, for it was understood that these were the unluckiest days of the year, when the universes were out of sync and our souls cast far apart. Many Regents undertook vows of silence and refused to leave their quarters for the entire five days.

The task was growing more urgent by then, for it was becoming clear that it was only a matter of time before the Grand Regent was lost to us. Molijc had told us it might be a matter of weeks, if not days. Everyone in the Hierarchy seemed to have the same understanding, for the Protectors' House was a hive of activity, with agents from various factions fanning out across the Church.

"We don't need proof they're all apostates," Lasinha said after I had expressed my frustrations about my failures to this point. "We just need something we can use as leverage. It has to be there."

"It's not," I said, thinking of all the things that might be used against me. "There's nothing there. And none of them has so much as jaywalked in the last year."

"It's there," Lasinha insisted. "Those three have been here since the beginning. You don't think they made some mistakes, committed some sins? Did some things for the Church they'd rather nobody found out?"

"If they did, I can't find it."

"Impossible," Lasinha said. "It just doesn't scan."

We were both silent, mulling our thoughts until I saw Lasinha's eyes brighten. He reached out to touch my arm.

"De Gofroy will have files on them all," he said. "When you were reporting to me on Molijc, I had to write something up and pass it on to Osahi. He passed it on to De Gofroy. It was the same with everyone we inducted into the Hierarchy. The Protectors were one of the first arms of the Church that De Gofroy established. All of them will have been observed. We just have to find the reports."

"I'll talk to Dejian," I said.

Molijc, when I managed to speak with him, did not know where the reports might be, and in fact seemed somewhat surprised that they would exist.

"They must be somewhere in his chambers," I said. "He wouldn't trust something that sensitive to the Protectorship, not even to Osahi."

"No, they will be somewhere there," Dejian said. "We can't exactly search the place, though. There's always someone there, and we can't trust them all."

"Could you ask him?"

Molijc nodded. "He might not agree to tell us."

"It's worth a try," I said. "We need to know where they are. We need to secure them. Who knows what might be in there?"

Dejian's eyes widened. "Right. I will speak to him the next time we awaken him."

A week following our talk, as the erratic Calgary spring began its slow turn to summer, the Acolyte awoke the

Grand Regent, and Dejian came to me with word of the location of the reports. They were stored on hard drives disconnected from any of the Church's servers and kept locked in a vault in the Grand Regent's chambers.

"He has given me the combination," Molijc said with a smile.

That still did not give us the drives, for Dejian could not simply take them without anyone noticing. Aside from Molijc and the Acolyte, both of whom seemed never to leave, at any point during the day there were always a handful of people present in the Grand Regent's chamber. Most of them, we knew, were agents working for various parts of the Hierarchy, so they would be watching for exactly the sort of thing we needed to attempt.

Only during the delicate procedures involved in awakening him did the Acolyte clear the room, leaving only he, Molijc, and whoever might have an audience with De Gofroy. We could not risk De Gofroy's health in waking him just to steal the drives—no matter how important they were, they were not as important as he. Nor did we want to chance leaving them in case he should perish before his next audience, which was not for another three weeks, the Acolyte having judged the strain of the last awakening to be too great on De Gofroy's feeble heart.

That left us trying to find a means of getting them out during De Gofroy's artificial slumber. We considered doing so during the nights, when there were fewer people around, but thought that might attract even more attention, for Dejian was rarely to be found in the chambers then.

"Better to do it when there is a crowd to provide cover," I said. "We just need to find a distraction."

The only one credible distraction was the Grand Regent himself. Molijc suggested as much. "If something were to happen to him," he said, "every eye in the place would be on him. It would be the perfect chance to get into the vault."

"What would you suggest *happen* to the Grand Regent?" Lasinha said with a raised eyebrow. We were in my quarters, all of us speaking in hushed tones, though I had swept it for bugs earlier. Osahi had people on us every moment we were on campus. The only time we lost them was when our duties took us elsewhere. Even then I could not be sure.

"Nothing, really. All the equipment the Acolytes have connected to him is alarmed in case there's any change in his stasis. We just need to make sure the alarm goes off and stays on for a good long while."

"How will you manage that?" I said, and Lasinha nodded.

"I won't. The Acolyte will," Molijc said with a pleased grin.

I leaned back in my chair, remembering the glance Dejian had shared with the Acolyte responsible for the Grand Regent. The Acolytes had long been their own world within the Church. Even the Protectorship had gained little headway in investigating them. All I knew of their work was what they did involving the Eye and Protocols of the faith. There were rumors that they were deeply involved in attempting to reverse-engineer the Travelers' equipment, but who knew what truth those stories held?

"He will do that for you?" Lasinha said.

He had gone very still at Dejian's words. I understood why. The only man in the Church to be allowed within their inner sanctum had been De Gofroy. And now apparently Molijc had gained their trust as well. The support of the Acolytes' Guild lay at the heart of the struggle for the Church we were engaged in with Osahi and the High Regents. Everyone assumed the Acolytes would support whoever became Grand Regent following De Gofroy's death, but nothing in that regard could be assured. They followed their own path in all things. If

Dejian had managed to gain their support, our influence within the Hierarchy was assured.

"I believe so," Dejian said, his smile growing.

Lasinha and I both broke into grins as well. I felt something like elation. We truly had been chosen by De Gofroy to guide the faith.

The plan was put into effect two days later. It was decided that I should be the one to steal the drives. There was no need to manufacture a reason for me to be present if it came to that. I was simply visiting Dejian, something I had done in the past. We also wanted the drives out of the chambers as soon as possible. It might look strange if Molijc left immediately following an emergency involving De Gofroy, but for me it would be perfectly explicable.

I came to the chambers at the arranged time. Dejian caught sight of me and made a show—too much of one, in my mind—of coming over to kiss me and say hello.

"How is your day?" I said, smiling and looking past him to scan the room. There were fifteen people present, all milling around in the vast space surrounding the Grand Regent and the Acolyte machinery. The Acolyte himself was nowhere to be seen.

"Good, good." Dejian sounded nervous, and I squeezed his hand to reassure him. He had not been a part of something like this before. He smiled, though it looked forced.

"Will you be able to come for supper tonight?"

He nodded his head, jerking it violently. "Yes. Yes, I should."

I had to hide my own annoyance. Where was the silver tongue that he used to dazzle all the faithful now, when we needed it most? His nervousness was starting to influence me as well. I felt overdressed and uncomfortable in the jacket I was wearing, which I was going to use to conceal the drives. I had the sense that people were surreptitiously watching us, and no doubt they were, and here we were standing and acting about as naturally as two teenagers in the middle of their first dance.

We were both saved by the alarm, so loud it startled both of us. There were gasps from those gathered, everyone moving quickly toward the bed where De Gofroy lay. Molijc did as well, calling for calm, saying that the Acolyte would be there momentarily. As he emerged and took charge of the scene, I slipped away from the main chamber to De Gofroy's study, where vault was, tucked in a corner beside a bookshelf. It was heavily built and bolted to the floor, made to look impregnable.

Knowing I had little time before my absence was noticed, I quickly punched in the combination and pried open the vault door, scanning the shelves for the hard drives. There were three, each about the size of a large cell phone, and I tucked them into the inner pockets of the jacket. After I closed the vault, I smoothed out my jacket, checking to make sure the bulges from the drives were not too obvious, and slipped out from the study to rejoin the group surrounding De Gofroy.

The Acolyte, noting my return, turned the alarms off and raised himself from the equipment to look at the assembled crowd. "There has been a minor failure in the stasis equipment," he said in grave tone. "It has been rectified for the moment, and no harm has come to the Grand Regent, but I will need time to set the systems right. I would ask that all of you leave for the time being so that I may concentrate."

A quiet murmur went through the crowd, with people looking at one another in consternation. How close had the Grand Regent just come to dying, I could see them wondering. One by one they began to trickle from the room, glancing back at De Gofroy as though it might be for the final time. I joined the flow of people, moving unnoticed from the room. The adrenaline that had seized me while I was stealing the drives eased, leaving only euphoria in its place.

As I went out the door to the surrounding corridors, I felt someone's eyes upon me and glanced behind me. There was a woman watching me, among the last of us to leave the chamber. She seemed familiar, and I nodded at her reflexively. It was only when I was down the corridor, almost to the elevator, that I remembered her. It was Osahi's agent, the one who had been waiting outside the Grand Regent's chambers after our audience when the future of the Church had been granted to us. Since that day I had noticed her about, always at a distance, always watching Dejian or I.

My hand strayed to my jacket and the hard drives. Had she noticed me leaving the chamber or when I returned? I didn't think so, but I couldn't say for sure. My euphoria vanished and my stomach twisted. Something would have to be done about this woman, I realized. First I would need to discover who she was.

20

The archives on the Grand Regent's hard drives were vast, providing exhaustive detail on seemingly every Regent who had set foot on the campus grounds. It was unbelievable to me that De Gofroy would ever have had time to review all these reports, let alone make any decisions based upon them. There were simply too many for one person to keep up with. They were insurance, then, to be used when necessary. And they were needed now, if De Gofroy's vision for the future of the Church was to be realized.

That I was one of the hands that was to guide this venture still left me thrilled when I thought about it, though I often had to remind myself of it when the tedium of reading through report after report had me wanting to delete everything on the hard drives. My first step had been to find my own file and read it. There were reports from Lasinha and Ana, both of which I had expected, and also from Dejian, which I had not. His had continued long after we had started our relationship, but then so had mine. De Gofroy had trusted neither of us, although to judge by the archives and who was reporting on whom, he trusted no one but himself.

I deleted my file, as well as Molijc's and Lasinha's,

though not before making a copy of theirs—who knew when I would need insurance of my own, after all. The other files I removed and made a copy of were Ana's and her father's. It seemed important to have their documentation close at hand, for I sensed somehow that my fate would be tied to theirs.

That done, I began my research on the three High Regents. There was little on there that was usable. Most of it was known, their exploits part of the history of the Church, part of De Gofroy's own tale. Anything questionable would implicate him as well as the three. I mentioned this to Molijc when he came to our rooms one evening and I was still engrossed in the files.

"Keep looking," he said as he massaged my shoulders while peering over my head at the computer screen. "There will be something there."

"Maybe," I said with a doubtful shrug.

"We need something," he said, his hands going still. There was the air of a command in his voice, which made me stiffen.

I turned to look back at him, irritated with how he had spoken. As if he realized it, he pulled me up from my chair and said, "Come to bed. There's time for that tomorrow."

Still annoyed, I opened my mouth to speak, before thinking better of it. It was just the long hours we were both putting in, I told myself. We were wearing ourselves to the very edge, until we were both sharp enough to cut. I forced a smile to my lips and followed Dejian to the bedroom.

The next day I had a meeting with Lasinha and I voiced my concerns to him. We met at his office, which by all appearances he had spent that night and many others at. There were shirts and pants littering the backs of chairs and the remains of meals spread out on his desk. Apparently we were all burning ourselves to the final ember. Somehow that gave me heart. All of us were absolutely dedicated to the task De Gofroy had blessed us with.

"It would stand to reason," Lasinha said, taking a sip of coffee from one of the mugs on the table. It looked cold, and I wondered how old it was. In spite of the signs of disarray in the room, Lasinha looked as he always did: vibrant and alert, his eyes unshadowed, his smile ever-present. "How else would they rise to such positions with blemishes on their records? Have you looked at Arajuano's?"

"I glanced through it," I said.

"Much the same, no?" Lasinha said, raising his eyebrow slightly.

"From what I saw."

"I think we don't need anything conclusive. No one knows what is in these files. Maybe the unknown is leverage enough."

"We need to have something," I said, echoing Molijc's words, hating myself for doing so.

Lasinha spread his hands expansively and smiled. "The fact that we have the files is enough. What did the Grand Regent have to declare Arajuano an apostate? His word and Osahi's. We just need to know what they fear is in those files. That should be what you are looking for."

I told Lasinha I would proceed with that in mind, though I didn't believe it would prove successful. From what I could see of the reports, the High Regents had nothing to fear from them. And we did not have the authority of De Gofroy to make them believe otherwise.

We discussed a few other matters, though I barely paid attention to what was said, my mind still on the files, and when I left I returned to my own quarters, where I resumed my study. Before I returned to the High Regents' files, I pulled up the file of woman who had been in the Grand Regent's chambers when I stole the hard drives. Her name was Meredith, and she was one of Osahi's newest lackeys.

One of my own agents had been looking into her, but so far had turned up only a few tidbits of little interest. There was very little in her file as well, for she had joined the Church only two years before. Her past was not so different than mine, and her rise through the Church had apparently been nearly as precipitous. Her file barely touch on that though, for as soon as De Gofroy had fallen ill, Osahi had ceased sending reports to him. I had no doubt reports were still being made, but Osahi was the one keeping them. I made a note to investigate that when time allowed.

Something about Meredith had caught Osahi's eye and led him to trust her. She was very good; I had to admit that. I had failed to pick her out of the crowd when I was in the Grant Regent's chambers. And I suspected she had noticed me slipping from the room and returning during the time when the alarms had sounded, though I couldn't say for sure. Something about her expression when I at last caught her watching me said as much. There had been an arrogance at her knowledge that she had bested me, which she had done nothing to hide.

It was more than that, somehow, I realized as I went over the moment once again. She had wanted me to see her, had wanted to let me know that she had seen me and that she would best me again. For no reason I could explain, I felt myself beginning to grin.

Meredith became my obsession as the Uayeb began with its attendant ceremonies, vigils and fasts. Dejian, together with Frederik and some of our other allies in the Hierarchy, started a vigil in the Grand Regent's chambers over the nameless days. As a Protector I was excused from such observances, for the faith had to be guarded at all times. In fact, there were many people about as the Uayeb began, all the various factions in the Hierarchy on alert after the alarms had sounded on the Grand Regent's stasis equipment, and knowing they needed to be prepared to set into action whatever plans they had made.

Lasinha and I, and all our agents, were busy with these preparations in the days leading into the Uayeb. They were a welcome distraction from the tedium of the Grand Regent's exhaustive and dreary secret files. Part of the distraction lay in the constant presence of my shadow as I moved about the campus to meetings. It became a kind of game between the two of us to see how long it would take me to discover Meredith in amongst the passing Regents and initiates as I went about my day. There were even times when I grew so tired of the files that I abandoned my work and walked about the campus, hoping that she would follow me. She never disappointed.

Sometimes I would try to catch her eye, to hold her gaze even for a moment, but she always resisted, smoothly looking past me, her expression unchanged. Other times I tried to lose her, even if I had nowhere important to go. Just to prove that I could, that her ability to follow me was because I allowed it. Sometimes I was successful, sometimes not. As our game went on, I thought I detected a hint of amusement in her expression during these wordless exchanges, the barest hint of acknowledgement of what we were both about.

It was undoubtedly foolish to indulge in such frivolity with one of Osahi's agents when the fate of the Church was still at play. De Gofroy barely clung to life, and he had asked me to protect his legacy and the faith itself. If I truly believed—and I was certain I did—in all that he had taught me about the universes and the Protocols, then I would not so willfully risk my and every Regent's fate in playing games with a woman, attractive as she might be. Yet I could not help myself: I was giddy with the thrill of it all.

As the Uayeb began, a stillness seemed to settle over the campus with so many people keeping vigil. The warm May days, which normally saw the pathways and streets of the campus teeming with initiates were largely quiet. Even those of us who moved about did so in a hushed and frantic fashion, scurrying about as though we were afraid to break the reverie that the rest of our fellow Regents were under. On the morning of the first day, I managed to keep to my rooms for the most part, locking myself within in my vain struggle to find anything that might be useful against Osahi and the three High Regents. By the afternoon I could no longer stand to read any more reports, my eyes aching from too long staring at a screen, and I locked up the hard drives and left my quarters.

I found my shadow almost immediately, but made a show of ignoring her, hurrying toward the Grand Regent's tower. My quarters were unguarded—normally I had one of the Protectors take up an unobtrusive watch whenever Dejian or I were absent—and I tried to put on a distracted air, as though I had just discovered something important and could not wait to tell Molijc. Whether Meredith believed my ruse or not, she could not dare to pass up such an opportunity to search my quarters for whatever she believed I had taken from the Grand Regent's study, and she soon stopped following me.

I continued on until I felt a new shadow take her place. By then I was at the Grand Regent's tower. I entered the elevator, making sure that I was alone in the car. Instead of going up to De Gofroy's quarters, I went below to the second level of the basement and locked the elevator, sending it to the top floor. My new shadow would be frantically reporting to Meredith that he could not follow me, and they would have someone else trying to pick me up to determine what I was doing and to intercept me if I was returning to my quarters. They would not have the chance.

I knew how long it would take someone like Meredith to break into my rooms and how long it would take her to break into my safe. It would give me enough time to return and catch her in the act, provided I moved fast. There were tunnels interconnecting all the buildings on campus, which once had allowed students to move about unmolested by the elements. They were locked now, and only the High Regents and a few in the Hierarchy, myself included, had access, and it was through them that I sprinted to confront Meredith.

My quarters were on the fourth floor of one of the old residences. Knowing there would be agents at the doors and the elevators, I took the stairs from the basement, to ensure that she would have little warning. As I exited the stairwell to the corridor and headed toward my door, I nodded at the woman standing watch, smiling slightly at her panic-stricken expression. I could hear her frantically whispering as I opened the door and entered, locking it behind me so that I would not be interrupted.

Meredith was in my study, standing uneasily by the safe. As I stepped into the room, both our eyes glanced down to the closed door and the equipment she had set atop it.

"I thought you might have been in by the time I got here," I said.

"Sorry to disappoint you," Meredith said. Her poise was impressive. Given my position in the Church, it would have been a simple thing for me to have her declared an apostate and taken from the Church grounds immediately. Not even Osahi would be able to protect her.

"What were you looking for?" I said.

A flicker of a smile danced across her face. "Not important now, is it?"

"I suppose not," I said, gesturing for her to leave the room.

She passed me warily, as though expecting me to attack. I watched her carefully as she paused in the living room, knowing that we were not through. She was more visibly nervous now, which I found surprising, and I glanced back to assure myself that the safe door was actually closed.

"What do you see in Osahi?" I said, not expecting an

answer and stalling for time as I studied her.

"You worked for him," she said, her equilibrium restored.

"But I always knew what he was. A blunt instrument. He has no insight into the faith, no matter what he might be telling you." I moved a step closer to her and she took an involuntary step back, raising her hands as though to ward me off.

"He's shown me the proof that Frederik is in league with an apostate who's betrayed us to the Society. That's enough for me," Meredith said. She jutted her face toward me to put more force behind her words, though her voice had an odd quiver to it.

I took another step toward her. "He showed me the same proof," I said in a calm voice. "It wasn't enough for me."

"That's because you and Molijc...just want to control the Church." She had been about to say something else, and I wondered what it was. Had Osahi told her we were in league with the Society as well? Did she believe it?

I smiled at her as if she were a wayward child. "The Grand Regent believes in Frederik and he believes in Molijc and me. He has asked us to lead this Church when he is gone. Isn't his word enough?"

A flash of doubt crept into her face, only to vanish as she set her jaw tight. "You have misled the Grand Regent. You are keeping the truth from him."

I was careful to keep my smile in place. "Is that so? Do you think someone like the Grand Regent, who could pierce the veil of the universes, would be misled by the likes of Molijc and I? We are his servants above all. Are you?"

Meredith flinched at my words, and the image of her standing poised above the safe as I burst into the room came again to my mind. I crossed the space between us and grasped her by the arm, pulling her near. Her scent was intoxicating, and I was momentarily distracted as I inhaled it deeply. Our eyes locked and I saw a mixture of fear, anger, and something else—was it desire, or was that my own reflected on her?

"Let me go," she said, though she made no move to struggle against me.

"No one is stopping you from leaving," I said, making no move to release her.

She smiled, and I felt my knees go weak. "What would Dejian say about this?"

"What would Osahi?" I countered, but I let go of her arm.

"He would say I'm doing my job," she said with a defiant glare.

She turned to go, adjusting her blouse as she went. Something about that involuntary gesture caught my attention, and I leapt at her, pulling her into my arms and pressing my lips upon hers. Meredith resisted for a moment, before returning my kiss, pressing her body against mine. My hands began to explore her body, moving from her hips to her curve of her breasts. She made a sound, somewhere between a sigh and a cry of protest, before surrendering to my touch. Soon enough I found what was looking for, the hard, angular shape of the hard drives taped between her breasts and on her stomach.

Meredith went stiff as my hands found them, but she made no attempt to stop me as I ripped them free. With them safely in hand, I released her, though my lips were still upon hers. I traced my tongue upon the lower half of her mouth, before moving to her ear, where I whispered, "You may go now," and bit down hard on her lobe.

Meredith gasped in surprise and pain, her face going red. She stepped back, her fingers touching her ear to see if I had drawn blood. She was breathing heavily, as was I, and she paused before going. "This is not over," she said.

I smiled, said, "I certainly hope not," and turned to go back to the safe, not bothering to look to see that she had left.

21

Lasinha came to see me first thing on the morning of the second day of Uayeb, a welcome distraction from my fevered thoughts. My kiss with Meredith, the warmth of her lips and the suppleness of her flesh under my insistent hands, had stayed with me through the rest of the day and haunted my dreams throughout that night. I was even restless as Lasinha talked with me, wanting our meeting to be at an end, so that I could find a reason to confront Meredith again.

I did my best to hide it, but I thought he could detect how distracted I was. He was always so perceptive, and so careful to hide his own thoughts behind that smile. I told him that I had found nothing of use, though I did not mention how close I had come to losing the drives, or that Osahi now likely knew what it was we had taken from the Grand Regent.

"It will have to do," he said, his smile never changing. I found myself wondering if he had people watching me as well, but dismissed the idea. We trusted each other and our secrets, and had since that terrible night we had exiled Arajuano. "I've just spoken with Dejian. He does not think De Gofroy will last out the Uayeb."

"That is a poor omen for us."

"Dejian will find the words for Frederik," Lasinha said.

I nodded. He would; it was his gift. After Lasinha left, I forced myself to spend the day with the files, refusing to give in to temptation, though I knew Meredith was standing somewhere near, watching my doorway. Although I did not stray from my task, my thoughts wandered continually, always returning to the kiss, my mind taking the moment further, imagining various scenarios, all with the same outcome: Meredith and I entwined in each other's arms.

That evening as I ate supper alone, Dejian messaged me that the Acolyte did not think the Grand Regent would make it through the night. I replied, asking if he wanted me to be with him as he kept his vigil, hoping that he would say yes and stop me from giving in to my own worst instincts.

Best to stay away. If you are here it might attract attention, and that we don't need. Stay home, but be ready. The next day will be a long one, I suspect.

I wanted to argue with him, but I knew he was correct. The situation was very delicate and had to be managed carefully. No one truly knew how the faithful would react to word of De Gofroy's death, especially if it fell, as it seemed it would, during the Uayeb.

I spent the evening alone, pretending to read reports, though I could barely read more than a sentence before losing my focus. I gave up eventually and went to bed, lying awake, my thoughts astir with all that was happening. It was just after midnight when my phone chimed with an alarm. I fumbled for it in the darkness.

"Yes," I whispered, expecting to hear word that De Gofroy had passed beyond.

"She is breaking into your apartment. Do you want me to send someone to stop her?"

It took me a moment to process what the Protector had said. Meredith was breaking in. She had to know that someone was watching my apartment and that I was within. She was expecting it.

"No," I said. "Let her come. I will deal with her myself."

I went to the common room to stand by the doorway, waiting for Meredith to finish picking the lock, not even bothering to dress. She showed no trace of surprise when she entered and saw me standing in the darkness awaiting her. We eyed each other warily, neither of us daring to move or speak. I was the first to break our silence and end the standoff. "What do you want?"

"I told you this wasn't over."

I shrugged and took a step toward her. "A word from me and half the Protectors' House will be here to exile you."

She made an attempt at a low, seductive laugh, but all I could hear was her nervousness. "Why aren't they here already?"

"The situation is well in hand," I said in a dismissive tone.

"Is it?" she said in a provocative voice, though I could see her hands trembling.

Osahi had put her up to this, I realized. She had reported the kiss and he had smelled an opportunity. I also knew I did not particularly care, nor, I suspected, did Meredith.

"It is," I said with a finality we both understood. Our eyes met and we both hesitated, understanding the precipice on which we stood, before we sent ourselves hurtling off, plunging into abandon.

I could still smell her on my hands over the aroma of the coffee I was brewing the next morning, the third day of the Uayeb. I had to close my eyes and take a steadying breath. The night before had been the night before. Now the day was upon me, perhaps De Gofroy's final day, and I could not afford to allow myself to be swallowed by these emotions. As I poured my first cup, I toyed with the idea of bringing one to Meredith in bed, watching as the sleep drifted from her eyes while I ran a hand through her tangled hair.

I had just pulled the mug from the shelf when there was a knock at the door. I went to it, slipping it open a crack so that I could peer out at the corridor. Lasinha was there and he burst past me, nearly knocking me to the ground. He did not appear to notice, pacing about the room, his agitation obvious. I closed the door behind him and watched, knowing that something must have gone wrong for him to come here without warning.

All I could think of, though, was my open bedroom door, where Meredith lay. Was she awake now? Would she reveal herself to Lasinha? All such worries disappeared with his next words.

"De Gofroy is dead," he said in a loud voice. "The Grand Regent is dead."

The words failed to register immediately on my consciousness, and I found myself staring at Lasinha as though he had spoken in a foreign tongue. The news was not unexpected, given all that Dejian had told me in the last days, and yet it still took me by surprise. De Gofroy was gone. The light of the Church had been extinguished, and his soul now labored to rejoin his other parts. Only we who remained alive could see it done. We had to break through the veils cast between the universe by the Society and their allies. De Gofroy's very being was at stake.

These thoughts flooded my mind and I stood overwhelmed, tears stinging at my eyes. Lasinha was watching me, and he saw the wave of emotion crest over me. He embraced me and we held each other for a time. When I had gathered myself, I stepped back and said, "What now?"

"Dejian is informing the Hierarchy as we speak," Lasinha said. "By this evening we will need to have a formal declaration to all the Church via simulcast. We'll name Frederik as De Gofroy's chosen and ask for three days of mourning, so that we are beyond the Uayeb when De Gofroy is laid to rest. Frederik will be anointed the day after."

As Lasinha spoke, I heard sheets rustling from the bedroom. There could be no doubt that Meredith was awake and trying to listen to what we were saying. My anxiety must have been evident in my expression, for Lasinha looked behind him in the direction I was staring and turned back to me with a cocked eyebrow.

"I was just thinking of the reports, is all. Would you like some coffee?" I said, heading toward the kitchen, where it would be more of a challenge for Meredith to hear what we said. I poured him a cup in the mug I had grabbed for Meredith.

"Expecting someone?" he said as he accepted the mug from me.

"I thought Dejian might come by," I said as I cursed myself for taking the mug down and for coming up with such a flimsy and easily discredited excuse. "Milk? Sugar?"

He waved me away and I gestured to the table where we sat down. "Osahi will try to stop us from making the formal declaration," I said. "It's their only play."

Lasinha nodded. "Yes. Dejian will see to that. One of the three will be making a rival declaration. We need to find out who and find a way to stop them."

"It will be Des Rosas," I said. "She is the only one they would trust with that."

Lasinha nodded in agreement. "Where is she now? Do we know?"

"Morris will," I said. "Let me get in touch with him."

"Good. Don't trust the comms or your phone," Lasinha said. "Osahi has it all, I think. Face to face only. We can't be too careful."

I had a vision of Meredith pressing herself against the edge of the doorway to my bedroom, thrusting her ear as near to the opening as she dared to better hear what we said, her naked form silhouetted in shadows. I pushed it away as quickly as I could, feeling blood rush to my face. Lasinha was staring at me, and I wondered just how long I had been lost in my thoughts.

"Is there something the matter?" he said.

"No," I said. "Just thinking about who I can trust to be a runner if I need to get you a message."

"Call in everyone who you trust. If they can be here in a couple of days or less, we will need them. We have to assume there will be fighting."

I nodded, gulping at my coffee and wincing as it stung my throat. Lasinha glanced over his shoulder, as though he had heard something, and I felt panic seize me. Had Meredith made some sort of noise? I had heard nothing, but now I could not be sure. Lasinha was looking at me again, and I wondered what he could read on my face.

"Are we alone?" he said, raising an eyebrow.

"Of course," I said.

He nodded, his face betraying none of his thoughts, though he leaned closer and lowered his voice. "Osahi needs to be removed."

"Cut off the head of the hydra," I said.

Lasinha gave a shrug that indicated his agreement. "The Arajuano stuff, everything else he knows. We can't have him in the Church once Frederik is Grand Regent. The High Regents are less important. They will fall in line when they see which way the wind is blowing."

I looked past him toward my bedroom, where Meredith stood, no doubt hanging on our every word. "If we can find evidence that he is conspiring against Frederik, or catch him in the act today, we would have the grounds to exile him from the Church as an apostate."

Lasinha shook his head. "That's not enough. We can't let him live. He knows too much."

"What do you mean?" I said, though I knew exactly what he was saying.

Lasinha gave me a look that said as much. "We'll do it today, during the declaration. He'll try to seize the Grand Regent's chambers to stop the declaration. There will be fighting, and that is when we can make sure he is taken care of."

"How do we know there will be fighting?" I said. I felt my chest begin to tighten. Not just at the thought of openly talking of murdering someone—a step that, as far as I knew, no one in the Church had ever dared to contemplate before—but at the fact that Meredith was overhearing all our plans. If she brought word to Osahi of our plot, we would have to act against him, for he would know that he would never be safe within the Church. Who knew what he might decide to do then?

"We will have to make sure there is fighting," Lasinha said, his eyes holding mine. "Find me this afternoon and we will make our plans."

With that, he left and I sat at the table, staring at my coffee, gone cold in its cup. What we were embarking on was almost too terrible to contemplate. Yet it seemed there was no turning back now. If we wanted to seize the Church, to do as De Gofroy had asked, this is what we had to do. Osahi would never stand idle against us, especially once he heard that Lasinha intended to have him killed.

That thought spurred me to my feet, and I went to my bedroom to find Meredith. I would have to stop her from reporting what she had heard to Osahi. Perhaps she could be brought to our side somehow. I was running lines in my head as I stepped into the bedroom to confront her, but the room was empty. I searched the whole apartment, convinced that she must have secreted herself somewhere, but it was empty and Meredith was gone.

22

There was only one thought in my mind: I had to find Meredith before she spoke to Osahi. Now that she was gone, and the thrill of our entanglement had evaporated in the light of day, I was overwhelmed by regret. How could I have been so stupid? And at the very moment, when the fate of the Church was in the balance. De Gofroy had entrusted us with his legacy, with the future of all the Regents, and I had allowed myself to be distracted from it as he lay dying. Now Osahi would know what we planned, and that Lasinha intended to murder him, unless I could find Meredith.

My only hope was that I knew Osahi was not on campus at the moment, if our intelligence reports were to be believed. He had removed himself at the beginning of Uayeb, once it became clear that De Gofroy was in his final days. We had been unable to locate him as yet, but I knew he would be nearby. Someone like Osahi would not trust any comms. If he had managed to penetrate ours, he would assume we had done the same. He would only communicate face to face. If I was right, Meredith would lead me to him. Finding her would solve all of my problems at once, assuming I could do it in time.

My first step was to send out a bulletin to my people to have a rotating watch set on Meredith's quarters. She would not go there, but I hoped she would believe I expected her to. Next I called Morris Loverne to join me in my quarters and updated him on what was happening now that the Grand Regent was dead.

"I need you to let everyone know. But stay off the comms. We can't trust them."

He nodded. "Of course."

"We also have to find Des Rosas. She is going to be giving the alternate declaration. We need to find her, or, failing that, where the declaration is going to be."

Morris frowned. "That's tricky without the comms."

"I know," I said with a sigh. "But we know they won't trust the comms either. So it will be somewhere nearby, somewhere they can easily get a message to and from. You've tracked her the most. My guess is it will be somewhere she is familiar with."

"I'll talk to the others who were observing her regularly. We'll come up with a list of likely candidates."

"Good. Our other problem is Osahi." I stood up to get myself some coffee, hoping to disguise my agitation. I offered some to Morris, but he waved me away, his lips pursed in thought.

"You don't think he'll be with Des Rosas?"

I shook my head. "Too risky. He'll want to be somewhere that he can use to plausibly deny his involvement."

Morris snorted. "He can't seriously expect to be able to deny he was involved."

"Not to us," I said. "But most of the Hierarchy doesn't know what has been happening. Osahi was De Gofroy's black hand for a long time. There will be enough people who will believe that he is loyal no matter the evidence we present. The same goes for the three High Regents. We cannot discredit them, not now at least. We just need to stop them. The rest can be worked out in time."

"How do we find him?" Morris said.

I sipped my coffee, taking care to make sure the gesture looked casual. "Meredith."

"Okay."

"She will take us to him. She has a message to deliver. For his eyes only."

Morris raised an eyebrow but did not ask the question that was on his mind. He knew I would not answer. Instead he asked another: "Where is she now?"

I could no longer hide my distress. "I don't know. She was here this morning, but we lost her."

I had checked with the Protector assigned to watch her that night. He had replaced the woman who had notified me she was breaking in about an hour after she had entered. For some reason, he had become convinced Meredith had slipped by him during the night, most likely during the changeover of the watch, and had gone to her room, so he had not been there to see her leave in the morning. It was both infuriating and an immense relief in the same instant. Either way, Meredith was in the wind and we had to find her.

The eyebrow went up again. "What was she doing here?"

"The reports," I said. "She doesn't have them, but she tried to get them again."

Loverne nodded, knowing from what I had told him and what I had left unsaid that she had found something else, something that we could not let Osahi find out.

"How do we find her?" I said, holding my hands open to him. We both considered this question, the silence growing heavy.

"We know that Osahi is not on campus. So she'll need to leave if she wants to get a message. We're already watching all the exit points on campus. She can't slip out without our knowing."

"I don't know that I trust that," I said. "Osahi wouldn't leave without having a safe channel set up."

"No, I suppose not. Would she trust the message to anyone else, someone that we don't suspect?"

"Maybe. But they would have to assume that we've identified all their agents. They'd want something more secure."

"What if we're looking at this the wrong way?" Morris said, his eyes widening. "They have to organize everything by tonight, just like us. They don't want the risk of having Osahi and Des Rosas on campus, but they also can't afford the time it would take to run messages to them. They won't use the comms, but that doesn't mean they won't use some other system."

I felt a shiver of electricity go up my spine through my neck. Meredith was still here somewhere. "What kind of system do you think?"

Morris shrugged. "It could be anything. Something rudimentary, I'd guess. Something no one would notice. I say we start with the high ground."

I nodded and set aside my cup of coffee. "Let's go," I said. There was not a second to waste.

There were three buildings on campus higher than ten stories. One was the Grand Regent's tower at the center of campus. We controlled it. The second was the Protectors' House, a divided land over which neither side could expect to maintain control, or keep secret their activities. The third tower, set on the southern edge of the campus, was where we focused our attention. Once the Acolytes had occupied its rooms, but they had left for what had once been the computing and engineering buildings. Now several different arms of the Church used the rooms for their work, with people always coming and going, making it easy for Osahi and his people to take over an office without anyone noticing or asking questions.

A quick search of the Church facility records gave us two likely candidates, one on the tenth and one on the thirteenth floor. Morris sent one of his people to do a quick reconnaissance. The woman reported back in less than half an hour, saying that the tenth-floor office did not have outward-facing windows, while the thirteenth-floor room looked out over Nose Hill. We sent her back with two others to keep a discreet watch on the office, which she thought was unoccupied, telling her to report anyone who entered it, and sent another two off campus, where they could find a clear view of the windows to the office and hopefully intercept whatever message Meredith was sending. Though I had no intention of giving her the chance to send it.

Morris and I went to the fourteenth floor of the tower, to the same corner of the building that the mystery office was located. There was a large office there, occupied by a team of writers who put together the books on the faith and the Protocols intended to reach out to the untouched and bring them into the fold. De Gofroy had written most of the early texts for the Church, such as the one that brought me to the faith, but he had been unable to continue that work for some time now, and it fell to this team to continue those efforts.

They looked surprised to see us when we entered the office. Apparently there were few visitors to their workspace. Their mouths went tight and their faces paled when I showed them my Protector's seal, and they offered no protest when I asked them to leave for the rest of the day.

"Can we take our work with us?" one of them dared to ask, while the rest made a show of looking anywhere but toward Morris and I.

"No," I said, offering no further explanation. If there were stories about this, I wanted them to be about what was being written here, not about what we were actually doing.

As soon as they left, Morris and I availed ourselves of the view. There was a scattering of houses from what had once been the Brentwood district of the city, now largely fallen into dereliction. Beyond that lay Nose Hill, a vast protuberance on the landscape. A few airships idled above, the airport lying to the east of Nose Hill. For so long a park lined with bicycle paths, with tables for picnicking, in the last difficult years it had been allowed to fall back into wilderness, the long native grasses overwhelming its trails. They were a vibrant green on this warm day, the sun shining gloriously above in a sky with only a scattering of clouds.

We ignored the hill—there was nothing but vagrants there—and focused our attention on the remaining houses. Those that were still standing and had not been obviously stripped for materials were presumably still inhabited, and could be Osahi's safe house. Even with so few potential candidates, it was impossible to make any determination as to which one we should focus our attention on. The only possibility was to sit and wait for Meredith to send her message and see which of the homes responded, assuming we were able to.

I sent Morris to see to tracking Des Rosas, knowing our time was short, and told him to let Lasinha know where I was. The next hours passed without incident, an excruciating passage of time, as I found myself contemplating all manner of disasters that might befall me. I was convinced that somehow we had guessed wrong and that Meredith and Osahi had found another means of passing messages to each other. Maybe they knew we hadn't cracked their comms and were using them freely.

If that were the case, I had wasted the last two hours, on top of letting Osahi know exactly what we planned. The thought made me sick. On the very day De Gofroy had died, I had utterly betrayed his trust in me, and to this point I had been able to do nothing to make up for my mistake. If anyone should come to know what I had done...

I could not finish the thought. It was too much to bear.

I was still lost in these thought and my self-recrimination when one of the team of the rotating watch below burst into the office, startling me from my chair.

"She just went into the office," he said, out of breath.

"She didn't make you?"

He shook his head. "I don't think so."

I turned back to the window and motioned him to stand by me. "Keep your eyes on the houses and be ready to move as soon as we pinpoint the location. Is the rest of the team in place?"

He moved beside me, peering out on the houses below. "They're waiting for me to return."

Seconds ticked by, turning into minutes, as both of us strained our eyes to pick out the signal from one of the houses. Nothing was visible, at least not anything that appeared to me to be a response to Meredith. Had she started her message? Were they simply not responding? I swore under my breath, wishing I knew what mechanism they were using to communicate. My head began to ache from the strain of watching.

I desperately wanted to go to my phone and call the two agents who were observing the tower from off campus. They would know whether Meredith had started communicating, but I knew that doing so would only tip off Osahi that we were here and watching. That would add to the unfolding disaster whose wave I was engulfed in. The longer we went without identifying the safe house where Osahi was coordinating his people, the better chance Meredith had to tell him all she knew, to say nothing of the fact that the two agents I had on the ground would also have the message, assuming they could break the code.

I was contemplating whether I should just order everyone into the office to seize Meredith—was it more dangerous if Osahi got her entire message, or if we didn't find out where he was located? Both were awful to contemplate—when the agent with me said, "Fuck me. The airship."

He pointed at the forgotten vessel floating lazily in the sky above Nose Hill, and I saw the flash of light. A series of flashes, more accurately. We watched it until the flashing stopped.

"Get her out of there," I said. "I'll be down in a second."

I grabbed a scrap of paper and a pen from one of the desks and scribbled down the signals while I still remembered them, hoping that I had it correct, before I followed him downstairs. Two men were wrestling to control Meredith in the office, as she tried frantically to return to the signal lamp bolted to the windowsill. She bit one of them and he let out a cry, causing a gasp of consternation from the gathering crowd in the hallway who were watching intently.

"Go to your offices immediately," I said, with what hoped was an air of command. "This does not concern you. It is Protector business."

That was enough to get everyone to disperse. I went into the office, motioning to the other two members of the team to take up positions at the door, which I closed behind me. The two agents had managed to finally to get hold of Meredith, and she glared at me, a snarl of rage on her face.

"How much did you get sent?" I said, ignoring her stare and going over to look at the signal lamp.

Meredith did not answer. I could feel the derision in her stare and I turned to face her, smiling. "Nothing to say? You've bet on the wrong horse, you know. It doesn't matter what you told Osahi. Frederik will be Grand Regent. It is De Gofroy's last wish. Everyone knows it. Would you defy the Grand Regent?"

She offered no reply, but I had not expected one. What I had said was for the benefit of my agents rather than Meredith. Word of De Gofroy's death would be spreading now, and all sorts of rumors and talk of his final intentions would begin to emerge. It needed to be said and said again as clearly as possible what the Grand Regent's wishes were. We could assume no one's loyalty, not with Osahi's involvement.

I turned my attention to the signal lamp again, looking out the window to see if the airship had resumed signaling. It had not, and I glanced back at Meredith. "I don't suppose you're going to tell me what the code is, are you? I assume Morse."

I pulled the sheet where I had jotted down the airship's earlier signal and unfolded it on the desk. As I did, I noticed a book with an innocuous grey cover on the corner of the desk. I picked it up and began to flip through it. I could feel Meredith going stiff beside me and I looked up at her, raising an eyebrow. She would not meet my eyes, and I knew that I had discovered the code book.

It was, I saw as I went through the pages, a variety of different codes, to be used at different times. There was no indication of which one was in use today. I sighed. Nothing was ever simple. On a hunch, I pulled open the drawers to the desk, looking for any scrap of paper. There was only one, and it was marked in pencil with a series of dashes and dots. I looked through to the final section and compared it to what I had written. The ending was the same. I had Osahi's replies, then, presumably in their entirety.

There was no translation of the Morse, although Meredith had made a few markings indicating letter, word, and message breaks, so I would be able to figure out which code they were using eventually, given time. But time was not something I could afford. Meredith had marked the top of the page with a large "3." I stared at it a moment, trying to divine her intention, before nodding to myself and turning back to the code book.

"You can take her away," I said, already engrossed in the citations. "I will deal with her later."

I looked up as they left, and nodded at one of the agents standing watch to close the door. Before I had a chance to return to the code book, I noticed that the airship was signaling again, and I began to mark it down. When they had finished, I realized it was the same message as the last one. No doubt they were awaiting a response from Meredith. I would have to give them one.

Returning to the code book, I searched the pages for a Morse code that had been shifted three letters. There were two, one shifting it forward, one backward, and a quick run through the last message showed that the code had been shifted forward. Leaving the message aside for the moment, I put together one of my own and began to signal a reply. "Halt all signals. Believe under observation. Will confirm with SOS."

I watched the airship for a moment to see what it would do, but it remained floating above Nose Hill as innocuous as ever. When I had assured myself that they were awaiting my response, I returned to the message and translated all that Meredith had recorded. It read: "Do they know our location?... Who knows what you have heard?... Follow emergency protocols. Laila will seek to neutralize. Rendezvous at section 2 at 1800. Confirm receipt."

I stared at my translation for several seconds before the full force of the words and their meaning hit my body, a wave cresting and falling upon me with all its incredible weight. My legs seemed to have lost all sensation, and I staggered to the floor. Fury came next, overwhelming the shock, and suddenly I was back on my feet, throwing a chair against the wall and punching the desk as hard as I could. "Fucking cunt. Motherfucking cunt." I continued shouting until I remembered the two agents outside the door, and I forced myself to be calm. I leaned against the desk, my hands pressed painfully into it—it was agony, and I wondered if I had broken my hand—drawing in deep and ragged breaths until I could see again.

When I had at last regained my self-control, I turned back to the signal lamp and began to send another message: "Rendezvous at section 2 at 1800. Confirmed."

I waited as the airship signaled its own confirmation, though I hardly noticed. All I could think about was Osahi. He knew about Meredith and I; he knew that I had failed De Gofroy, Molijc, and Lasinha. He knew everything and could see me destroyed. How could I have let this happen, to have him hold such power over me?

I put that question aside, forcing the bile in my stomach down. It was done. The question now was how to handle the fallout. Lasinha wanted Osahi dead, as he now knew. If I could get to him before Lasinha, perhaps there was a deal there to be made. A life for his silence. It was my only hope.

23

It was approaching five in the evening when I met with Lasinha in his office, my thoughts edged with exhaustion, my body feeling numb. I had yet to eat that day, but hunger did not burn at me, my stomach too twisted by worry and fear. It was one hour until Meredith's rendezvous with Osahi, and three hours until Frederik was set to address the faithful.

Word of De Gofroy's death had already begun to spread across campus and the other Protocol Centers, and soon would reach the faithful everywhere. Next would come the wild rumors and conspiracies. I could hear them even now. Perhaps it would even become necessary for us to start some of them ourselves. No doubt Osahi would be considering the same tactic.

There would be stories of the various claimants to the Grand Regent's throne, all of whom were conspiring together, while simultaneously betraying each other, in order to remove De Gofroy and seize control of the Church for themselves. Behind every maneuver would lurk the dark and hidden hand of the Society of Travelers, who, in these stories, had placed people at every level of the Church in order to ensure that power was transferred to their chosen Regent.

The great irony, of course, was that the rumors could almost be true. Osahi was leading a conspiracy to thwart the Grand Regent's final wishes. He would say that it was the case that the Society had agents within the Church, and that one of those had influence over Frederik. By ignoring it, we—Molijc, Lasinha, and I—were, for all intents and purposes, allying ourselves with the Travelers. And we were contemplating the murder of a fellow Regent, to ensure that what he knew of Frederik never came to light.

Where was the faith in all of this, the word of De Gofroy? It was hard to see amidst all we were doing, and yet all of us would have sworn on our lives that what we were doing was essential to the faith. I myself had no doubts on that matter, and nor did Lasinha. We were both palpably aware of the significance of this day, and of all that remained to be done to assure that we triumphed. I could see it on his face when he stepped into the office and said, without preamble, "What do we know?"

"Osahi hasn't left the airship. It hasn't set down and we have people watching it. They haven't signaled anyone else. Meredith won't tell me anything, and we haven't figured out where the rendezvous point is."

Lasinha sighed. "And Des Rosas?"

"I still haven't heard back from Morris."

"We're running out of time."

"I know," I said, "I know. Are we ready to broadcast?"

"Everything is as secure as I can manage. There's only people I trust around the tower. But even then we can't be sure. Osahi has his people everywhere. He's so deep into things we may not even know."

"Speaking of Osahi…" I let my voice trail off.

Lasinha nodded. "If we could find a way to keep him in the airship and keep him out of play, that would be useful. Then we could deal with him at our leisure."

"What if we take the ship down?"

Lasinha shook his head. "We don't have that kind of

firepower. And who knows who is on board? We don't want to be killing people indiscriminately, not if they can be useful."

"I wasn't thinking of that, exactly. I'm not sure that he needs to be killed." Lasinha raised an eyebrow and was about to argue with me, but I held up a hand to forestall him. "We just need to take the ship out of play. Force it to land at the airfield and have everyone detained for a couple of days. Then we can deal with them at our leisure."

Lasinha thrummed his fingers on his desk. "Do we know anyone in the aviation authority who we could press to do that?"

"No," I said. "I wouldn't trust them even if we did. Osahi might be able to buy them. What we need is to get the Society involved. They can ground the ship. They can seize whoever is in there."

Lasinha stiffened at my mention of the Travelers. "I don't want them involved," he said. "The situation is precarious enough without bringing them in. Besides, we don't want them talking to Osahi."

"Osahi won't talk," I said. "We know he has people in the Society too. He'll wait for them to get him out. All we need is to make sure that he stays grounded for the rest of today."

"I don't like it," Lasinha said, still shaking his head.

I shrugged. What other choice did we have?

At last he relented. "Damn Morris. Why hasn't he found Des Rosas? Fine. I will talk to number seven and see what she can do."

We referred to the agents we had in the Society by numbers, based on how deep they were in the Travelers' hierarchy and their location. Only Ana did not have a number, and we did not speak of her. Not that there was anything to be said, as she remained incommunicado. I could not even say for certain she was still alive, though I desperately hoped she was.

Seven was based in Calgary, well placed to bring the full

weight of the local apparatus to bear on Osahi's airship without attracting attention to herself.

"It's our best option," I said.

Lasinha waved a hand, his face clouded with anger. "Just find Morris. We need to know where Des Rosas is."

"Send me word when you know the ship can be grounded," I said as I got to my feet. Lasinha nodded, his displeasure still evident. I knew why. If Osahi was under Society watch, it would be difficult to ensure he was killed, which would give me the chance I needed to speak to him before Lasinha could act.

I did not bother with Morris. He would find me when he knew something. Instead I returned to the cell where we were keeping Meredith. She had said nothing to this point, and I did not expect her to reveal anything else now. She knew time was on her side. Our only advantage lay in the next hour, before she was supposed to rendezvous. Once she failed to arrive, as expected, Osahi would know we had intercepted her and would alter his plans. Unless we managed to ground the airship before then.

She was sitting cross-legged on the floor, her eyes closed, as though in meditation. As I sat in a chair across from her, she opened her eyes only slightly and closed them again, a smile stirring briefly across her face. "You cannot stop us," she said. "De Gofroy is on our side."

"You know that's not true," I said. "No matter how you might pretend otherwise, you know that we're doing what De Gofroy has asked of us."

"He was led astray. By Molijc."

"How could De Gofroy be led astray? Listen to yourself. Such a thing is not possible and you know it. His is the chosen vessel."

"That doesn't mean he cannot be led astray," Meredith said, her eyes flashing open.

I saw fire in them, and I felt something stir within me. "Tell me which is more likely. That De Gofroy was led astray, or that Osahi is wrong?"

She blinked and looked away, not saying anything. I stared at her, waiting. When it was clear she was not going to speak, I said, "I'm not asking you to betray him. I know you won't. I'm just asking that you think about your own future in the Church after today. You don't want to tie yourself to him. Not now."

"Why? Will I get killed too?"

"No one is getting killed today," I said.

"That's not what I heard this morning," Meredith said.

I took her hand in mine, holding it tight as she tried to pull away. "Listen to me," I said. "I know what you heard, and I am here to tell you that I will not allow any Regent to kill another Regent. Osahi is a problem for us, but he is only doing what he believes is right. That is no reason for him to die, and I swear to you I will do whatever I can to keep him alive."

Meredith stared at me, not speaking again, but I could tell she was considering what I had said.

"Listen," I said, still clutching at her hand, "you and I have started something. I don't know what, but I know you feel it too."

"We can't keep doing this," Meredith said, pulling her hand away and shaking her head. "It's beyond stupidity."

"It's madness," I said, nodding in agreement. "But I don't care. And I don't think you care either. I want to see it through. There is a way to do that. If you join us, I will make sure that Osahi is protected. I will bring him back into the fold. Molijc will listen to me, and Frederik listens to him. It can be done."

"And what about Molijc?"

I could not look at her. "That is my problem to deal with. If it comes to that."

She raised an eyebrow, but did not ask the question that I could see shadowing her face. I answered it anyway. "His first bride is the Church. I will always be second for him."

I had never allowed myself that thought before, let alone spoken it aloud, yet as soon as the words were said, the weight of their truth settled upon my shoulders. I would always be second for Dejian. The Grand Regency would always come first. If the two ever came in conflict, it would be me who would be set aside. It did not change the fact that I had betrayed him with Meredith, and that I had put all of us at risk this day in doing so. He would never forgive me if he knew, and yet I did not care. It was madness.

I found Meredith's eyes again. "What do you say?"

She almost spoke, her mouth open and her lips wet, but no words came forth. Instead she stood up and folded herself into my welcoming arms, her lips finding mine to give me her reply.

THREE:

MORRIS

24

The room I step into is much smaller than the one I left on the other side, with none of the vast array of equipment, nor any corridors leading off it. Instead there is a small transfer unit, similar to the one I managed to construct in the other universe, set in a corner, its lights flashing out of sequence now that the channel is closed. There is a single door behind me and the room has no windows. But for the transfer unit it is bare, with only a fine layer of dust on the floor suggesting it is still a part of some universe.

I am alone as well, though I still find myself glancing over my shoulder, half expecting to see the Travelers approaching, pulse weapons at the ready. My own gun I dropped to the floor in my transfer. I walk over to pick it up, but my hands are shaking so badly I can't even manage to grip it. I collapse to the floor, blinking against the lights that swim up from my unconsciousness, until I manage to return to a semblance of equilibrium.

In spite of my struggles, I feel a sense of exhilaration at what I have achieved. Rather than trying to balance the transfer to hide the signal as we normally do, I crossed over, using the signal from Sebastien's transfer to disguise my own. I sent him to what I knew to be a Society transfer point in the universe I am now in. It will take them hours to sort out my signal from the other and pinpoint where I crossed to. That is enough time to clean me of my signal, and to disappear so that even the Seeker will have trouble finding me. Here we have the technology to manage that. Here I will not be so on the run.

I try to stand up but am not able to manage it just yet, the aftershocks of my latest ordeal lingering. It is strange that I am alone here. Where are Morris and the others? The message in the Humboldt volume told me to transfer here, to this basement. It seems unfamiliar, though I was here before. This is where it all began, my resistance to Molijc. Only he would appreciate the irony of me using this place against him, though not any longer. He is long past appreciating such things.

I cough miserably and blink back the lights that threaten again to overwhelm me. Aeida, too, is disturbed, reacting violently. Something is the matter with me. The result of the transfer, maybe.

A just consequence, given what I did to Sebastien. I used him. Sent him to his doom among the Travelers. They will never let him from their clutches. He will disappear as so many others have, never to be seen or heard from again. It is not what he deserves, but the fate of the universes is at hand. Molijc cannot be allowed to pervert De Gofroy's work any longer. The true faithful must reclaim the Church if we are to ever find the One Universe.

My thoughts ring hollow, sounding like lies even to me. All I want is to see Molijc pays for what he has done to me and to reclaim the body that is mine. And I will do whatever it takes, sacrifice whoever must be sacrificed, in order to see that done.

Why is no one here to greet me yet? They have to be expecting me—they told me when to come across and where. This is our safe house. Maybe they are staying above to keep watch. If the Society and Molijc's people are both closing in on them, and they will be after our earlier failure to cross, then every moment we stay in one place could be perilous.

Add to that, the house is no longer safe now that I have crossed to it. We will need to leave very soon and start the process of removing my transfer signal and cloaking the fact that this flesh is not of this universe. This is what gets me to my feet at last. No matter my state, we can't afford to waste any time now, or my transfer will all be for naught.

I stand, wavering slightly, and when I feel steady enough, I walk to the door. My hand shakes badly still, the handle rattling as I turn it. My grip is so flimsy that I can barely turn it, and for a second I think the door is locked and that I am trapped here. The door at last clicks open, though, and I see that my situation is infinitely worse than that. The Seeker is on the other side, there to greet me.

25

"We meet again, David Aeida. Or should I call you Laila?"

There is no expression on the Seeker's face, but I could swear he is smiling. Something about the way he stands looking at me betrays his amusement. That he stood on the other side of the door, letting me savor my presumed triumph before revealing that he has ensnared me again, tells me all I need to know. He is enjoying this. He wants me to know that, wants me to realize that all my earlier victories against him were fleeting. In the end, he found me. In the end, he is victorious.

I don't reply to his question, trying to steady myself. The shock of seeing him there is so overwhelming that I think I might be ill. If I am, I am going to be certain it is on his immaculate grey robe and spotless boots.

"Do not look so surprised, Aeida," the Seeker says. "We knew sooner or later you would try to return to this universe. And once we had determined who you really were, we knew it would be sooner rather than later. It was just a matter of directing you so that we could be certain you would arrive in our hands."

How, I wonder, did they manage to figure out who I really am? Someone betrayed me, or was made to. There is no other explanation.

The thought leaves me cold. They will have everyone now. All of those who dared to stand against Molijc and Lasinha and their reign of terror will find themselves in the clutches of the Travelers. The cruelest of fates. The Grand Regent could not have planned it better if he tried.

"Why bother with the team on the other side if you compromised our communication?" I say, bitterness leaching into my voice.

"You have proven most elusive, David Aeida, as I know firsthand. It seemed better not to underestimate you. Besides, if there had been no pursuit, you might have suspected that your people had been compromised."

I try and fail to search for a way I could have avoided capture. If I stayed on the other side, the team they sent across would eventually have found me. Them, or Meredith, or some others working for the Grand Regent. It was all too inevitable, and I was only fooling myself to believe otherwise.

Defeat seeps through my body and sits like a weight upon my limbs. It is over, I think, struggling not to weep. I will be trapped in this flesh forever, sent off to some prison in some lost universe, there to stay in the darkness for what remains of my days, punishment for the crimes I have committed against the Society. That is after the Seeker has taken all the information on the Church I possess. I can feel the pull of his eyes even now, and I almost surrender to them. What is the point of resisting?

"What about Sebastien?" I say, wondering if I can at least spare him my fate. What I did to him was unconscionable, and only justifiable in the event that I succeeded in destroying the Grand Regent and restoring myself to my body. All impossible now.

"He will be questioned and returned to his universe," the Seeker says. "He is no more than a pawn in this game. As, for that matter, are you. But you we have use for yet."

I am unable to stop myself from looking at him, and I

fall into the terrible orbit of his eyes.

This time he does in fact smile. "Come along, Aeida, and I will tell you what we want."

26

They don't take me to that industrial street near downtown Calgary where, in another lifetime, it seems, Lasinha and I dropped off Ana's father, handing him over to the Society and exiling him from the Church. Instead I am brought to another neighborhood, somewhere to the south of downtown. Another anonymous building, perhaps once a warehouse or a factory. Now only the skeleton of its former existence remains, empty corridors and rooms, blank walls, and only rudimentary furnishings here and there. The Seeker and his Society men lead me through its warren of hallways, like a condemned prisoner being ushered to the gallows.

In a way, I am. I will never emerge from this place again. I won't remain in this specific location, of course. I will be ushered from black site to black site, all places that look more or less like this. Where exactly they are doesn't matter. What does is that I will be removed utterly from this world and put in another, hidden from the universes. This is its own universe, with its own laws. Only there will be no channels across which I can go to escape.

I cannot help but recall the building Osahi brought me to when he captured me at the market. That was a near thing all around. His people hadn't realized who Meredith was, and so he failed to make the connection to me, to realize my true importance. That meant they were new to the Church, if they had failed to recognize her. I am unsure what this might mean, given that we have been hemorrhaging faithful since Molijc created the Watcher's Order.

Of course, Osahi believed Laila was still at Molijc's side, lobotomized by the Acolytes. I was very careful to keep him from realizing what I was attempting against Molijc, which in the end might have been a mistake. In the predicament I am in, I need allies. I don't trust him, though, and never have.

I am left alone in an empty room at the center of the building. It smells vaguely of mildew, and the floor is covered in a thick layer of drywall dust. A naked fluorescent bulb glares down at me from above. In spite of the unwelcoming surroundings, I lie on the floor, trying not to breathe in the dust, and attempt to go to sleep. I don't know when I will next have the opportunity, and it feels like days since I have done so.

It is difficult to fall asleep. Aeida seems hyperactive within me, trying again and again to wrest control of my consciousness away. Crossing over did something to us, it seems, upsetting whatever precarious balance existed previously. My hands have still not stopped shaking, and as I lie there I have to clasp them together, my fingers interlocking with one another, gripping hard, to still them. It does no good: they seem to vibrate of their own accord. I will never be whole again, they seem to be telling me, and that I no longer doubt.

Footsteps outside the door wake me, and I rise from the floor in time to see the Seeker enter. He is alone, though I glimpse one of the Black Robes standing watch outside the door. He looms over me, waiting until I at last give in and stand up to face him, being careful, as always, not to meet his eyes. I can still feel those strange orbs upon me, can feel the pull of them, their awful gravity. I resist, though I can't say why. Soon enough I will have to face them, and I will tell him everything. It is inevitable.

He waits, as though expecting me to speak first. I hold my tongue, not wanting to give him the satisfaction of seeing me crumble. As our standoff continues, I try to guess what questions he might ask me. What does the Society want to know about the Church? And what do I know that those already taken don't? Perhaps there is a way to turn the Society upon Molijc and Lasinha, to purge the Church without destroying it. The Seeker is a blunt instrument, as are the Black Robes generally, so it seems unlikely that I will do anything but destroy the Church utterly. But I have to try. I owe that much at least to those who remain.

"Tell me, Aeida, what do you know of the Seekers' Guild?"

His words startle me, our silence, uneasy as it was, persisting so long that I am surprised when it is broken. I risk looking at him, but his expression, implacable as always, tells me nothing.

"You are a guild, like any other. Like the Society. Like the Acolytes. You can supposedly be hired by any state or person who can afford your fees, for any task allowed by your guild law. Is that enough, or would you like a historical analysis as well?"

The faint outlines of a smile touch the Seeker's lips. "Do you remember the last time we spoke? I talked of how fate defines our lives. Well, fate has brought us together again, David Aeida."

"Is that what the Society calls torture now? I wonder if my friends feel the same way."

"And it has given us an opportunity," the Seeker continues, ignoring my interjection, "to see where a shared path might lie."

I can feel his eyes on me, judging my reaction. "Is that

an offer?"

"It is. I think you will find our goals have a certain synchronicity to them at the moment."

"I doubt that very much."

"Do not be so quick to judge Laila," the Seeker says, pulling back his hood to reveal his long hair, which is pulled back into a bun at the back of his head.

I can't resist a closer glance at him, and am surprised at how androgynous his features are, in direct contrast to his cavernous voice. It is partly because he looks so young, his face without any of the stubble that is perpetually upon Aeida's, much to my annoyance. I have, I realize, never looked at him before, my focus always on those eyes, fighting to avoid them, yet always being drawn to them.

"You desire the removal of the Grand Regent and the destruction of the Watchers' Order apparatus. Along with the restoration of your body. We want the same thing."

"You want the destruction of the Church itself. You deny our very reason for being," I say.

He gives something of a shrug. "You are perverting all reasonable understanding of the nature of the universes, with the result that they are being polluted with billions of lives being sent astray. You deny these people their proper and rightful existence in their own worlds. That is, in my mind, a heinous crime, one for which all those in the Church should be punished. Or at least those who have passed from belief to action in the matter."

"You deny our right to practice our faith," I say, my hands beginning to shake again. I clench them tight, but not before the Seeker notices.

"Your faith and its followers are deluded. Which is why you and your ilk are dangerous. You can so easily be led astray."

"De Gofroy understood more of the nature of the universes than you could ever hope to. He saw through the clouds that the Society has erected to hide their crimes, their attempts to deny our true fragmented and false nature, and he saw the path to our return to our true selves."

"You ,of all people, should know that one can be fragmented, Laila Aeida. There is nothing false in that," the Seeker says, watching my hands, which continue to tremble, in spite of my best efforts to stop them.

I turn away, unable to face him anymore, tears streaming down my face. "There is nothing true in me," I say. "I am a simulacrum, nothing more."

The Seeker takes a step toward me and presses his hand upon my forehead. His fingers are cool and dry, like any others, somehow not at all what I expected.

"That is not true," he says. "You were something else before. Now you are different."

"I don't want to be this," I say. "He destroyed me and I will destroy him."

The Seeker doesn't reply, and I turn around to face him. His eyes are just eyes, the power of them absent for the moment. "As I said, our goals are synchronous for the moment. There is much to discuss."

27

Before he continues, the Seeker takes me down the hall to another room, where there is a table and chairs for us to sit at. One of the Black Robes brings in a plate of sandwiches cut into halves and two cups of coffee and sets them between us. The Seeker gestures for me to help myself, and I do, devouring several halves as quickly as I can. While I eat, the Seeker speaks, sipping at his coffee now and again.

"Now, as to our aligned interests, here is what I propose. You do not take anything in that, do you?" He gestures at my coffee and I shake my head. He continues, "We will allow you to go free, to return to your people and to continue your work against Molijc. We will discuss the specifics of that in a moment. We will help you in whatever way we can in this endeavor. That, too, we can discuss. Our information on the inner workings of the Church has become clouded since the purge by the Watchers."

"You lost your assets there," I say, and the Seeker nods.

"Yes, many innocents were swept up, as were a few of our people, in that whirlwind. So I suppose you could say it was worth it."

"I would not say that," I say, speaking around a bite of egg salad.

"No, though both of you played your part in it."

I look away from the Seeker, Aeida's memories competing with my own in my thoughts. "There is blood on my hands. I told myself it was worth the price."

"Was it?"

There is no hint of mockery in the Seeker's voice, though I look hard to find it. "No, certainly not. Maybe if I can restore myself and restore the Church, I can tell myself that those losses were worth it. Their lives had meaning. But I'll be lying to myself. I'll probably believe it."

"We always do believe the lies we tell ourselves," the Seeker says, and takes a sip of coffee. "To return to our proposal. We will set you free and return you to your people. This rebellion of yours. Many of them are still in place, though I think they are suspected by the Grand Regent. Still, you should be able to continue with your plans and see to the overthrow of the Grand Regent. We will be able to help you more then, as you might guess, removing certain individuals from play and that sort of thing. In return, we want to know what you know about the Church. What the Watchers' Order is doing."

"And if I succeed," I say, "what then? Am I still to provide the Society with whatever information they desire?"

The Seeker gives an ambiguous shrug. Either he doesn't care what happens after Molijc is overthrown, or he does not expect me to succeed.

"Our alliance would be finished at that point," he says. "Our goals would obviously diverge, and possibly even stand opposed. This should be familiar to you, given your past with the Society."

He is talking about Ana, but I ignore that. "Wouldn't they be opposed of necessity? The Society stands against everything we believe."

"Not necessarily," he says. "Things are more complex than you realize, Laila Aeida."

Understanding begins to dawn on me. There is a reason why we are meeting here at this site and not the one Lasinha and I dropped Arajuano off at. And there is a reason the place appears empty but for the Seeker and the Black Robes with him.

"You aren't working for the Society, are you? That's why the extraction team was in the other universe. That's why you can't offer me any support. You never had anyone in the Church to begin with."

The Seeker shakes his head. "Obviously we have someone with your people. That is why we were able to intercept you. You will meet soon enough, should you agree to our proposal."

"But you don't work for the Society?"

"The Society is a multifarious thing. Not all our beliefs are uniform."

"Great. I've joined up with an even more hopeless rebellion. Not just the rebellion, but the rebellion's hired guns. Why don't you just turn me over to the Travelers or Molijc and be done with it? I'm surprised they haven't offered you a better deal."

One of the Black Robes enters the room and kneels to whisper in the Seeker's ear. He listens to what is said with a distant expression on his face. Once his message is delivered, the Black Robe leaves the room and the Seeker turns his attention to me.

"I asked you before what you knew of our guild. We are not the same as other societies. We do not go to the highest bidder. Everything we do is with an eye to the proper order of the universes. That is why we have worked in concert with the Society of Travelers for years in order to ensure the universes are properly policed. But not everyone agrees on how this must be done within the Society."

"What does that have to do with the Church?" I say.

"Your Church, with the power it has gained, is the greatest threat to order in the universe," the Seeker says. "If it were up to me, the Grand Regent and all your believers would be removed from the earth. But for the time being, it suits my purposes to use you against the Church. If nothing else, you can cause some havoc. If you do as I say, work in concert with our allies, you may be able to regain your Church and your body."

"And if I refuse to be your weapon?"

"You won't," he says, and smiles.

28

The Seeker is right, of course. I cannot refuse. Even if he intends to use me to destroy the Church, as seems evident whatever he might say about shared designs, I am willing to be his implement if it means I can have my revenge upon Molijc for what he has done to me. I am willing to set the whole thing to fire, if only to deny him. In truth, I am little better than he, working only toward my own ends with no care for the faithful or the Church.

After our conversation, the Seeker leaves me alone. I finish the last of the sandwiches and my coffee, ignoring the acid biting my stomach. As I am taking my last bites, one of the Black Robes comes in. Without preamble, he sits across from me.

"We have made arrangements with one of our remaining agents in the Church to make contact with you and help you in your rebellion," he says, not even bothering to ask if I have agreed to join causes with them. "He has been involved with your cause for some time. You know him quite well, in fact."

"Morris," I say, the realization coming to me suddenly.

"Yes," the Black Robe says. Aeida curses me for a fool, and I wonder how I missed it. It seems impossible and yet

I am unsurprised. There is no betrayal remaining that can cut as deep as Dejian's and Meredith's.

"Why even bother pretending that I was Aeida on the other side?" I say, giving voice to my bitterness. I have an endless number of questions, foremost among them how long Morris had been one of them, but this is the one I give voice to.

"He did not inform us of the nature of your situation until after you reported the destruction of the transponder you stole. He judged that the only way to get you across was to involve us. And since we want your little rebellion to continue, we acted."

The Seeker enters as the Black Robe is speaking. He looks at me, and I shiver in spite of myself. "I suspected your true nature from the moment we met," he says. "But I did not know for certain. Morris has existed in deep cover for some time. He cannot inform us of all that is happening, for reasons which you will no doubt be aware, given your own experiences. He took a great risk in reaching out to us, because he thought you were important to your cause and ours. Let us hope he is correct."

I resist the urge to ask any further questions. I don't trust the Seeker or the Travelers, and I will not believe what they tell me anyway. As the Black Robe outlines how I am to make contact with Morris, my mind goes back to that shared memory, one side of it Aeida's, the other my own, when I met Morris in the bar in the other world to prepare for my insurrection. That was before I realized just how far Lasinha had stretched his tentacles and just how much he knew. Before my nightmare truly began.

"Suspicions will be aroused with you turning up without any provenance, so to speak," the Traveler says. "Morris has been laying the groundwork for this, so that you can re-enter your movement without issue. But you will have to trust him."

To hell with that, I think, but don't say. I will play their game only as long as it suits my purposes.

The Seeker seems to sense my thoughts on the matter. "He is your conduit to me," he says, emphasizing the last word. It is both promise and threat. "When the time is right, I can create chaos that will provide you some cover. Remember that."

I nod, but do not answer. When the time is right, I plan to create chaos of my own.

A Black Robe drives me across the city in silence, not even glancing in my direction. It is after three in the morning and the streets are barren. I have long since lost all sense of how many hours I have been awake. Exhaustion is burning at the back of my eyes, and yet sleep, I know, will elude me. My mind cannot stop whirring with thoughts.

I don't believe for a moment the Seeker's claims to be working at odds with the Society. He is doing the Travelers' bidding, setting us one against the other, hoping to sow whatever chaos he can in our ranks. Not that he needs much assistance with the Watchers' Order at work, staining the whole Church with Molijc's paranoia.

It amuses me, in a twisted sort of way, that his seeing betrayal in every face has been its own self-fulfilling prophecy. Only after he suspected me of unfaithfulness did I betray him, after all. Though that was not the first betrayal. Our duplicity against each other was seemingly without end, and the trust we had was that we would betray each other eventually. Now he has made me an apostate to my own faith, willing to sit down with my enemies if it will bring me closer to revenge.

The Black Robe takes me into downtown, which is a ghostly terrain this far into the night. A hundred glass buildings glowing with light, and all of them empty. We sit at intersections listening to the car idle, waiting for the lights to change. I find myself running through the conversations I will have with Morris once we meet again. Sometimes I am white hot with fury, incandescent with emotion. Other times I am distant and cold, all calculation and disdain.

Even as these thoughts echo through my mind, I know I won't act on them. I need Loverne. He is my conduit to everyone in the insurrection now. He has been with me from almost the beginning, one of those indispensable people who knows people at all levels of the Church and can move about without being seen. A man who can disappear and be everywhere, seemingly. That is why it is no surprise he is with the Society. He is the sort they look for and appeal to.

I am so lost in thought I don't notice we have arrived until the door to the car is being opened by the hotel concierge. I glance at the Black Robe, but he continues to stare straight ahead as though I have already left the car. The concierge smiles at me, unsure what the delay is. I get out and he leads me into lobby and gestures to a seat on one of the long couches arranged opposite the front desk. But for the concierge and the woman at the front desk, the place is empty and hushed. I wait.

Ten minutes pass before there is a phone call at the front desk. The woman speaks to the caller in a low voice. I watch, intent, as she hangs up the phone and comes around the desk to approach me.

"You are Joseph Aurellano?" she says in the same murmur. I nod. "Your party is waiting for you in 320."

She gestures toward the bank of elevators across the lobby, and I nod again and head toward them.

The lighting in the elevator is odd, making me feel as though I am under interrogation as it ascends. My trepidation only grows as I approach the room. If Morris, one of my oldest compatriots in the Church, can betray me so completely and for so long, what can I trust now? Not myself, not with Aeida within and this false flesh without.

I pause in the hallway outside the room and close my eyes to gather myself. I've gotten myself this far. I can go the rest of the way. Taking a deep breath, I knock on the door.

Morris Loverne opens it and motions me in. I follow him inside, taking care not to let him out of my sight. He walks past the two beds, one of which has rumpled sheets, and sits under the window in one of the room's two chairs. After taking a moment to survey the room and look in the bathroom to assure myself that we are alone, I join him. The curtains on the window are drawn tight, and the only light comes from above the table, bathing the room in shadows.

"I'm sorry that—" Morris begins, but I cut him off.

"Motherfucker," I say. "How long?"

He swallows and is careful to avoid my eyes. "I've always been with the Society. I don't know who else, so don't bother asking. They don't tell us that."

"What do they tell you?"

He shrugs and smiles. "You know what the Society says—you have agents with them, right? They say the same thing you say to yours. We're sending hundreds of you, we're not going to tell you who else, trust no one, and get as deep in as you can. And then you hope someone is able to."

Morris is staring at my hands, and when I glance down I see they are shaking violently. I put them in my pockets to still them. I can barely contain my rage.

"How many Regents did I send to their doom because of you?" There are tears in my eyes. I don't want him to see.

"None," he says, concern etched on his face. "None, I swear to you. All your agents were kept in play. You know that. We just made sure they were kept out of the loop. Fed them false information."

"For now," I say with a bitter shake of my head. "But what happens when you decide that I am done? That I'm not getting my body back? What use is there in keeping those people in place then? None. And we both know what will happen to them then."

"We're getting your body back," Morris says. "We're getting the Church back."

"Is that what you told your masters too?"

Morris stands and goes to the bathroom. I let him go without following him to make sure he isn't trying anything. There seems no point now. I hear the tap running, and he returns with two glasses of water in his hands. He holds one out to me.

"You look like you could use some water."

I refuse to take the glass from him, in part because I am afraid I will drop it, my hands are shaking so badly. He sets it down on the table in front of me and resumes his seat.

"You haven't answered my question," I say, trying to land the words like a fist to his jaw.

"I've told them what they need to know. Look, you won't believe me, but I've been embedded long enough to know that all the Regents would be far better off with you leading the Church, not that madman."

"Spare me," I say with a vicious shake of my head. It seems my mind is losing command of my body. Is Aeida taking over? That does not appear to be the case. He has no more access to my motor controls than I do.

Morris is staring again, and I look away at the curtains, as though I might peer through the window. "Look," he says in a gentle voice, "maybe I can't fix this. I thought you would understand, but that was wishful thinking. And it doesn't matter. We have to work together, whether we like it or not. There's no choice."

I meet his eyes, my whole body seeming to vibrate. I refuse to say anything, even though I know he is right. The silence stretches on between us as he waits.

"We can't stay here," he says at last with a sigh. "It's not secure. I've established another safe house. I'm the only one who knows about it. Let's go there and we can talk about this more, once you've rested."

I nod, once, still not willing to say anything to him. He looks relieved and gestures for me to follow him. I stand up, feeling my legs quiver under my weight, and take an unsteady step forward. The room spins and the light and colors blur around me, whirling into darkness.

29

I can feel my eyes blinking, but the void still engulfs me. I fight against it, remembering those awful days when it held sway. Hands hold me down and a distant murmur reaches my ears, the words indistinct, but an obvious attempt to soothe me. I redouble my efforts and throw them off, lurching up, or at least where I think up is, for my sense is that I am lying down. But everything is confused. I am not where I think I am, not exactly, and my attempts to raise myself end in me sprawled on the floor.

"Fucking goddamn idiot," I can hear Morris say over my gasping breath.

"You try living in a body that's not yours," I manage to say.

"Are you going to let me help you up?"

I hold up a hand to forestall him while I regain my breath and let my eyesight return.

"Your eyes were in the back of your head," Morris says.

"I'm aware," I say.

When I can see clearly and I feel more or less myself, I extend my hand to him and he helps me to my feet. I stand, taking in my surroundings and getting my sense of myself. The room is unfamiliar, a bedroom with sun streaming in through a window. Outside there is a tree with bright green leaves that draws my attention. I don't yet feel confident enough to risk taking a step, my equilibrium still not quite returned.

"Do you want something to eat?" Morris asks.

After a moment I nod and he takes me by the arm. I consider refusing his help, but think better of it and let him lead me out to the kitchen. He sits me at the table and busies himself making some scrambled eggs and toast.

"Something bland would be best, I imagine," he says as he works. "How's your stomach?"

"I don't know," I say. "Where is my body?"

Morris stops whipping the eggs and glances back at me. "With the Grand Regent. You're rarely seen anymore. Only official functions, that sort of thing. There are rumors that something has happened. There are rumors about everything."

I watch as he pours the eggs into the frying pan and begins to stir them, refusing to look at my hands, which are twitching atop the table. "Who is left around Molijc?"

"Just the Watchers' Order. The Acolytes. We can't get anyone even to the tower. Osahi and some of the other High Regents have disappeared. Officially, they are conducting a review of the faith."

"Osahi is back? Did the Seeker turn him too?"

"No," Morris says, glancing from the eggs. "He made it across during that whole mess, apparently. The High Regents who are not with Molijc are with him. Everyone is in hiding."

"I am through with hiding," I say with force.

Morris nods. "What do you have in mind?"

"Who is still left on the inside?"

"Darien and Valeria are still in the Order, but they are not in this universe. I don't know how much use they'll be to us."

"No one else?" I say.

Morris shakes his head as he slides the eggs from the frying pan to the plate he has set on the counter. The bread springs from the toaster as he does so, and he sets it on the plate as well and brings it over to me.

"So there is no one left," I say.

He will not meet my gaze. "Most of them were picked up after we tried to bring you back across. Some of them by the Society because of the stink from the transfer we had on us. I think the Watchers only took the ones they were interested in. The rest they let the Travelers deal with."

I want to weep as I think of all my friends who have followed Ana and myself and so many countless others into the Acolytes' chambers. But I won't do so in front of Morris. I won't give this Traveler the satisfaction of seeing me break again. The fate his kind have consigned my friends to is nearly as terrible.

"Do you want salt? Pepper?" he says, and I shake my head. "We could recruit others to the cause. We did before, remember? There are untold numbers of disaffected within the Order. Everyone is looking over their shoulders, waiting for Molijc or Lasinha to find them lacking."

"They won't stop until the Acolytes have operated on everyone," I say as I start into my eggs. They taste flat, as though my tongue and the food are not quite aligned in the same plane of existence somehow. Perhaps I have not come all the way over.

"How many will be thinking exactly that?" Morris says, pointing at me. "There is an opportunity here. It will just take some effort."

"Who in the Church is going to trust us after what Meredith did?"

"True," Morris says, going very still.

"I am not wasting my time sowing insurrection, no matter what you and the Seeker want. I need my body back. That's the first order of business. And the person with the means to do that is Osahi. We have to find him."

"He won't want to work with us," Morris says, a little too quickly, I note. Interesting, that.

"And I don't want to work with him. But we have no choice, and neither does he. This is bigger than both of us now. Even he can see that. The Church cannot survive so long as Molijc is Grand Regent."

"No one knows where he is," Morris says, holding his hands open.

I push the eggs aside, unable to get past the taste, or lack thereof. There is something very wrong with me. I can only hope it is the aftereffects of my transfer, and that they will eventually fade as time passes, as the balance of the two beings within me is restored. Morris has not mentioned it, and I am loath to bring it up, but it lies between everything we have said so far. I do not have the weeks or months needed to institute any grand designs we might come up with.

"Then you and I will have to find him," I say. "And soon. So let's get started."

He nods and will not meet my eyes.

The smell of coffee brings me from the realm of sleep. For a moment I am between two worlds, awash in visions of Ana and her impossible beauty, of Meredith and her expressions I can never quite read, but that draw me ever deeper, and of Molijc, implacable Dejian, who cannot abide anyone who might stand against him. How did I not see it all those years? Osahi, I always knew I could never trust. Even Meredith, I never entirely gave my heart to her, not until the end. But Dejian, for all his faults, seemed as true to the Church and De Gofroy as I.

He would say he still is, that he follows De Gofroy, is guided by him in all things. I can hear the arguments, can imagine myself being almost persuaded by them until I begin to doubt myself and lose my resolve. He was always so persuasive. A madman, he is a madman, I tell myself, as

I pull myself up from the bed, the sheets in a tangle around me.

I go to the bathroom and wash my face. Looking up in the mirror I do not recognize myself and fall to the floor, my whole body shaking with tremors. The world goes black for a moment and then returns. I am not myself, but perhaps I never was.

There are those people I murdered. Osahi's people. I have tried not to think of them, but they haunt the edges of my vision, in the same places Aeida lurks. He is a monster, even if he does not realize it. And I am as well. There can be no denying it.

Why do I still pretend that I follow this faith? It has been months, perhaps even years, since my last protocol or observance of faith. I am willing to do anything, including killing people, this thing I am not even sure I believe in. Which makes me no better than those I oppose. Molijc. The Society. We are all apostates. Only the faithless can rule.

This train of thought can only lead to revulsion, or worse, so I force myself to feet and head downstairs. Morris is already up, sitting at the kitchen table, frowning over a cup of coffee. He barely notices as I enter the room and pour myself a cup and sit down across from him.

Mornings are still the worst. Aeida is most present as I wake up, his thoughts and his being coming to the forefront. Sometimes I even find myself receding, slipping away as he takes command. It is only for the briefest of instants before I manage to reassert control over this flesh that is not mine, but each time it happens it is terrifying beyond measure.

I cannot bear the thought of ever losing control of myself again. Every one of my nightmares now is of that very thing. I can remember when I lurked behind the half-Aeida, watching and seeing everything, but unable to do anything. I must do whatever possible to return myself to my own flesh and to exact whatever measure of vengeance

I can against Molijc. If it means allying myself with the Seeker and the Society and this snake Morris, so be it. If it means the destruction of the Church itself, then, De Gofroy forgive me, I will see it done.

Apostate. The thought echoes through my mind and I force it aside.

Morris is watching me as these thoughts cascade through my mind, and I wonder what he has seen flitting across my face. The last three days, most of which I have spent in bed recovering under Morris' care, have seen the worst of the tremors that have afflicted me subside. I am almost myself again, but I am still not as good as I once was at controlling my emotions and keeping my face unreadable.

"No one can find any trace of Osahi," Morris says, and clears his throat. He still has difficulty looking at me, I notice, knowing that it is me, but seeing only Aeida. "It's just like the last time. He is very good."

"We found him the last time," I remind him. "And this time he is not alone. The High Regents, the rest of the Hierarchy, they are with him. All of them can't have vanished without a trace. There has to be a trail from one of them."

"We are looking," Morris says. "But if there was, don't you think Molijc and Lasinha would have found it?"

"They are not worried about Osahi," I say, and take a sip of coffee. "They know Osahi and the rest will have to come to them, come to the campus and the tower if they hope to take command of the Church."

Morris shrugs, as though he doubts what I am saying, but he does not reply.

"I know what I am talking about," I say, pointing at Morris. "No one knows him, knows the both of them, better than me. What fucking good is it to be working for the Seekers if they can't find a fucking person? That's what they do."

Morris winces at my shouts. "You know they will have

tech to hide them from the Seekers. It will take time."

"Time is what I don't have."

We stare at each other, hatred in my eyes, frustration in his, the silence simmering to a boil.

Morris leaves the safe house later that morning, though he will not say what for. I cannot leave; the risk is too great if the wrong person were to see me in this world. Vancouver, with its Protocol Center, which I used to launch my revolt against Molijc, is a hub for the Church. Too many members of the Hierarchy come here too often. I think of my days watching Arajuano in this very city, hidden but observed, the sword dangling above his head at every moment. Had he known?

Would I know if it is the same for me? I would not, if only because Molijc will not sit idly if he knows where I am. He will bring me back and put the Acolytes back to work. I know far too much.

I pace from room to room, resisting the urge to peer from behind the shutters drawn tight on every window. This is a Seeker safe house, Morris told me—not even the Society knows about it. So long as I remain here, I am safe. I do not feel it. I feel helpless and trapped, filled with rage. I was Molijc's plaything and now I am the Seeker's. My life is not my own. Can it ever be again?

There is food in the kitchen, enough for several days, and when I get hungry, I eat. Morris does not return that evening, and eventually I grow tired of waiting for him and go to bed. The next day and the day after are the same: eating, pacing, and waiting. I alternate periods of frenetic energy, the desperate need to act, to do something, with hours of lethargy and despair that sit like a weight upon my chest and squeeze at my thoughts until there is only darkness there.

On more than one occasion I find myself contemplating the knives in the kitchen, imagining what I can do with them, the release that is there. I am very tired of all this. Wouldn't it be easier for everyone? Dangerous thoughts, and I always find a way to escape them, but the longer I stay here trapped and alone, the more they linger.

Morris returns the morning of my third day there. He is not alone.

30

It is still dark when I awake to a clatter of furniture being stumbled against and muffled curses. I remain in my bed, frozen by indecision. Is this Morris returning, or the Seeker come to check in, or someone else who has found me? I fumble to look at the clock on the bedside and see that it is four thirty. No good can come of this, I think, and slip out of bed.

I am creeping to the door to try to see if I can peer out without revealing myself in some way, when the lights flick on in the main room and Morris calls out, "Aeida, get out here."

The mention of the other within me nearly pulls him to the forefront of my being, and I experience a moment of vertigo before I am able to respond. When I emerge from the bedroom, I see Morris crouching over the prone figure of a woman who is breathing very rapidly, her face drenched in sweat. She looks very familiar, and I try to place her as I take a cautious step toward them both. Morris has his hand pressed against her side, his own face damp with perspiration, his expression grim.

"Get the fuck over here," he says when he glances back to see me standing, unsure of what to do. "We don't have a lot of time here."

I nod, as much to myself as to him, and come to stand beside him, hovering over the familiar-looking woman. She is older than the last time I saw her, her hair sprinkledwith grey she has not bothered to hide, her face getting fuller. Where have I seen her before? Why can I not recall her name?

"Make yourself useful," Morris says, interrupting my thoughts. "Put some pressure on this."

He gestures with his head to where his hands are at her side, and for the first time I notice the blood that is on his hands and her clothes. The sight of it snaps me from my thoughts, and I take Morris's place, applying pressure to her wound, while he rushes to find the safe house's first-aid kit. As he frantically pulls out bandages and gauze, I study the woman's face. She is very pale, her eyes squeezed shut in anguish, her lips pressing together and apart as though she is trying to say something. I murmur encouraging things to her, nonsensical mostly. She is not listening, I know; her only focus is the pain.

"The bullet went through clean, I think," Morris says as he applies some gauze and disinfectant, causing the woman to gasp. "Fucking animals."

Her eyes blink open at his words, and it is then for some reason that my memory finds her. She is number seven. Lasinha's agent in the Society in Calgary. The one he had bring down the airship with Des Rosas, Annestol, and Hammelltharup aboard. What is she doing here in Vancouver, I wonder? I try to recall what happened to her following the final day. She remained with the Society, though there was a great deal of suspicion and she begged us to remove and hide her. Lasinha refused, though we had stopped using her as an asset. Perhaps things changed.

I understand now why Morris referred to me as Aeida and not Laila. Best that this woman not know who I really am. It would be dangerous for us both.

Morris works quickly, stanching the wound, so that we

can move her from the couch, now irreparably bloodstained, to the kitchen table, where the light is better. There we work together to stitch up her wound. At one point Morris pulls out his phone, and I can see on the screen the woman's internals made visible. Society or Seeker tech, no doubt. He catches me looking at it and quickly puts the phone away.

"No damage to any of the organs," is all he will say.

When we are finished, we carry the woman to my room to sleep, Morris giving her something for the pain. He stays to watch her, to make sure she falls asleep, while I go to try to salvage the couch cushions. I give up quickly—it is a hopeless task. There is a trail of blood on the carpet as well, leading from the door to the couch. I ignore that and return to the kitchen, putting the first-aid kit away and cleaning up what I can there.

Morris joins me and starts to make coffee and breakfast. It is light outside now, and glancing at the stove, I see the time is well after six. I didn't even notice the passage of these last hours, but now I feel them, the tiredness behind my eyes.

"We can't stay long," Morris says, as the smell of coffee begins to permeate the air. "They'll find this place before too long. We'll eat and then go."

"And her?"

"Nicola? She'll have to be ready to go."

I nod, glancing back in the direction of my bedroom. "Who shot her?"

"Your husband's people," Morris says. The coffee is ready, and he pours us each a cup before turning his attention to the omelet he is making.

"She's one of Lasinha's," I say. "He placed her in the Society."

"She was," Morris says. "Not after that day. Not after he wouldn't get her out of the Society. They knew, of course, that she was compromised, but they kept her around, fed her false information, made sure she handled nothing important."

"We didn't use her at all after," I say.

Morris turns from the eggs to look at me, mild surprise on his face. "A waste of time all around, then."

"Who is she working for now?"

"Osahi," Morris says. He divides the omelet and slides it onto two plates. There is toast as well. He brings both plates to the table and we sit down. "He found her after he came back and turned her. She had enough access to be useful to him. She's the one who's been moving his people, making sure there is no trace. No one thought to look at what she was doing. Neither side trusted her, but they both thought they had her contained."

"But they found out," I say, pushing the eggs around on my plate.

"It may have been us; I don't know," Morris says. "The Seeker suspected, of course, but he couldn't investigate without drawing attention to her. So he sent others, all very discreet, but maybe not discreet enough. One of Lasinha's agents must have noticed and sent word to the Order. They almost beat me to her."

"They'll be wondering how you found out," I say, looking at him.

He nods. "Very suspicious, no doubt. Can't worry about that now, though. We just have to get moving before they track us down and hope that Nicola can get us to Osahi."

Though I do not know why, I find myself beginning to smile.

Nicola awakes with gasp, raising her hand as though to fend off a blow. "We have to go," I say. "Can you walk?"

She blinks, her eyes coming into focus. "I don't know."

"Let's try."

I help her up from the bed, but she doubles over as soon as she is on her feet, moaning softly, and I move quickly to support her. I slip myself under her arm and, with me carrying most of her weight, we make our way from the bedroom to where Morris is waiting. He purses his lips but does not speak, turning to lead the way out the door. I follow behind, moving as fast as I can, though I wince with each gasp from Nicola.

I worry she will lose consciousness, so I say, under my breath, "It's not far, just a few more steps. You're doing great."

"What's your name?" she says, each word sounding as though it has its cost.

I almost find myself saying "Laila," before I catch myself. "David."

Morris turns around to check on our progress and to raise a warning eyebrow at me. I just nod. We both help Nicola into the car, which he left parked in the alley behind the house, a war special, as they are known, from the twentieth century. It is somewhat appropriate that I have been staying in one, trapped as I am in a war that it seems will consume all my days. And, if the Seeker is to be believed, I have been but a cog in a larger struggle. It still seems hard to fathom, but I cannot lose focus on what my goals are.

Once we ease Nicola into a seat in the back of the car, Morris says, "Stay with her. Make sure she hasn't broken any of the stitches."

I climb into the back of the car while he climbs into the front, and watch as he proceeds down the alley and onto the road. He drives with care, staying near the speed limit and taking no chances on lights. We cannot afford to be stopped. He also watches the mirrors intently, and I can see him calculating whether the cars behind him are just random or if the Watchers have enough vehicles in play to switch off.

"How are you?" I say to Nicola, pulling up her shirt to check her stitches.

"I'll be fine," she says, her eyes closed. She takes one deliberate breath after another, exhaling slowly. I catch

Morris's eye in the rearview mirror and nod at him.

We drive for an hour, aimlessly, doubling back on our route several times, until Morris is satisfied we are not being followed. Then he heads south and we cross the Fraser River and pass out of Richmond. For a time I am certain we are headed out of the country to Seattle, but instead we take the turnoff to the ferry to Victoria. He parks the car at the park and ride and gets out of the car. I join him, leaving Nicola in the car for the moment.

"How are we going to get her on the ferry?" I say. "Somebody will notice."

"I'm sure they will, but not in time to make a difference." I look at him, and he says, in answer to my unasked question, "We're not getting off in Victoria. Nicola is going to tell us where Osahi is, and then she's going to take us there."

31

The sky is cloudless, the sun bright and warm, with only a slight wind on the ocean, so most of the passengers on the ferry move out onto the decks of the vessel to enjoy the weather. There are whales surfacing just off to the starboard of the boat, and at various points as Morris and I sit watch over Nicola, who has drifted off to sleep, we hear gasps of awe.

A few people still remain aboard, and all of them glance in our direction at various intervals. Nicola is clearly not well, and the way Morris and I stand guard by her makes it look as though we are escorting a prisoner, which, in a way, I suppose we are. Morris appears unperturbed by the attention we are receiving, but it makes me jumpy and nervous. I have to remind myself that I do not need to fear the Seeker finding me. I am in his employ. The members of the Watchers' Order, even Society agents, however dangerous they may be, are still mortal. I know how to handle them.

We maintain our vigil for the first hour of the journey, which Morris says will take four hours. After the first hour has passed, Morris sends me to the commissary to buy lunch for all of us. When I return, Nicola is awake. She takes the food I offer wordlessly and eats slowly, wincing from the effort. Morris and I do the same, casting our eyes around at the scattered few people still left in the passenger area.

When everyone has finished, Morris nods at me and I help Nicola to her feet, and we head to the lower level of the ship, just above the car hold. Ignoring the *Employees Only* sign, Morris leads us out of the passenger hold and down a set of stairs deep within the ferry. The corridors are narrow and the ceiling low, and I have to remind myself to keep my head lowered. Aeida is much taller than I. When we reach what I judge to be the stern of the vessel and the end of the hallway we are in, Morris pulls out a key and unlocks a door that has *Specialized Personnel Only* on it. He steps within, flicking on a light, and motions for Nicola and I to follow.

The room within seems as though it should be on another vessel entirely. There are rows of screens set into one wall, which blink awake as Morris taps at a keypad attached to the wall below them. There is what appears to be a server, but what I know is a cloaking device. Why Morris would want to hide us from the Seeker's gaze I cannot say. There are pieces of equipment bolted to the floor and the roof. Some of them I recognize: a channel beacon, a transfer engine, both far more elaborate than anything the Church has been able to acquire from our Society agents. Others I do not, and those I study hungrily, wondering what their purpose might be.

Morris notes my curiosity but says nothing, offering a chair for Nicola to sit in, which she slides into with a heavy sigh. Morris turns to the keypad and screens, turning on the equipment and letting it warm up. I watch him while Nicola sits with her eyes closed, a slightly pained expression on her face.

When everything is on, he turns back to face us, his expression severe. "Now," he says, "you're going to take us to Osahi."

Nicola shakes her head without opening her eyes. "I don't know what you're talking about."

"Don't play games," Morris says. "Give me the channels for the universe Osahi is in and we'll go there. It's your only hope."

"I don't know what you're talking about."

Morris shakes his head sadly, as though Nicola is a willful child he does not want to discipline, but will if it comes to that. He glances at me to catch my eye. "Nicola, we have an hour and a half before we dock in Victoria. Molijc will have people there waiting for us. You know that, right? You can't be on this vessel when we arrive. Lasinha will not be as gentle as we are. The Acolytes will get Osahi's location from you."

Nicola sighs. "I won't let the Travelers find him either. That is no better a fate."

"We are not Travelers, Nicola," I say, putting a hand on her shoulder. "We are Regents, just like you. I was once a member of the Watchers' Order. I worked side by side with Lasinha. It will not go well for any of us if the Order gets their hands on us."

She nods as though she understands what I am saying. "I will not take you to Osahi."

I remove my hand and step aside with a sigh and a shake of my head. Morris takes my place, looming over her, putting a hand on either side of the chair and thrusting his face into hers. "You will or we'll leave you on this boat to be captured by the Watchers. We want to help him. Our goals are the same as his. The end of Molijc and this reign of terror. Let us help him."

Nicola looks from Morris to me, silently pleading with us to stop and let her be. "I'm so tired," she says, with a shake of her head. "If I sleep…"

"No, I'm afraid we can't let you do that," Morris says. "At least not until you give us the channels for Osahi's location."

"I can't." Her voice is pathetic and mournful.

I try again. "Yes, Nicola, of course you can. We are not your enemies, or Osahi's. We are your friends. We have information that can help him. We just need to find him. Please help us."

She stares again from face to face, still pleading. I smile at her in what I hope is an encouraging manner and squeeze her shoulder. Morris has drifted away, almost out of her range of vision. She looks into my eyes and I can see the moment when she surrenders to us. As she opens her mouth to speak, there is a loud knock at the door and all of us turn to face the door.

"Open the door immediately," is the command that is issued, and all of us go very still in response, not even glancing at each other.

Another knock follows, and another command. Still none of us move. I hear something, a whisper to whoever is with the woman issuing the command. The dull thud and reverberation of the battering ram striking the door follows.

32

Each impact by the ram sounds louder and shakes the door even more. It seems it must be only seconds before the door gives way under the force of the blows. Nicola moans, and I can feel my hands starting to tremble. I look to Morris, who seems paralyzed as well. I start to say his name, but he comes to himself with a shake of his head and turns back to Nicola.

"Those are not our friends," he says. "We don't have much time. Tell me the channels for Osahi's location. We have to go through now."

Nicola shakes her head. "I won't. I can't risk them being able to follow us."

"Keep going," a voice shouts on the other side of the door, following a momentary pause in the barrage, which begins again following the command.

"If they capture you, they have the location," Morris says. "I can scramble the channels. You know that as well as I. They may be able to follow, but they would have to be very, very good."

Nicola's thoughts war in her mind, a battle made visible by the expressions that flick across her visage, all shadowed by her doubt and fear.

"We don't have much time," I say to her, as gently as I can manage under the circumstances. "You have to trust to someone. Why not us? We are after the same thing."

The clamor from the door grows louder, with shouts from those behind it sounding as well. It is difficult to say whether they are cries of frustration or triumph. The door groans at its hinges, and Morris and I both look to Nicola, pleading with our eyes. She bites her lip and sits up in the chair, wincing at the effort, and looks at Morris.

"I will do it," she says. "But I will enter the channels and scramble them. Not either of you. I'll take you there, but I don't want you seeing anything."

"You can't even stand up," Morris says, throwing his hands up in frustration. "How are you going to do this? We don't have time."

"You'll have to make time for me," she says, getting to her feet. She wobbles as she stands straight and has to grab the chair to support herself, but she brushes me aside when I move to take her arm. "You both worry about the door and what's on the other side. I will do this."

I look at Morris, and he shrugs helplessly. He turns to the door, which sounds as though it is beginning to buckle, though the lock seems to be holding well. Behind us Nicola begins to shuffle toward the screen and enter the channel information. I resist the urge to turn around and see what she is doing.

"Is there anything we can do to stop them?" I say.

"The door isn't coming down without a lot of effort," Morris says, his voice pitched so only I can hear it. "The question is, do they have anything else besides that ram to bring it down?"

As he finishes speaking, the ram stops and we can hear whoever is using it tossing it aside. There is some muffled back-and-forth from those outside, most of which I cannot make out. The final phrase is quite clear, though: "They are bringing down the saw."

"Shit," Morris says.

"Not good?" I say.

"No," he says. "Get ready—we're going to have to brace the door."

I nod, though I am unsure how we are supposed to hold the door against these invaders while simultaneously making our escape. I swallow the question and join Morris bracing myself against the frame. We are quickly running out of good options.

"Nicola, how much longer?" Morris calls to her. "This room is going to be crowded in about five minutes."

"I'll be ready," Nicola says, though her voice sounds dim and weak. Morris and I glance at each other, and he sighs.

"Don't worry, Nicola," I say. "Get it right. We'll keep the wolves at bay."

Her reply is interrupted by the metallic snarl of a saw starting up. Morris nods at me, and we both move to put our shoulders against the door. An awful, screaming hiss sounds as the saw blade begins to cut through the hinges. Both Morris and I grit our teeth at the agony of the sound, heads turned to watch as Nicola moves among the equipment at what seems a glacial pace. I want to scream at her to hurry, but there is no point. She would not be able to hear me over the saw anyway.

I feel when the top hinge gives way. The stench of burnt metal is overwhelming, the air within our small room clouding with dark, thin curls of smoke. The door groans as the saw begins to cut at the bottom hinge. I shout something at Nicola, but she does not hear me. On one of the screens I can see the channel lights beginning to blink in unison. There is a timer above, but I cannot read what it says. Beside me, Morris coughs.

The last hinge gives way, and both Morris and I push hard against the door to hold it in place. The saw quiets and the woman on the other side shouts, "Take it down."

Two bodies crash against it from the other side, sending us momentarily reeling. We recover before they can knock aside the door, and put it in place and brace ourselves before their next charge. It comes, and this time we meet their surge with our own, grunts and swears all that passes across the threshold.

Out of the corner of my eye I see Nicola step awkwardly to the center of the room, which is gone in a blink, the walls vanishing to be replaced by a scene of immense splendor. There is a mountain or outcropping of rocks, down which tumbles a waterfall into a tangled forest. As my mind tries to comprehend all that I am seeing, I do not even notice as Nicola steps across the channel to the other side.

Morris shouts something, but I do not hear him. I am still focused on the rushing, coruscating waterfall, imagining myself engulfed in its thunder. The image of it begins to waver as the channel starts to close, bringing me back to myself. The force on the door behind me is overwhelming, our pursuers now exerting a steady and growing pressure that, it is clear, will inevitably win out.

"Laila," Morris says, at last getting my attention. "You have to go."

"What about you?" I say.

"Go," he says. "You have to get across. I'll hold the door and be right behind you."

I hesitate, knowing that he alone cannot withstand the forces on the other side of the door for long.

"Go," he shouts, slamming himself against the door with a possessed fury.

I spring into motion, running to the already draining image, so magnificent it seems it must be a painting set in some museum, not a real and tangible place. Behind me I can hear Morris shout with pain, but I do not dare pause or look back. I step across to the other side. Already the channel is beginning to degrade. I can feel the gravity of each universe pulling strangely at my body, first one and then the next.

My feet touch earth, the air now with a crispness to it

that tells me we are at a high elevation. The waterfall thunders nearby. It is both much larger and farther away than it had appeared from the cramped room in the vessel. The river that it is a part of curves around behind me into the forest that surrounds us. It all takes my breath away.

Remembering myself, I turn back to look through the disintegrating channel. I am in time to see that the door has fallen, Morris leaving it behind. He is running for the channel, three others in pursuit, their faces vague. He is almost there when one of them grabs hold of his arm and another falls upon him. The third makes for the channel, but it is too late—it is gone and I can see no more.

FOUR:

ARAJUANO

33

"Mas cafe?" the waiter said lifting up the large carafe from which he had just poured an inch or two of the thick, viscous liquid into my glass.

I shook my head, having learned the day before how strong the coffee within was. He nodded and smiled and stepped over to the next table, and was replaced by a woman with a jug of warmed milk. She filled the rest of the tall glass with milk, the dark black of the coffee mingling with the white of the milk and settling into a dull brown. Though it seemed like far too much milk for my taste, the resulting mixture was, in fact, a perfect amalgam of coffee and milk. I took a sip and closed my eyes in delight.

When I opened them, I spotted Meredith moving across the broad plaza to join me under the awning of the cafe that spilled out onto the square. The *zocalo*, they called it here. She sat across from me, and the waiter with the coffee came by promptly to serve her. She asked for a fruit salad as well, and the waiter turned to me to see if I also wanted something to eat, but I shook my head.

"He is here," Meredith said, without preamble once the waitress had finished pouring in the milk for her cafe con leche. "Or nearby, at any rate."

"Will he see me?" I said, looking past her, out onto the zocalo. It was largely empty at this hour, a few old men and women with their children sitting on the benches beneath the trees at its center, trying to hide away from the afternoon heat. Unlike some of the other plazas I had been to in Mexico, the one in Veracruz was filled with empty space, with only the very center of the zocalo having the usual trees, benches, and gazebos where anyone could wile away the hours.

"I think so," Meredith said after a moment's hesitation.

I turned my attention to her. She looked nervous, I thought, and I tried to smile. "You think so."

"He said he would. But not here. He's worried about a trap."

I frowned. "Where, then?"

"Cempoala."

"And where is that, exactly?"

Meredith took a sip of her coffee. "Apparently it's an old ruin. Not Mayan," she said, to forestall my question. "About an hour north of here. There's beaches nearby."

"Wonderful. It will be a relaxing trip, I'm sure. So he wants to go to an old ruin, in a small town, no doubt, where we'll stand out even more than we do here. Easy place for him to set up a trap for us."

She shrugged. "It's the only place he will meet us. He won't agree to anything else. I know him."

I sighed, holding back my reply as the waiter brought Meredith's fruit salad, a large plate filled with bananas, mangoes, papaya, and other fruit, sprinkled with granola and drizzled with honey. I stared at it enviously and she pushed the plate toward me, gesturing that I should help myself.

"Do you think he's planning something, or is this just an abundance of caution on his part?"

Meredith considered the question as she took a bite of the salad, chewing slowly. "Caution, I think. We know he still has his supporters in the Church, but there aren't that many. And he won't have that much money. He can't afford to set up any sort of elaborate sting and buy off half the town or whatever."

"He may not have to," I said, plucking a piece of papaya from the plate with my fork.

"He doesn't know there are only two of us," Meredith said. "He has to assume there are more than just us. That Lasinha and Molijc are part of this. Until we can prove otherwise, at least. He would be a fool not to."

I considered this, taking another bite of the salad, this one a melon of some kind. Exquisite. "All right," I said, looking hard at Meredith. "Send the word. We'll head up tomorrow."

Meredith nodded. "As soon as I'm done here. What are we doing tonight?"

I smiled. "Tonight is about us."

Meredith grinned as well, raising one eyebrow slightly, and I had to take a sip of coffee to still the throb of desire that surged through me.

Cempoala had been a Totonac city, of perhaps thirty thousand souls at its height, before the arrival of Cortes. Their chief, Xicomecoatl the Fat, forged an alliance with the Spaniard, and the Totonacs stood with the conquistadors when Tenochtitlan fell. All this I had gleaned from the interpretive center, which Meredith and I had spent an hour wandering through, before heading out into the glare of the midday sun to wander the remnants of the city.

The structures were far less impressive than those the Mayan and the Aztecs had left, and the encroachment of the forest only served to diminish what remained further. The temples were squat and low to the earth, hardly the towering buildings we had seen at Teotihuacan, north of Mexico City, as our airship passed over. We made our way to the Place of Accounts, a series of fortresses and squares where tribute was collected. I had no doubt Osahi had carefully chosen this place for our meeting—the symbolism of the name alone would have called to him.

But which of us was giving tribute to the other? Hard to say, even now that I seemed to be ascendant in the Church and he cast out, for all intents and purposes. I never trusted my footing when I was around him. The ground could always shift in an instant. Today would be no different.

The fact that we were utterly alone, the only guests at the site, did little to ease my worries. There were two interpreters, but both of them were in the main building, and given the heat of the day it seemed unlikely either of them would be leaving there anytime soon. My more paranoid self whispered that they would not be stepping outside because Osahi would have been sure to pay them off, to make sure that whatever happened here in the Place of Accounts was unseen by anyone.

Meredith was fidgeting in place, glancing around at all the various structures, red-stoned and crumbling, as though she thought Osahi would emerge from the earth. She knew that my trust in her, earned over this past year since De Gofroy's death and the terrible events of that day, would evaporate the moment it became clear that Osahi had betrayed us here. She was vouching for him in this, and in everything that would follow.

"Stop that," I said, as she began to pace. "You're making me sweat."

I walked up the steps to one of the fortresses, and she followed behind me. The top of it was grass-covered now, though the walls of the building still remained, and I passed within, hoping for some shade. There was none, and the air seemed even stiller here, the heat more oppressive. We both moved outside in time to see Osahi coming down the gravel path from the entrance. Neither of us moved as he came to the foot of the fortress.

Our eyes met, and I glanced at Meredith, waiting for

her to speak and break the spell of tension. She seemed paralyzed by the moment, biting her lip nervously. My mind cast back to the night before, when I had watched her biting her lip, but for very different reasons. I swallowed and turned back to Osahi, his expression arrogant as always.

"Might I suggest lunch?" he said. "I know a place in town."

"Probably a good idea," I said, trying to keep my tone light to match his.

He turned and waved for us to follow. "We'll take the bus, if you don't mind. Your vehicle will be fine here for an hour or two."

"Fine," I said, and glanced at Meredith. She shrugged: *I don't know why*, she seemed to be saying. I nodded and started down the steps after Osahi.

The town was hardly that, only a scattering of houses and the main street we found ourselves on. There was a cantina across the way and a few other stores, along with the one restaurant we now sat in out of sight of the street. We roused the woman who ran it from her house behind it, where she was watching a very loud game show. We were the only customers, the only people even on the street. The others on the bus with us had all been locals heading home for siesta, if such a thing still existed.

No one spoke until after the food arrived and we began to eat. Osahi took a bite of enchiladas verdes and a pull on his beer and said, "So, Meredith tells me you want to welcome me back into the fold of the Church."

"I do," I said, uttering the words with care. Meredith picked at her dish, a whole fish fried and stuffed with olives, garlic, and chiles, not looking at either of us.

"Let bygones be bygones," Osahi said in an ironic tone, refusing to make the first move.

I would have to, I realized, as I studied him. He was dressed like a tourist, in a cotton shirt and long shorts, his face marked with stubble. His hair had grown out as well and his dark skin had gone even darker in the sun. All of his usual markings, his ostentatious dress and his precise grooming, were absent. I took a swig of my own beer, already warming, the bottle damp with perspiration.

"Lasinha and Dejian don't know I'm here," I said, getting that out of the way.

"You assume."

I nodded. It was a fair statement. Lasinha, I knew, had people watching Meredith. He had no trust for her and, I suppose, by extension, me. Dejian, so far as I knew, remained oblivious. He would not, I thought, ever suspect me of having an affair. It would not enter his head. Betrayal of another kind, certainly, but sex for him was as much about hierarchy as anything else, and he could not imagine anyone leaving him for some lowly, untrustworthy Protector. He, after all, was the man beside the Grand Regent. The Grand Regent in all but name.

"We were careful," Meredith said, her first words since Osahi had arrived. Neither of us glanced in her direction.

"I'm sure you were," Osahi said in a dismissive tone. "Now, I suppose you're going to tell me that you can promise me Lasinha and Molijc will simply welcome me back with open arms at your word."

I shook my head. "Lasinha still wants you dead, so far as I know."

"I know far better than you," Osahi said. I was unsure whether he was talking about his last year in hiding, or about the events of that terrible day. The fire on the airship, which had killed all aboard. Osahi had not been on it, but the three apostate High Regents had been.

"No doubt you do. I can show him that you are more valuable to us alive. Your resources and contacts are essential to the Protectors. And to the Church. He has to see that. And you cannot damage Frederik now, not after a year. The Regents have chosen. Even you can see that."

Osahi did not reply, focused on his enchiladas, his eyes

narrow. I resisted a smile. "What I need is to be able to demonstrate to him that you will not be plotting against us. That you will be working with us. We know that De Gofroy trusted you more than almost anyone. I want to be able to show you that same trust."

"Why, exactly?" Osahi said, looking at Meredith as he spoke.

I nodded. "There is that. There is what you both know about that day. And because I do think you can be useful to the Church. It is a better place with you in it, not fighting against it."

"So your price. then, is my silence on matters concerning you two?"

"And on what happened the final day," I said. "Whatever accusations you think you have, you will let them lie."

"So it was a lightning strike that hit the airship and killed the High Regents," Osahi said with a vicious smile.

"A tragedy we all still are reeling from, I can assure you," I said, not taking my eyes from his.

"You are going to tell me you had nothing to do with what happened."

"I did not. I swear upon De Gofroy and all that is sacred. I would never kill a Regent. Not you, not them. There Lasinha goes too far, which is why it would be good to have you back. Another voice at the table."

"You may not like what I have to say," Osahi said.

"I don't expect that I will always. I certainly didn't before."

Osahi leaned back in his chair, stirring the cheese into his refried beans, as he considered me. "I have one condition, assuming you can convince me that Lasinha has buried the hatchet."

"Your welcome back into the Church will be very public. The rumors, as you know, have been considerable," I said, looking past him now at the woman who sat by the kitchen door watching the television set up in the corner, which blared the same baffling game show at an obscene volume.

"If something were to happen to you, he would be the first person anyone would look to," I continued. "And once you have proven yourself, I don't foresee any difficulties. Lasinha is a pragmatist, above all else. What is your condition?"

Osahi nodded, as though he accepted what I had said. I had my doubts on that front. "Frederik is still seeing Arajuano?"

I nodded. I could feel Meredith stiffen beside me. She had not known about that.

"He hasn't attempted to have him reinstated?"

I winced. "It has been explained to him that it is impossible to do. We cannot go against what De Gofroy has decreed."

"Of course not," Osahi said. "But he will not stop trying. And you have not forced him to end the relationship?"

"Dejian has judged it," I said, choosing my words with care, "*imprudent* to halt the relationship, given we allow the Grand Regent so few other freedoms."

"In the name of De Gofroy," Osahi said with a bitter smile. I did not reply. I did not have to.

The game show ended, and the woman stirred from her seat, disappearing back into the kitchen. I followed her movements until she disappeared from sight, and reset my gaze on Osahi.

"My condition is that Frederik can no longer be Grand Regent, not even in name."

I was careful to control my face, but I could hear Meredith's intake of breath. "I cannot promise that immediately, but I think you know that Dejian has long had designs on that chair. If you are amenable to him taking that seat, then I think you can be assured that Frederik will not be long for the job."

"In the name of De Gofroy," Osahi said again.

I shrugged. "The Church will always follow the path he set. He chose Dejian and I and Lasinha, and entrusted us with its most sacred mission."

"Of course," Osahi said with some derision. "I will accept that. My price for that is that I be named a High Regent."

I smiled and nodded. "I think it is only fair, given your service to the Church, that you be so elevated."

"Good," Osahi said, standing abruptly and pushing aside his plate. "I will await your word when it is all arranged."

Without waiting for a reply, he turned and walked out of the restaurant to the street. I watched him go before turning back to Meredith. Her face was unguarded, as though she were still processing all she had heard. So, for that matter, was I.

"Your fish is getting cold," I said, gesturing with my fork to her mostly untouched plate of food, before turning to my own, as I wondered about what I had just done.

34

Every morning with Molijc began with us joining in prayer to remember the three High Regents and the dozen others who had perished aboard the airship on that final day nearly two years before. Dejian had not witnessed it; he had been too busy coaching Frederik on what he needed to say in his speech. He knew that the ship had been brought down under Lasinha's orders, that the blood of that day was on all of our hands, yet he saw nothing strange in bearing witness to those lost.

Every word I uttered during those prayers felt like a lie to me—*was* a lie. I couldn't bring honor to the dead, not when I had played a part in their murder. Dejian did not see the lie in it. He could never understand why it made me uncomfortable, and I had given up trying to explain it to him. He had reconciled himself to the lies we had put forth to the faithful and now believed them himself. We had to honor the dead each day, remember the tragic accident that had marred De Gofroy's passing and Frederik's ascension to Grand Regent, for Dejian, through Frederik, had said so that very day in his speech to all the Regents.

When our prayers were finished we had breakfast,

which passed largely in silence, both of our thoughts on the duties that awaited us. I was thankful for the silence. Conversation with Dejian had become strained since that day. Since Meredith, I told myself. I was forever trying to hide my relationship and my actions on that day, afraid that some expression, some gesture would reveal all that I had worked so hard to keep secret.

Dejian was apparently oblivious to all of this, which in so many ways was the worst of all. He had to sense the growing distance between us, yet he did not appear to care. The lie was enough for him. He would talk as though what we showed to Lasinha and the Hierarchy, to the Church, was the reality, when he had to know it was a false front, and that what lay behind was hollow and empty.

Lasinha suspected, I thought. He likely knew about Meredith, though I could not be certain. I had to assume, though. Lasinha, after all, was truly dangerous.

That was why I went to Dejian first with word that Osahi wanted to return from exile. He saw the reason in it. He was nothing if not practical. Osahi had led the Protectors, knew more of the secrets of the Church than anyone, and had done more than anyone to keep us free of the Society. We all knew that. So long as he was outside the Church he was dangerous. Within the Hierarchy he could be contained, reasoned with, compromised.

That was the argument I made to Dejian, and it was the argument we brought to Lasinha. To my surprise, he agreed.

"But he knows we cannot just remove Frederik? Not so soon after he has been anointed. We would lose all the trust we have built in ourselves in the past year. It will have to be done carefully."

This was Lasinha's only concern, one that I agreed with. I had promised to talk to Osahi, to explain how it would do none of us any good to so quickly overthrow the Hierarchy we had established. It was Dejian who disagreed.

"No, it can be done quickly," he told us. "In fact, it should be done quickly. The longer he remains in that chair, the more secure he becomes. The more secure he becomes, the less he will need us. I know how to do it, so leave it to me."

And so we had. Lasinha and I met with Osahi and made our promises, forged our alliance, and he returned to his old office in the Protectors' building. Many of his old allies were still there, for we had made no move to purge them after the tragedy of De Gofroy's final day. It would have drawn too much attention to the truth of what had happened.

With Osahi back, we all slowly worked our way into a new equilibrium and waited for Dejian to let us know what he had planned for Frederik. The months ticked by with no sign of action on his part and I began to fret that Osahi would grow frustrated and renege on his part of the agreement. Surely Dejian was seeing to the matter, I told myself, even if he was not informing me of what he was doings. There were many things these days we were not informing each other of.

As I pushed aside my breakfast and stood to go to the Protectors' building, where I had meetings planned with some of my agents, Dejian glanced up from his own meal and said, "Actually, I'd like you to come with me this morning. I have a meeting with Frederik."

I blinked in surprise and nodded, not saying anything, and he offered no further explanation.

We met Frederik in the Grand Regent's chambers. It was still difficult, even after more than a year, to stop myself from looking for De Gofroy's bed and the attendant Acolyte. Instead I saw Frederik, who had ensconced himself in his father's chair, which he had moved back into the vast main room that overlooked all of the campus. There were a few other chairs in a loose semicircle around him, where a group of young men idled, speaking in hushed tones.

They all went silent as we stepped into the room, turning to look back at us with guarded faces, even as Frederik stood and welcomed us with a broad smile. I thought of what Dejian had said about him becoming more secure and no longer needing us. It had already begun, and he had witnessed, had felt the power beginning to slip from his grasp and decided he needed to act.

"We need to talk, Frederik," Dejian said, striding toward him with me following in his wake. His tone was brusque, and I noted the lack of honorific. Molijc never let the boy forget that he owed his place to us.

"Of course, Dejian," Frederik said, gesturing for him to sit in a chair that one of the youths vacated for him. They were all staring hard at Dejian, eyes filled with daggers, thinking I could not see their anger.

"I think it would be better if we were alone. This is a matter of some delicacy," he said, glancing back at me as he spoke, implying that I had brought the matter to him.

"Anything you have to say to me you can say to these gentlemen," Frederik said, after a moment's hesitation. "I trust them."

"Indeed," Dejian said. He remained standing, staring hard at Frederik, as though they were the only two people in the room.

At first, Frederik made an attempt to stand as well, to face Molijc, but eventually the silence and tension, and all the eyes upon him, wore at his confidence and he slumped into his chair. Dejian did not move, and the youth who had given up his seat to stand awkwardly off to the side slunk back into it, as though he were hoping to avoid drawing Molijc's attention. I watched all this from behind the circle of chairs, wondering what Dejian was playing at.

"You have failed in your duties as Grand Regent. You have failed to honor the memory of your father," Dejian said. I blinked in surprise at his words, and the young men surrounding Frederik looked shocked and horrified.

Frederik was taken aback, his face gone white, his lips

drawn. "What are you talking about, Molijc?" he managed to say, though his voice had none of the force he had obviously hoped for.

"You have forsaken the Protocols of the faith. You have forgotten all that your father taught us. You have betrayed me, you have betrayed the Regents, and you have betrayed our faith. Do you know the damage you have done?"

Something like terror seized Frederik, and he had to fight to quell it. His hands, I saw, were shaking. Was he thinking of Arajuano now, of all their conversations and what had been said and who the apostate might have repeated them to? No one had ever spoken to him of the relationship, in spite of what I had told Osahi. We had monitored it and let it proceed, knowing that it could be used when the time came. Apparently Dejian had decided that now was the time.

"What are you talking about?" Frederik said again, his voice empty, almost pleading. The room had gone very quiet. The youths hushed and shrank into their chairs, desperate to escape.

Molijc took a threatening step toward Frederik. It looked as though he were about to strike him, and certainly the Grand Regent ducked and braced himself for a blow. Not the first, I thought, though I could not have said how I knew that. But it was true. I looked at Dejian and saw the fire in his eyes, half mad and barely contained. It was familiar from any number of arguments we'd had had over the years, though he had never been as unhinged as he was in this moment. This was not a game he was playing, I realized—he truly believed Frederik had betrayed us. And yet he also knew this was all a setup, to find the means to remove De Gofroy's son from power. Why else was I here, after all?

"Do not play your games with me, Frederik De Gofroy," Molijc said, emphasizing the family name, the better to land the blow. "You know who this is, don't you?" he said, turning to point at me. "She is one of the Protectors of the faith, and she has been watching you. She is the one who your father entrusted his files to. She knows everything. Do you think you are above the Protectors? You are not. I am not. None of us are. Only the faith stands above them. The faith and the truth."

Dejian had turned his back on Frederik and was facing me as he spoke those final words. Our eyes met, and I felt the disorientation Frederik had under that gaze, the fury that threatened to explode and the cold calculation that kept it in check. Molijc had not needed me here to confront Frederik. He needed no props. He had wanted me to hear this.

35

Frederik became erratic in the days that followed Molijc's confrontation. He was late and inattentive for his duties as Grand Regent, or skipped them altogether. The agents Lasinha and I had sent to watch him reported that on those occasions he did not leave the Grand Regent's chambers, locking himself in his quarters. They would overhear him in hushed conversation with someone when they approached the door, but could make out nothing that was said.

Our comms had no record of any of those conversations, which meant he was using a separate system that had been carefully firewalled from our own. That set Lasinha into a panic, for we had not realized Frederik might suspect we were observing him. He had always been so oblivious, except in one regard, and that was why I was not concerned about the unmonitored calls. It was obvious whom he was talking to, especially given what Molijc had said to him.

"Do we bug the chambers?" Lasinha said when the three of us gathered to discuss the situation.

It was a difficult question, given the general reluctance the Protectors had toward deploying listening devices on campus or in the homes of Regents. Such actions were only taken in cases where evidence of malfeasance or apostasy was near incontrovertible. To do so in the Grand Regent's chambers would rouse suspicion in us, meaning we would have to place the bugs and do the listening, or risk the specter of an investigation by the Protectors into our actions. Osahi, newly returned and still harboring resentment toward us, would relish such an opportunity.

"That is not necessary," I said.

"No," Molijc said. "We know who he is talking to. We can listen on the other end of the conversation, can we not?"

"Arajuano is very careful," Lasinha said.

"Still," I said, "we know where he is. We can make it happen if need be."

Lasinha nodded reluctantly.

"Then let's do it," Dejian said, making a sharp motion with his hand. "And in the meantime, keep up surveillance on the boy."

Lasinha and I both nodded, and Molijc left without a word, determining the meeting had reached its conclusion. Lasinha raised an eyebrow at me, and I shrugged. Dejian had not spoken to me since the day of his confrontation with Frederik and his message for me. He knew about Meredith, that much seemed evident, though how much he knew I could not say.

The knowledge sat at the bottom of my stomach like a stone that seemed to grow heavier every day. I longed for him to confront me about her, to yell and scream with the same cold fury he had shown Frederik. His silence persisted, though, with both of us finding excuses not to spend time in each other's company. He was waiting for me to address him, it seemed clear, something I had no intention of doing, at least for the moment. A reckoning would follow, though, regardless of what I did—of that I had no doubt.

"The people we have watching him will begin to ask

questions soon," Lasinha said.

I shrugged. "It won't be long now, I don't think. He's clearly planning something, and it's only a matter of time before he carries it out."

"What do you think he does?"

"I don't know. Is he foolish enough to try to remove any of us?"

Lasinha considered this. "No. Those kids he has around him don't have the guts to stand beside him in a fight. He has to know that."

I thought about the others there that day, how they had all cowered as soon as Molijc and I entered the room. "You're probably right," I said.

"Let's hope," Lasinha said.

"All the same," I said, "let's put some eyes on them as well, just to be sure."

Lasinha nodded his agreement and we set about expanding our watch of those in Frederik's circle, unaware that everything had already changed irrevocably.

I spent that night in Meredith's room, providing only the flimsiest of covers as to why I was not in our quarters. It seemed pointless now to even pretend. I knew that Dejian would not be there. He was otherwise engaged, spending as much time as possible in Frederik's orbit, continuing to intimidate and put pressure on the Grand Regent and waiting for fissures he was certain would soon appear.

Meredith could sense the growing friction between Dejian and I, as well as the general tension resulting from the situation with Frederik. She knew me too well not to be aware of it. I could sense her wanting to ask about it, to find out what was happening, even as she knew I would tell her nothing. At every turn, I had refused to discuss our future. Part of the thrill of our being together was the secrecy and risk of discovery, the very tenuousness of our arrangement, paradoxically strengthening the bonds between us.

It was not yet morning, the light just beginning to show through the darkness, when Meredith woke me, her lips warm on mine. Although sleep still held part of my mind, darkness and visions swimming through the stirrings of pleasure, I responded to her with an embrace. Her lips sought out every contour of my form, her fingers following in their tracks, and I surrendered to her touch. She traveled my body from toes to my long hair, which she grasped firmly in her hands as she nipped at my neck.

"Are you going to tell me what is wrong?" she said, whispering in my ear as her teeth found my lobe.

"No," I said, pivoting our bodies so that she lay beneath me. I began my own journey of her body with my lips, while she laughed with bitterness and desire.

Before we could proceed any further, the lights in the room burst on and Lasinha entered. Meredith let out a shriek of surprise, and I barely contained one of my own.

"Come on, Laila," he said. "We need to go."

His face was closed, betraying none of his thoughts. Would he tell Dejian? Had he already? It did not matter, I realized, as I put on my clothes, carefully avoiding looking at either of them, as they studiously avoided looking at each other. Dejian already knew. He needed no confirmation.

Lasinha waited until we had left the room to speak. "Frederik is missing. He slipped his tail."

"How did he do that?"

"He must have had training." Lasinha glanced at me.

"Osahi will have a field day with this," I said.

Lasinha did not reply, and we spent the rest of our journey in silence as we made our way to the chambers where Dejian awaited us. He was pacing in a state of agitation, muttering to himself, his hair disheveled and his eyes worn from lack of sleep. He seemed to have aged a year in this night.

"Do we know where he is?" he said as soon as he

caught sight of Lasinha and I.

Lasinha shook his head. "Not a trace yet, but he'll show up."

"We know where he's going," I said. "Do we still have sightlines on Arajuano?"

"As far as I know," Lasinha said. "I'm checking now."

"No one," Molijc said, his voice rasping with anger, "can find out about this. No one can know that we have lost the Grand Regent."

"All right," I said, holding up a reassuring hand. "Who knows right now? And can we trust them? We'll keep the circle to those people, and deal with anyone we think is a problem."

Lasinha rattled off the list of agents who had been watching both Arajuano and Frederik. There were ten in total, all highly ranked Protectors, all people whose discretion we trusted. Among them was Morris, whom Molijc had taken a disliking to in the months following the deaths of the High Regents. There was no reason to his aversion, but he had never needed one, and at the mention of his name, Dejian pounced.

"Loverne," he said, as though uttering the name of some particularly noxious plague. "He's not to be trusted."

"Don't be ridiculous," I said. "He's been with me for years."

"I know," Molijc said, his tone heavy with insinuation.

"Do you not trust me now, too?" I said. "Is that what you are saying, Dejian? Because the three of us are in this together. De Gofroy anointed us, and our fates will forever be tied because of it. The only path forward is together."

Molijc stared at me, practically vibrating with fury, yet he was somehow aware of himself enough to realize the sense in what I had said. Whatever lay between us would have to wait. For the time being we needed to stand united, to ensure that we could survive this crisis.

"I want him watched," Molijc said, pointing to Lasinha.

Lasinha nodded. "I suggest we look into all of them.

Let's be certain of our allies. The last thing we need is questions about who we can trust."

He looked from Molijc to me, his expression suggesting we put the matter to rest. We both nodded. "Now what are our next steps?" he said.

"We find Arajuano. If we've lost them both, we're in trouble," I said. "And we'll need to find a reason for Frederik to be gone for a few days."

Lasinha rubbed his jaw. "I'll see to Arajuano. Laila, you look at Frederik's circle and see if any of them know what is going on. Was he stupid enough to tell them anything? Let's hope so. Dejian, you think of the cover we can use for Frederik's absence and look at what events need to be covered for the next few days."

We all agreed, and Lasinha and I left the tower. Better that we not be seen there, given the rumors and suspicions that were bound to grow in the days to come as Frederik's absence led to more and more questions. We were in the service elevator, descending to the basement, when Lasinha's phone buzzed. He listened to what was said, saying little himself, his jaw tightening as the call went on.

"Find him. Bring in the others. This is our top priority."

He hung up and I glanced at him. There was no need to say anything. We both knew what the call had been about.

"Should we tell Dejian?" Lasinha said as the elevator reached the basement and we exited the car.

"Let's wait until we have something more concrete to tell him. He has enough on his mind right now. And there's nothing he can do anyway."

Lasinha did not reply—in fact, it did not seem he had even heard me. He was lost in his thoughts, trying to piece together how we could have been so badly fooled by these two men who we had watched so carefully these last months. It was something I had to wonder as well. What had we missed?

36

It seemed there was no trace of Frederik anywhere. No one could pick up his trail. We did not even know how he had left the campus, let alone Calgary, as we assumed he must have. For all we knew he was still in the tower, hidden away in some room we did not know of, laughing as we desperately tried to manage a situation that rapidly threatened to spiral beyond our control.

Lasinha was convinced Osahi was involved in the Grand Regent's disappearance. "There is no other explanation. Neither Arajuano nor Frederik have the resources or know the people to be able to disappear so completely. Osahi does. He's done it before."

"We found him," I reminded him, but it did not placate him.

"After more than a year," he said. "We cannot survive like this for a year."

"I don't know if we can survive another day," Dejian said. "Too many people are asking too many questions, and the answers we are giving are starting to not make sense."

"He'll surface eventually," I said. "He has to. He's not Osahi, and Osahi would never do anything to help

Arajuano. Or to hurt the Church, for that matter."

"Maybe this is the Society's doing. It has all their fingerprints," Dejian said, running a hand through his hair, which seemed to somehow have grown thinner in the three days Frederik had been gone.

It had been hard on us all, Lasinha and I frantically searching for any sign of Frederik or Arajuano and coming up empty at every turn, while Molijc tried to project a calm front to the faithful in the face of the continued absence of the Grand Regent. Agents in the Protectors had already begun to notify me of the rumors that were beginning to spread among the Regents everywhere. Frederik's absence was the result of a debilitating illness, or there was a power struggle within the Hierarchy for influence over the boy. The longer he remained out of sight, the more credence would be given to those rumors.

"We know Frederik has no power here," Lasinha said. "But does the Society? Doubtful, I would say. Arajuano will be trying to make himself seem essential. From the Travelers' perspective, Frederik going AWOL is a disaster. They just lost the one person they were certain they could influence. No, I don't see it from their end."

"I don't either," I said with a nod.

I stood to get myself some more coffee. We were meeting in Dejian's and my quarters, the first time either of us had been here since Frederik had disappeared, something we were all careful to avoid acknowledging. I lifted the pot to see if the others wanted more as well, but they both shook their heads.

"They would want him to stay in place," I continued, "for the same reason we did. So something changed for the two of them. What?"

Dejian looked over to where I stood, meeting my eyes for the first time that morning. "We wanted him removed."

"But he did not know that," Lasinha said.

Dejian shrugged, and I said, "Are we sure?"

"He would have suspected something was up after my little tirade," Molijc said, a smile touching his lips. "I implied we knew things, hoping he would draw the obvious conclusion that we knew about Arajuano. I did not expect him to be able to escape without our noticing, though."

"They'd obviously been planning for this for some time," Lasinha said.

"Where would they go?" I said. "Let's assume for the moment they have no intention of returning. There is no nefarious plot. They've given up on the Church, Frederik has decided Arajuano is worth more than being Grand Regent, and they're just going to run and find someplace to live out their days."

"Why give up the throne?" Molijc said.

I shrugged. What did it matter?

"They'd need money to go somewhere where we couldn't find them, to hide their trail and to make a new life," Lasinha said. "That's a lot of money."

"Maybe we need to look at that a little more closely," I said. "Where would he have gotten it from, and how is he getting it now?"

"We've looked at the accounts already," Lasinha said. "Nothing has been active."

"We're missing something," I said. "We've been thinking he's on the run, that he'll make a mistake, that ultimately he's planning to come back. But if he's not, if this is something they've planned to do, then there might not be a mistake. We need to find the money and go from there."

Silence followed as Lasinha and Molijc considered what I had said. A silence that grew awkward as it became clear that the two had reservations about looking too deeply into the Church's accounts, but did not know how to express them without implicating themselves. The wordless way they glanced at each other was implication enough. What, I wondered, had they been up to?

"Unless there is some sort of problem with looking through the accounts, that is," I said, gritting my teeth.

"There is no problem," Dejian said, staring at me levelly. "Lasinha will help you investigate."

I nodded my agreement and watched as the two men shared a glance again, a confidence shared, and my disquiet began to grow.

How many years had I been a Regent in the Church, a Protector at that, and now was the first time I gave any serious thought to the money, untold sums, in our possession and what was done with it. Money had never been a question; it had always been there, seeming without limit. All those months traveling by airship with De Gofroy—and he had spent years doing such things—to say nothing of his care by the Acolytes, or their various unspoken of experiments.

There had been money for all of it. Now there was apparently none, or very little. How had it happened? How had I failed to notice? Lasinha sat with me, grim-faced, as I reviewed the accounts. By his manner, I knew none of this was a shock to him, as it was to me. He had seen it all before.

"How is this possible?" I said.

Lasinha gave a little shrug, betraying none of his thoughts. "De Gofroy spent a lot, and his care cost even more. The Protectors, the Acolytes, the maintenance of the campus—it all adds up. It all wasn't a problem so long as the Church was growing, but it hasn't been. We've lost hundreds of members since De Gofroy died."

And the deaths of the High Regents, he did not add, but he did not need to. Something had been broken that day, a trust that the Regents had in the Hierarchy. We had done little to regain it in the year since.

"Without their tithes, without De Gofroy to sell his works, there is very little for the Church to exist on. Frederik is not a charismatic leader, no matter that he is his father's choice."

"This is why Dejian is so worried about Frederik disappearing."

Lasinha nodded. "If he could have controlled his downfall it would have been one thing. This...all the rumors, I'm sure you've heard them as well. More will be leaving the Church. And there will be fewer and fewer people taking the Protocols."

I closed my eyes, unwilling to believe what I was hearing. Yet I knew it was true. I had not realized, or had allowed myself not to realize, but it had all been there to be seen if I had wanted to. But I had been too caught up in my burgeoning relationship with Meredith and all the maneuvering to meet my promise and see Osahi returned to the Church to bother with what had seemed mere minutia.

"It gets worse." Lasinha cleared his throat.

Why had he and Dejian not bothered to tell me any of this, I wondered? This was fundamental to the survival of the Church and the faith. De Gofroy had entrusted all of us to ensure his vision survived. Meredith, I realized. Whether they had always known the nature of our relationship or not, they did not trust our closeness. They thought she was still Osahi's agent. Even I was still not entirely certain of her loyalties. She loved me, I knew that, but she still felt an obligation to Osahi that went as deep as her feeling for me.

"How can it get worse?" I said, rereading the accounting, hoping that it would appear better somehow.

"Frederik has access to the accounts," Lasinha said.

"You haven't taken him off?" I said, feeling ill.

"We can't. He's the Grand Regent. So whatever is left in all our various accounts, he can take out. He hasn't yet."

"But he will," I said. Lasinha nodded. "What about the properties?"

"There's nothing he can do with them. He would need one of the High Regents or Dejian to sign off on any sale."

"Can we get him taken off the accounts?"

"We're working on that," Lasinha said. "It is difficult."

"We need to hurry that along, if we can," I said. "Otherwise, we wait. They must be using Arajuano's money, or maybe Frederik has accounts we don't know about. But they'll know that we're trying to get him off the accounts, and they'll know they need to act soon. If they have all the Church's money, that is a lot of leverage to be used."

Lasinha sighed. "Dejian will not be happy."

"Do you see any other choice?"

Lasinha shook his head as I stared at him pointedly, as though to suggest that their failure to confide in me on this matter had somehow led us to this point. In truth, my involvement would have made no difference, and I knew it. We had all underestimated Frederik, had assumed his ultimate allegiance lay with the Church and his father, not his lover. We were wrong.

37

Ten days passed before the remaining money in the Church accounts vanished. The exchange was done at five in the morning, and Lasinha called me ten minutes later to let me know it had happened. I left Meredith sleeping and went to join him in the Protectors' building. Since Molijc had made it obvious he knew about Meredith and I, there had seemed little point in attempting to hide our relationship from him, and so I had returned to her bed. A reckoning was still to come, but at least I would be able to take solace in pleasure in the meantime.

Lasinha was on the phone when I arrived. He put a hand over the mouthpiece and mouthed to me, "They're in Toronto." He returned to whoever was on the other end of the call. "Yes, just make sure. Neither of them gets on an airship. If they leave, they leave by car. I'll be alerting the local authorities to watch for them. We're going to run them to ground."

"Well," I said as he got off the phone.

"Emptied. Completely. There's enough money to last them both for quite a while."

I shook my head and sighed. "You've let Dejian know?" He nodded. "How exactly are we going to be paying for all the favors you're calling in, or our trip across the country, if we've got no money?"

Lasinha shrugged. "I don't know. We're just going to go and hope that we can sort things out on the way."

"Leave Dejian to deal with the creditors."

Lasinha laughed. "He said the same thing."

I did not smile, and we left for the airfield, where the De Gofroys' airship was already idling and ready to launch. There was not a moment to waste. It would take us nearly two days to reach Toronto, and I had no doubt that by then Frederik and Arajuano would have found a way to make themselves absent. We could only hope that the network of agents we both had to call on, as well as whatever local authorities we could enlist in the search, would be able to point us in the direction we needed to go.

So long as he did not take flight we had a chance, I thought—we just needed to find a way to increase our odds and bring more pressure to bear against the two of them. And as to that, I had some thoughts of my own.

Dejian remained on campus to attend to Frederik's duties. The High Regents had named him acting Grand Regent in Frederik's absence, which we had finally been forced to admit when our various evasions had failed to stanch the flow of rumors. Lasinha and I had attempted to start our own, having our people suggest that Frederik had simply gone on a secret voyage, not unlike those that his father had undertaken in earlier days.

We left it to the imagination of others to fill in the details as to why the Grand Regent would do so. Though it did not quiet any of the darker rumors, it at least became a part of the larger conversation. And it gave us something to build from once we had captured him and determined what to do with him.

He could no longer be Grand Regent, that much was clear. And not only because Osahi had made that a condition of his return from exile. We could no longer trust him, and he would know that we did not and would, in turn, never trust us. He could not be declared an apostate and exiled, the preferred fate of those who ran afoul of the Protectors. The son of De Gofroy could not be an apostate.

It was an impossible situation, and one that I put to Lasinha late on the first day of our travel. "Dejian has a plan," was all he would say.

When I pressed him, he elaborated further. "Internal exile. The Church has some land in Saskatchewan—I think De Gofroy had some idea that a second campus could be built there if we were forced out of Calgary for whatever reason. There's some basic buildings there already, apparently. We send Frederik there. Say that he is withdrawing from all daily concerns to focus on the spiritual guidelines of the Protocols to better help guide the Church. Something like that—Dejian will say it better—and we keep some Protectors on site to make sure he stays put."

"Imprisonment," I said, thinking of what De Gofroy had asked of us.

"Napoleon on Elba," Lasinha said with a nod.

This was De Gofroy's son, and we were, in effect, putting him in chains. For some reason this bothered me, though I had felt no qualms about removing the boy from the Grand Regency. It needed to be done. So did this, Lasinha and Molijc would say, and perhaps they were right. It felt like a line was being brushed aside again, just as Lasinha had with the attack on the airship.

How long would Frederik be allowed to live, I wondered? For now, we needed him alive—he was our connection to the past, to De Gofroy. But once Dejian had consolidated his position as Grand Regent, Frederik would no longer be necessary. More than that, he would be a threat to Molijc and us, for he would stand as a potential symbol to whatever opposition might be developed against us. Lasinha had proven that he would do whatever he felt was necessary, and I had no doubt

Molijc would be the same once he had his long-coveted position.

These qualms I kept to myself, for the more immediate concern was to return Frederik to the Church. If we failed in this task, if he somehow managed to escape, the Church was in all likelihood doomed. It would be a disaster even Dejian, with his mellifluous tongue, could not hope to navigate. We would be cast aside and others would take up the broken mantle of the faith, but it would be but an echo of what had come before, and the Protocols of the faith would be emptied of meaning without De Gofroy's chosen hands upon it.

On the second day of our journey, as Lasinha and I stood watching the sun rise, word came that Frederik was no longer in Toronto. There was no indication of where the two had fled, beyond the fact they had checked out of the hotel they were staying in and their car had been spotted on a freeway heading north out of the city by one of the local police who belonged to the Church.

"Get one of our locals on the road, see if they can track them," Lasinha said to the Protector who'd delivered the word. The man scurried away to make the call, and Lasinha turned to me. "They could be anywhere by the time we get there."

"I have an idea for how to flush them out," I said. "You won't like it."

Lasinha gestured for me to continue. I took a deep breath to steady myself. "We go to the police. In Canada and the Northern Union. We file reports saying that we are looking for two men fitting Arajauno's and Frederik's description who have stolen funds from the Church."

"You're right," Lasinha said. "I don't like it. Dejian will hate it."

"We need to run them to ground," I said. "And soon. How long can we keep the airspace closed to them?"

"A day or two in Toronto. Depending on where they go, if we can find that out, maybe a day or two. Maybe not," Lasinha said with a shrug.

"And we don't want to involve the Society, I am assuming."

"No, although I would be interested to know what their feelings are on Arajuano ghosting," Lasinha said. "Has he ghosted on them?"

"Do you think they are after him too?"

Another shrug. "Maybe. Maybe they wait, let chaos reign, and try to reestablish a connection later. This may not be exactly what they wanted, but it damages the Church significantly, and they can try to get an agent placed highly later on."

I turned from Lasinha to look out the vessel at the passing landscape. We were at that moment above one of the Great Lakes, those vast inland seas. I could make out ships plying the waters below, and in the far distance, along the horizon at the sun's edge, the barest contours of a tree-swathed land.

"We report them to the police," I said. "It will get more people than we can afford looking for them. It will save us the trouble of phoning a thousand hotels. We just stay on the police comms and we'll find them."

"And if they get arrested?"

"Then we know where they are," I said, turning back to Lasinha. "We can get them out. We either pay off the cops or drop the charges or something."

Lasinha pursed his lips. "What if they identify Frederik?"

I shrugged. "I'm sure Molijc can think of some way to explain that. It's not as though any Regent trusts the authorities anyway. We've all been harassed at some point or another."

"They may alert the Society as well."

"If the Society is pursuing Arajuano, then they will find them before we have a chance to," I said. "They have far more resources at their disposal."

Lasinha did not reply, his eyes half closed in thought.

The fact that he was considering the suggestion at all told me I had won the day.

"Make the call," I said.

He looked at me and nodded.

38

My plan was put into action within the hour and bore fruit by the time we approached Toronto airspace. Frederik and Arajuano had been arrested at a hotel in Montreal and were being held for questioning in response to our charges. We changed our flight plan, and Lasinha negotiated with the Montreal police to ensure neither Frederik nor Arajuano would be released before we arrived with evidence of their malfeasance.

"Just hold them till nightfall. We'll be there," he shouted into the comms. "We can explain everything to you then, and I'm certain we can come to an understanding."

I watched Lasinha, his forehead shining with sweat, and his eyes wild, as he continued to argue with the constable, only half listening to their conversation. An understanding could be reached, I knew. It was just a matter of price, and it would be high, for police and governments everywhere had a natural distrust of the Church of Regents. We had created an authority apart from the world, our own codex of law, and we paid little mind to the various powers of the wider world, viewing them as adversaries to our own goals. Some, such as the Travelers, were explicitly, while others merely served that purpose in their inflexibility and their refusal to recognize our beliefs as valid.

We found our way through such boundaries, and we would find our way through this one as well. The real trick would be getting the police to release Frederik to us, without alerting them to who he really was, and not getting ourselves further entangled in the law, while also getting the Church's funds back. Could they be seized as evidence, I wondered? Certainly the police would argue so.

"It's done," Lasinha said, slamming down the receiver.

"Should we notify Dejian that we have him?" I said. Neither of us had informed him of the plan we had put in motion, for we both knew he would have refused to go along with it.

"No," Lasinha said. "Not until we actually do."

His caution proved prescient when we arrived that evening over Montreal and the airport authority refused permission for us to land.

"They say we haven't paid our landing fees and they won't let us set down until we do," the pilot told us.

"Tell them we're out of fuel. We have to land," I said.

"I tried," she said. "They say we can go to Saint Jerome. It has a landing strip."

"Where is that?" Lasinha said.

"Two hours' drive from the city."

"We don't have that time," I said. "Find out what they really want."

The pilot made a face as though to say that we knew what they really wanted, but she did not say anything and turned to the comms to call the airport authority back.

I turned to Lasinha. "I thought we had arranged this."

"We did," he said, frowning and watching the pilot as she spoke into the receiver. "Things have changed."

"Do you think they used the funds to buy the airport authority?"

Lasinha shook his head. "Why not buy their way out of jail? We just confirmed they are both still there."

"Maybe that's what they're doing right now," I said.

"I don't think so. The police have them. They may even have the money. They can certainly get it. And if they do, they won't want those two out in the world where they can blab about what went down. This smells like the Society."

"One last favor for Arajuano?"

Lasinha ran a distracted hand over his shaved head. "Yes. Or we've been wrong and all of this has been to plan."

I felt a chill at his words. "You think they mean to destroy the Church?"

"That's always been their goal, more or less. Control it, or destroy it. Maybe when they realized Frederik was going to be frozen out and Arajuano wouldn't have any more influence, they decided it was better to ruin the Church than try to put another agent in place."

"We know how difficult that can be," I said, unable to stop myself from thinking of Ana, wondering what had become of her. "They have to know that they can't destroy faith. The Protocols will outlast us all. Whether the Church has money or not, no matter what, the faith will go on. So long as our souls cannot find their proper rest in the One Universe."

"Of course," Lasinha said with a nod, though he did not look as though he had my belief in the eternal nature of our faith.

The truth was that I had my own doubts. The son of our prophet had abandoned the Church he led for the love of an apostate. An apostate who had once been one of the chosen, a High Regent, second only to De Gofroy, and, evidently, a Judas, agent of our sworn enemies. His daughter, someone I had cared for deeply, and who had sworn her eternal belief to me, had gone to be our agent for the Travelers and had disappeared without a word. Had she betrayed us? Had she lost her faith?

If these people's faiths could be bought and sold,

pretended or abandoned, then anyone's could be, even Lasinha's and Molijc's. Even my own. Look at everything we had done in the name of the faith—lives had been destroyed on any number of levels—at a cost to our own souls, to say nothing of the others we had damaged, and to what end? We were no nearer De Gofroy's dream than when he had been alive. We were no closer to the One Universe. We could not even cross between the universes.

It all seemed pointless as the pilot continued to argue with air traffic control for permission to land and we floated above Montreal, the minutes ticking by, each one allowing Frederik and Arajuano the time to slip from our grasp again.

"They will not give permission," the pilot said again, her voice edged with tears as her frustration came to a boil. "We've offered them everything."

"Keep trying," Lasinha said. "Don't stop until they say yes."

The pilot looked to me, pleading with her eyes, in the hopes that I might be an ally, but I ignored her and turned to Lasinha. "What else can we be doing now?"

Lasinha shrugged. "Do we know anyone else in Montreal?"

"Not that could help us here," I said, biting at my lip. "What about in the Society? Can we use one of our people there?"

Lasinha pondered the question for a moment before shaking his head. "No, I don't think so. Who knows how high up in the Society these orders come from? We'd just be burning one of our agents, and they might not be able to do anything to help us."

"So we wait," I said.

"We wait," Lasinha said. We both turned in unison to look at the pilot, who continued her interminable request-and-deny conversation on the comms.

"I'm going to go and try to get some sleep," Lasinha

said. "I have a feeling it's going to be a long night. Let me know if there's any news. Come and wake me in two hours regardless."

I nodded and watched him go from the flight deck, before turning back to the pilot, listening as she continued to battle with air traffic control. The night sky bloomed around us, with the insinuation of clouds surrounding us in the darkness, the city below glimmering with fractious lights thwarting the night inch by inch. As I stared down at the city, seemingly so alive, while we lay moored in the vast endless sea of darkness, I was overwhelmed by despair. This, I felt, was the end. Doom, in one form or another, awaited us off this ship, and I did not want to face it.

As I stood there, trying to master my emotions, trying to ward off the melancholy that threatened to reduce me to tears, I saw the pilot had stopped talking on the comms and had turned to face me. I looked at her, expecting news of some kind, but she only stared at me, holding the comms receiver in her hand. I swallowed all the terrible thoughts swimming through me and stepped toward her.

"Let me try for a moment," I said, taking the receiver from her.

An hour later we were finally allowed to land. As the pilot tried again to request permission, claiming, with some real urgency now, that we were running short on fuel and needed to set the airship down, she was cut short and turned very still as she listened to what the authorities below were saying. I noticed the change in her attitude and moved from the back of the flight deck, where I had banished myself when I had exhausted all my reserves of patience arguing with airport control, to stand beside her.

She finished the conversation without uttering another word and set the receiver down. "They're granting us permission to land," she said, turning to look at me.

"Did they say why?" I said.

She shook her head. "No. They didn't even mention

our unpaid fees."

I gave a bitter laugh. "I imagine those have been settled. Take us down. I will go wake Lasinha."

He was already awake when I arrived at his cabin near the loading docks of the ship, carrying on a conversation on his phone. I paused at his door to listen for a moment and heard him say, "This is unacceptable. Everything we've worked for here is in jeopardy and no one is able to notify me when we're about to get royally screwed. What is the point of having people on the other side if not for that?"

There was a pause as whomever he was speaking to replied, and then he said, "Fuck open channels. We're playing for keeps here, not to establish some kind of détente."

I decided I had heard enough and knocked on the door. Lasinha opened the door, looking irritable, holding up a hand to forestall any words from me. "I have to go," he said. "Keep me posted on what's going on for a change."

I raised an eyebrow in question and he shook his head in disgust. "A Traveler I've been cultivating. He seems to not understand that our relationship is predicated on him providing us with useful and timely information."

"Maybe he's playing you," I said.

"Of course he is," Lasinha said. "And I'm playing him, but obviously he's doing a better job of it."

"They've given us permission to land," I said, and as I spoke I could feel the ship lurching into motion.

Lasinha grimaced. "No explanation?"

I shook my head.

"Fucking Travelers. Arajuano's fucked us, I'm sure."

"I assume so," I said, leading the way back to the flight deck.

We both silently watched as the pilot managed our descent, each second more agonizing than the last. Once we had safely docked, we left the airship, half expecting to be detained by the authorities as we emerged. There was no one there to meet us as we stepped to the ground, so we found a taxi that took us to the jail, Lasinha phoning ahead to confirm yet again that Arajuano and Frederik were still being held.

"They say they are," he said, after hanging up the phone.

"Do you believe them?"

"Not for a second."

The city jail where they were purportedly being held was in the derelict Old Montreal alongside the river, where at one point the docks had been. The jail was an old factory of indeterminate use, with a stern and blank visage that lent itself to its current occupation. Within the building everything had been stripped, removing any traces of its past existence.

Past the entrance a wall of caging wire had been erected, separating us from the rest of the prison. There was a tall counter on the other side of the cage, behind which sat two officers who had not even looked up at our entrance.

"We are the representatives from the Church of the Regents," I announced. The two officers glanced at each other, suppressing grins. "We spoke to you on the phone."

"We remember you, all right," one said, getting to her feet and coming to the counter to look us over. "I understand we've got your Grand Regent here."

I felt the blood leave my face, but I maintained my composure. "What would make you say that?"

"That's what the other one said." She looked from Lasinha and I to judge our reactions. "He said the kid would be worth quite a lot to you and we shouldn't just release him."

"Is that so?" Lasinha said. "And he is still with you as well?"

"No," the officer said. "He has some juice downtown. Took a while, but it finally came through. We let him out about half an hour ago."

I could see Lasinha's jaw go tight at her words. He swallowed and kept his composure. "Did you release him to anyone?"

"No."

"Was there anyone here to pick him up?" Lasinha said, leaning forward so that he was almost pressing his face against the cage wire.

The officer shrugged. "We don't care what happens to them once they're released. Not our department. I think you'd be more concerned about your Regent in here. Isn't he important to you all?"

Not anymore, I wanted to say, but held my tongue.

"Can we see him?" Lasinha said, the tone of his voice indicating he was nearing the end of his patience.

"Depends," the officer said with a smirk.

I could feel that Lasinha was about to explode, so I stepped past him to speak directly to the officer, peering through the cage wire. The last thing we needed after this unfolding disaster of a day was to end up in prison ourselves, and if Lasinha lost his temper that was certain to happen.

"We are the ones who asked that he be held," I said. "You are bringing charges against him for us. Should we not be able to talk to him to assess whether the charges are warranted?"

"We determine whether charges are warranted," the woman said.

"Fine. Keep him," Lasinha said. "We have more important things to deal with."

I shot him a look, which he returned with force. "Arajuano is gone," he said. "I guarantee you he has the money. We have to find him before he's out of Montreal."

The officer watched our staring contest with amusement and curiosity. It felt wrong to abandon Frederik to his fate, but I knew Lasinha was correct. Arajuano was the more important one now. But how to find him in the city?

"Come on," Lasinha said, turning to leave the jail. "They'll get tired of him taking up space once they realize there's nothing in it for them."

I nodded, still feeling the eyes of both officers on me, and we left the jail and stepped back into the night.

39

We rode the taxi back to the airport in silence, both of us lost in thought. There was little chance that we could find Arajuano now that he had a half-hour head start and we had exhausted most of our resources. Even if we could pick up his trail, there was no guarantee that we would be allowed to leave by the airport authorities. The landing fees that had mysteriously disappeared might just as mysteriously reappear.

"How do we know he'll take an airship?" I said, breaking our silence at last.

"The Travelers will have one waiting for him, whether he wants it or not," Lasinha said. "There's no running for him."

I glanced over at him, unsure of what he meant by that last phrase, but he did not elaborate, lapsing into silence again. The city was a blur around us, the streets darkened and empty, with hardly any other cars on the road. Exhaustion began to weigh on me, and I tried to remember when I had last slept. It felt like days, and perhaps it had been.

Our airship still sat in its dock as we arrived, with no sign of any guard or other officialdom in sight. The whole airport was quiet, our cab the only movement along the tarmac that could be seen. I took that as positive news. If need be, we would be able to take off before anyone could respond and stop us.

Lasinha was on the phone as we entered the tarmac area and were waved past by a bored guard who glanced at the docking slip for our airship that I held up to him. He was on the line with whoever was on duty in the air traffic control tower, asking if there were any recent arrivals or ships getting ready for takeoff. To my surprise, he received an answer and directed the taxi past our own airship to the far terminal, where the guilds and other officials docked their ships.

We were stopped at a gate by a guard, this one far more attentive than the last, who demanded to see our papers. Lasinha passed a document, which the guard studied for a long time before handing it back.

"It's very old," he said. "But I will let you through this once."

Lasinha thanked him and we went through. He turned to me and grinned. "Something from an old life with Osahi. I always carry it just in case I need it again."

He flashed it to me before returning it within his jacket, and I could just make out an official-looking seal from the Airship Guild. Membership in the Guild would give you access to every airport in the world, which made me wonder why we had not been availing ourselves of his membership before this.

Sensing my question, he said, "I'm not on the Guild list. We were found out. And the name here doesn't match my own. So it's always a risk, but here it seemed worth it."

He spoke hurriedly, as though trying to convince himself of the truth of what he was saying. Why would he be lying, I wondered?

That question was immediately put aside as we drove around a hangar and came upon an ship preparing for takeoff. There were three people walking toward the stairs leading to the airship, two of them flanking the third in a way that suggested an escort. One of them wore the unmistakable black robes of the Society of Travelers. The other was dressed in grey. I did not need to see her eyes to know it was a Seeker. I felt a chill ripple through my body at that knowledge. Between them was Arajuano, his long, dark hair making him immediately recognizable.

How many days had I sat watching him? It seemed years ago now. This felt like an ending.

Lasinha was very still beside me, watching the three as they progressed to the airship. The driver had pulled to a stop, sensing our reluctance to go any further. He turned around to look at us for further instructions.

"Should we get out and try to stop them?" I said to Lasinha.

He shook his head. "He's gone," he said. "There's no point."

As he spoke, the Seeker turned around and leveled her gaze upon our car. All of us stiffened in response, feeling the weight of that strange gaze upon us. The Seeker took a step toward us, cocking her head slightly, while the Traveler and Arajuano paused in their march and looked back at her. The air seemed to go out of the car, all of us holding our breath, not daring to so much as exhale. The Seeker took another step forward, raising her hand to the Traveler to signal that he should wait where he was.

"Get us the fuck out of here," Lasinha managed to say, his voice pitched high with terror.

The driver seemed unable to move, staring straight ahead at the approaching Seeker. I, too, could not take my eyes from her, fear paralyzing me and overwhelming all my thoughts. It was Lasinha who acted, reaching around from behind the driver to take hold of the wheel.

"Drive," he shouted, breaking the spell the Seeker had us under.

The driver startled back into awareness, slammed on the gas, and took hold of the wheel, spinning us around so that we were headed back the way we had come. As we sped away, I saw the Seeker come to a halt, her gaze still lingering on us, and I could feel its terrible pull. Behind her I could see that Arajuano had turned to look as well. His expression was oddly empty of thought or emotion, though I told myself it was just a trick of the docking lights.

We had the cab take us back to the jail, where the same officer greeted us behind the cage wire with a sardonic smile that made Lasinha burn with anger.

"Back so soon?" she said.

I stepped past Lasinha, not wanting him to say anything that would antagonize the officers, and knowing that he desperately wanted to do so, given the day we had just had. "Please let us see the Regent," I said. "We have reason to believe that he was not a part of the conspiracy to defraud the Church and that the man who you released was responsible."

"You are questioning our competence?" the woman said.

"Of course not," I said. "New evidence has come to light. And as I'm sure you know by now, the boy has no money. Neither, for that matter, do we."

The officer looked disgusted. "Typical. Your kind doesn't know when it's getting taken, does it? Lucky for you, you have some friends higher up, at least. We just got the order to release your man."

I nodded my thanks and could hear Lasinha taking a deep breath and exhaling slowly. We were buzzed through and taken to a windowless visiting room, where we waited for some time before Frederik was brought before us. He was still in shackles when they brought him into the room, but the officer released him and he sat across the table from us attempting a defiant stare. There were bruises around his eyes and on his neck.

Neither Lasinha nor I said a word, the silence growing

heavy, until at last Frederik crumbled, throwing his head into his hands and beginning to sob. When he was done, he looked up at us and said, "He said we would be together. He told me that he loved me and that we could escape all this madness."

Still Lasinha and I kept our silence. I found I wanted to throttle him, to choke the miserable life from his neck.

"I didn't want this. I don't believe any of this. My father was just making stuff up, and I thought I could too. And Arajuano said he could keep me safe from you. He told me he loved me."

Lasinha stood, reached across the table, and slapped Frederik in the face, the blow causing me to wince and the boy to gasp. "Do not speak ill of the founder. It is by his word that we all guide our lives. Even you, you miserable piece of shit. Now, where is the money?"

Frederik turned to me for sympathy, but my face was stone. He began to sob again. "He took it all. He took it all."

Lasinha and I stood in unison and went to Frederik, pulling him to his feet and escorting him from the jail, back to the airship. The light of the day was coming into the sky by the time we arrived. As we approached the staircase leading up to the airship, an unfamiliar figure emerged from the cabin to watch our approach. I was taken aback at the sight of someone I did not recognize being on the vessel, and I believed for a moment that we had been boarded by the authorities, for I was certain I had met everyone on the vessel.

As we started up the stairs the man's face became visible through the dim morning light. It was the Acolyte who had kept De Gofroy alive. As we came to the top of the stairs, he took Frederik by the arm, and together they disappeared into the bowels of the ship.

EXCERPT:

THE ACOLYTE
VOLUME THREE OF THE
SOJOURNERS CYCLE

After crossing the universes to join with Toma Osahi's group of renegades in their battle for control of the Church of Regents, Laila finds herself in a precarious position. While they both share the same goal—the destruction of the Grand Regent—Osahi doesn't know who Laila really is. What will he do if he finds out?

While Laila struggles to keep her identity secret, Osahi and his people pull her deeper and deeper into a search for Ana that promises to shed light on the dark secrets of the Watchers' Order and the Acolytes. Before she can find those answers though, Laila will have to face what lies within.

Crossing the universes has unsettled the already shaky equilibrium in her mind. If she wants to return herself to her own body, she will have to act fast, for the consequences of what Acolytes did to her are still reverberating. And Aeida hides somewhere, waiting for his time to come.

1

It is some time after the channel vanishes—leaving the ferry and the tiny room where Morris Loverne has just been overwhelmed a memory—before I can find it in myself to move again. I feel adrift. Events have conspired again to leave me alone, with no one I can turn to.

Though I can no longer trust Morris—he is a creature of the Seeker and a Society agent after all—his familiarity, our shared history, was a comfort to me. There was something like trust there, no matter how illusory it might have been. He was a friend once, however false he proved to be. Those are the only kind I have.

How pitiful it all seems now. The illusion of trust. That is all I have—illusions and lies. Even my body is not my own. My mind seems less and less so with each passing day.

Especially now, as I am reeling from the aftereffects of the transfer. My hands are shaking and my legs are trembling. It takes all my effort to keep my feet under me. I have to close my eyes against the sun, painfully vivid against the cloudless blue sky. My head aches. Everything hurts, actually, and, as I take a first tentative step, I collapse onto the rocks.

A swirl of thoughts and colors assaults me. I try to blink them back to no avail. Somewhere, lurking behind this internal cacophony lies Aeida, waiting for his chance to take control. He is still so dangerous. No matter that he is not what he was, this is still his body.

A terrible coughing fit assaults me, bruising my lungs. I don't know if I can survive another crossing, not in my current state. It was never like this before. But I was never like this before either. This remade mind, stolen and tamped, was not intended to be sent across the channels. It was supposed to stay lost in a universe known only to the Watchers Order and myself.

If I am to restore myself to my body I will have to attempt another crossing, especially now that I am here in another lost universe. It is inevitable. The thought terrifies me. Will entropy work further upon me each time, until there is nothing left of me and Aeida but a twitching mass of limbs?

That thought is almost as disturbing as those I have about what has become of my body. I imagine it, hidden somewhere in the endless universes, suffering under whatever tortures Molijc can devise. He will not win, I tell myself, as I work to steady my breathing and still my body. I will not allow it.

The Seeker has asked me to become his agent for the Society, or whatever faction of the Travelers he serves, and foment revolt within the ranks of the Regents. I have no doubt I will have to account for my failure to do so some day, but hopefully when I next stand before him, it will by my own eyes that meet his terrible ones.

I do not have the luxury of worrying about him. My time is short, I can see that clearly now. It is only a matter of time before Aeida gains command or this constructed mind collapses in on itself and neither of us survives in any form. I must restore myself before that happens. I must destroy Molijc and end the tyranny of his faith before that comes to pass.

My urgency brings me to my feet. There is no time to linger. As I rise, the colors grow brighter and brighter, at their center a pulsating orb that penetrates deep into my brain, lancing it like some doctor removing a tumor. Darkness is ascendant and I feel my legs go from beneath me again.

I do not know how much time passes before I awake again. Looking up at the sky I see that the sun has gone across the sky and is on its way to setting. I have no sense of how much time I have before darkness arrives, but a chill has already stolen into the air and I find myself shivering. I will need to find shelter soon and assess my options from there.

My first attempt to stand fails and I end up on the ground, dizzy and nauseous, but my second succeeds. I look around to reacquaint myself with my surroundings. The waterfall is before me, the thunderous roar of its descent swallowing all other sound. Beside the fall is a cliff of rock that looks, to my untrained eyes, nearly impassible. To my left the river passes, curling like a snake ready to strike. On every other side I am surrounded by forest.

There is no sign of habitation anywhere, no evidence that humans have ever passed this way. I have no sense of where Osahi and his people might be hiding themselves in this apparently vast wilderness and no idea of where to even begin in my search. A thought occurs to me as I ponder this conundrum: What happened to Nicola?

She came with me across the channel, but I did not see her after I came across and there is no sign of her now. Given the injury she was suffering from, she cannot have gone far and a quick search of the immediate vicinity reveals her prone form, hidden behind some rocks closer to the waterfall from where we had come through the channel.

I rush to her side, putting a finger to her neck. There is a pulse, though it is faint. I lift up her shirt and see that her wound has bled through the bandages Morris put on her. There is nothing I can do for her in that regard. I do not, I realize, a tremor running my hands, have food or even proper clothing for where we are. The chill in the air will only get worse once the sun sets.

I wonder how close we are to Osahi's refuge. We cannot be far, I reason. Nicola would have been well aware of how precarious her health was and that she was in no condition to begin an arduous journey. Surely she would have set the channels so that we crossed somewhere near our final destination. Yet that does not appear to be the case.

Is that the result of an abundance of caution? Or was she intentionally leading us astray? I cannot trust her—I cannot trust anyone, not entirely. Not even myself.

For a time I am paralyzed by indecision, unsure how to proceed in this new world. Finally I decide I will have to attempt some kind of search and I leave Nicola where she is, judging her to be safe enough for the moment, and start to reconnoiter the area. The only trace I can find of any human activity is a thin trail leading toward the rock face alongside the waterfall. I follow it along to the base of the cliff where it comes to an abrupt end. As I look at the cliff I can make out what might be a path to its summit.

"Motherfucker," I say to myself, the sound of my voice startling me and bringing me from a reverie I am not even aware I am in.

Along the base of the cliff wall I see a place where a small crevice has formed and I go to investigate it. It is near the waterfall, the mist dampening my face when the wind gusts. The noise is incredible as well, a ceaseless roar. The crevice is large enough to shelter two or three people and the ground in it has been lined with leaves and grass. There is a small depression at its edge where a fire had once burned.

I retrace my steps to where I left Nicola, finding her awake and trying to stand up.

"Don't," I say. "I've found a place we can camp in. I'll carry you there."

She looks as though she will argue with me, her dark eyes fierce, but relents in the end. I pick her up and carry her to the crevice, letting her settle herself there while I go in search of firewood. There is plenty of deadwood nearby and when I have collected what I think will be enough to last us for the night I return to the crevice. Nicola is asleep again, a slightly pained expression on her face, though her breathing remains steady.

Aeida knows how to light a fire without matches or tools from his youth in the Pacific Northwest. It is strange that he can remember this, when everything else from that time is vague and unrealized. His mother and father, all of that, has apparently been removed to allow space for me, though a few things seem able to bleed through to now.

How I long to scream at the Acolytes, to stand before them and ask why they obliterated two peoples' beings. For what purpose? How do they justify this to Molijc and themselves? I cannot fathom it. They must have their reasons, and I add that to my list of things I intend to do, if given the chance.

Nicola is awake by the time I get the fire going. She raises herself to a sitting position as I kneel over the flames, feeding branches in until the blaze is glowing healthily.

"I'm impressed," she says, her voice sounding weaker than before.

"Just a trick I picked up over the years," I say. "How's your stomach?"

She shrugs, wincing as she does so.

I nod. "We don't have any food. Is there some nearby that I can scavenge? I didn't see any, but this place has clearly been used for camping before."

"I don't know," she says. "I expect most people go on to the citadel. If they do camp here, they probably have supplies with them."

"The citadel," I say, hesitating over the word, "Osahi is there? It's up this rock?"

After a moment's hesitation she nods. "Climb the cliff and find the trail heading north. It's less than an hour's walk through the forest."

"You can't make it up the cliff, can you?"

A longer hesitation, before she shakes her head. "No," she says, with great reluctance.

"I'll go up at first light tomorrow," I say. "Osahi should be able to send someone down to get you back up here before the end of the day. Will you be all right?"

"I'll be fine," she says.

I nod and we both fall silent staring at the fire as darkness begins to envelope us. The air turns cold with nightfall and I can see Nicola beginning to shiver from the cold. I give her my jacket and add some more branches to the fire. She lays back down and falls into a fitful sleep, while I stay by the fire, keeping it stoked, my mind still racing from the events of the day.

What will happen to Morris, I wonder? The agents who came to intercept us were Travelers, I thought, from the brief glimpse I had gotten of them. They were not dressed as Black Robes, but they had that military bearing to them that was unmistakable. I had long since grown skilled at picking those sorts out of a crowd.

But I well knew that the fact that they were Black Robes, did not mean they were not ultimately answerable to Molijc. He has insinuated his agents within their infrastructure. I should know, I helped him do it. And the Society does not have any reason to pursue Morris—surely the Seeker would act to protect him even if they did— whereas the Grand Regent most certainly does.

I know what Molijc will do to him. He will have the Acolytes do their terrible work to extract whatever information they can and render him another of the half-things that wander about the campus, blindly doing whatever the Grand Regent bids. A terrible fate for anyone.

Will the Seeker act to spare Morris that, or will he decide that it is better to keep his involvement secret, provided he can trust Morris not to reveal it under the Acolyte's extraction procedures? I think I know the answer to the question, based on the final expression on Morris's face before the channel closed.

It is a long time before I can get that image from my mind and I am able to lie down beside Nicola, stealing a bit of her warmth, and sleep.

THE ACOLYTE will be available in November 2017.

ABOUT THE AUTHOR

Clint Westgard is the author of The Shadow Men Trilogy and the science fiction epic The Sojourners Cycle. In addition, he has published a work of historical fantasy set in colonial Peru, The Maleficio Chronicles, and a retelling of the Minotaur legend, The Trials of the Minotaur. Clint Westgard lives in Calgary, Alberta.

ALSO BY CLINT WESTGARD

The Acolyte
Volume Three of The Sojourners Cycle

After crossing the universes to join with Toma Osahi's
group of renegades in their battle for control of the
Church of Regents, Laila finds herself in a precarious
position. While they both share the same goal—the
destruction of the Grand Regent—Osahi doesn't know
who Laila really is. What will he do if he finds out?

While Laila struggles to keep her identity secret, Osahi and
his people pull her deeper and deeper into a search for
Ana that promises to shed light on the dark secrets of the
Watchers' Order and the Acolytes. Before she can find
those answers though, Laila will have to face what lies
within.

Crossing the universes has unsettled the already shaky
equilibrium in her mind. If she wants to return herself to
her own body, she will have to act fast, for the
consequences of what Acolytes did to her are still
reverberating. And Aeida hides somewhere, waiting for his
time to come.

The thrilling third volume of the Sojourners Cycle
continues Laila's incredible journey across the universes
against incredible odds, as well as exploring her past,
including the pivotal role she played in the rise of the
Grand Regent and her own downfall at his hands.

ALSO BY CLINT WESTGARD

The Double
Volume Four of The Sojourners Cycle

David Aeida now commands his body, having cast Laila aside. He has sworn fealty to the Grand Regent, who wants him by his side and sees that his loyalty is rewarded.

But the Grand Regent is not the man he was. He is paranoid and suspicious of everyone, isolated in his tower, and thirsting for vengeance against those he feels have wronged him. How long until he turns on Aeida as well?

That is only the beginning of Aeida's problems. For he knows the Seeker and the Society of Travelers remain to play their parts. Both desire nothing more than the utter destruction of the Church of Regents and all its works. And though Laila has been defeated, he knows better than anyone not to assume she has been vanquished.

The epic fourth volume of the Sojourners Cycle centers upon the many betrayals and lies at the heart of the faith of the Church of Regents and the devastation upon the lives of the faithful they have wrought. Desire and guilt, love and revenge, rage and despair will drive them all, with consequences for all the universes.

ALSO BY CLINT WESTGARD

The Sojourner
Volume Five of The Sojourners Cycle

Laila's strange and reluctant alliance with the Seeker continues, though she does not know where it will lead her. She fears it will place her in another prison, worse than the one she has just managed to escape.

But her escape is not entirely complete. For though she has been restored to her own flesh, parts of Aeida somehow still remain. Along with some other she does not recognize. Is this some aftereffect of the Acolyte's bizarre procedure? Or the result of the Seeker's meddling?

All this pales in comparison to what Laila soon discovers. That she has an unwanted part to play in an ancient struggle for who will rule the crossings between the universes and all that lies in them.

In the stunning conclusion to the Sojourners Cycle Laila will be faced with a terrible choice, one that will decide her fate and humanity's.

ALSO BY CLINT WESTGARD

Realm of Shadows
Volume One of The Shadow Men

Craitol and Renuih, two empires a world apart, divided by the desert that lies between them. A desert ruled by the Shadow Men.

An uneasy peace holds sway in both realms, hiding longstanding feuds and bitter rivalries. Until a Shadow Men raid on Renuih shatters the calm and sets in motion events no one can control.

Masiph id Ezern, unfavored son of the Imperial Vazeir, finds himself a hero following the raid. His father remains unmoved by his exploits and, in his bitterness, Masiph will find himself a reluctant participant in a plot against the empire.

As he finds himself drawn deeper and deeper into the conspiracy, he soon realizes there will be no escaping the realm of shadows, where intrigue and betrayal abound. And though the Shadow Men have gone quiet, they will not stay silent forever...

ALSO BY CLINT WESTGARD

Council of Shadows
Volume Two of The Shadow Men

Discontent continues to fester within the realms of Craitol and Renuih, fed by intrigues carried out in the shadows. As rivals and apostates struggle for supremacy, a long incubated plan begins to unfold.

Vyissan, a mysterious alkemycal practitioner arrives in Renuih, the latest strike in a long war over who shall control the secrets of alkemya and Craitol itself. He carries with him a secret that, once revealed, will reverberate across all realms. Before he can reveal it though, the conspirators against the emperor will strike their own blow.

But now, a new and more powerful menace looms on the horizon. The Shadow Men have gained the secrets of the Council Adept's alkemya and no one can be certain what they will do with it…

ALSO BY CLINT WESTGARD

Dance of Shadows
Volume Three of The Shadow Men

War with the Shadow Men looms in both realms as the consequences of the Gvers' Council in Craitol begin to make themselves known. A war that could end in glorious triumph or bitter disaster.

Doubt shadows everyone's steps, for they know there are no certainties in the desert. Especially now the Shadow Men have made the art of alkemya their own.

No one has more questions than Vyissan, for he is working in service to a cause he is no longer sure he believes in. And now he must undertake a journey with those who both loathe and fear him. Before the first sword is drawn, his life will be under threat.

But his will not be the only one, for somewhere in the desert the Shadow Men lie in wait…

ALSO BY CLINT WESTGARD

The Maleficio Chronicles

Luisa is always more than she appears. Rumor and mystery surround her. And strange events seem to follow wherever she goes.

Born in Lima, City of Kings, to a noble family, her father so fears her true nature that he banishes her to a convent. There she falls under the suspicion of the Inquisition and decides to flee.

Disguised as a man, she embarks upon a series of wild adventures, dueling, carousing, and gambling her way across colonial Peru. But everything changes when someone recognizes her for what she truly is, and soon she finds herself fighting for her very survival.

In a world where she will always stand apart, Luisa undergoes a strange journey, marked by betrayal and murder, terrible powers and mysterious strangers. *The Maleficio Chronicles* is her incredible confession and a story like no other.

ALSO BY CLINT WESTGARD

The Devious Kind

A Mystery

The body of a local woman is found in a coulee on a ranch north of Loverna, her head blown off with a shotgun. New to town and the job, Constable Martin Thomas arrives on the scene as a spring snowstorm begins to wipe out all evidence before his investigation has even begun.

There is no shortage of suspects to consider. A spurned husband. A jealous lover. A betrayed business partner. And family members battling over an inheritance. All have motive and opportunity. And no one seems to be telling him everything.

As he tries to sift the truth from the lies, the snowstorm continues to build, leaving Loverna cut off from the outside world. And Thomas alone to face a killer who will do anything not to get caught.